FACT &
FICTION

FACT &
FICTION

A Parker City Mystery

Justin M. Kiska

LEVEL
BEST BOOKS

First published by Level Best Books 2023

This novel is entirely a work of fiction. The names, characters and incidents portrayed in it are the work of the author's imagination. Any resemblance to actual persons, living or dead, events or localities is entirely coincidental.

Justin M. Kiska asserts the moral right to be identified as the author of this work.

First edition

ISBN: 978-1-68512-273-7

Cover art by Level Best Designs

This book was professionally typeset on Reedsy.
Find out more at reedsy.com

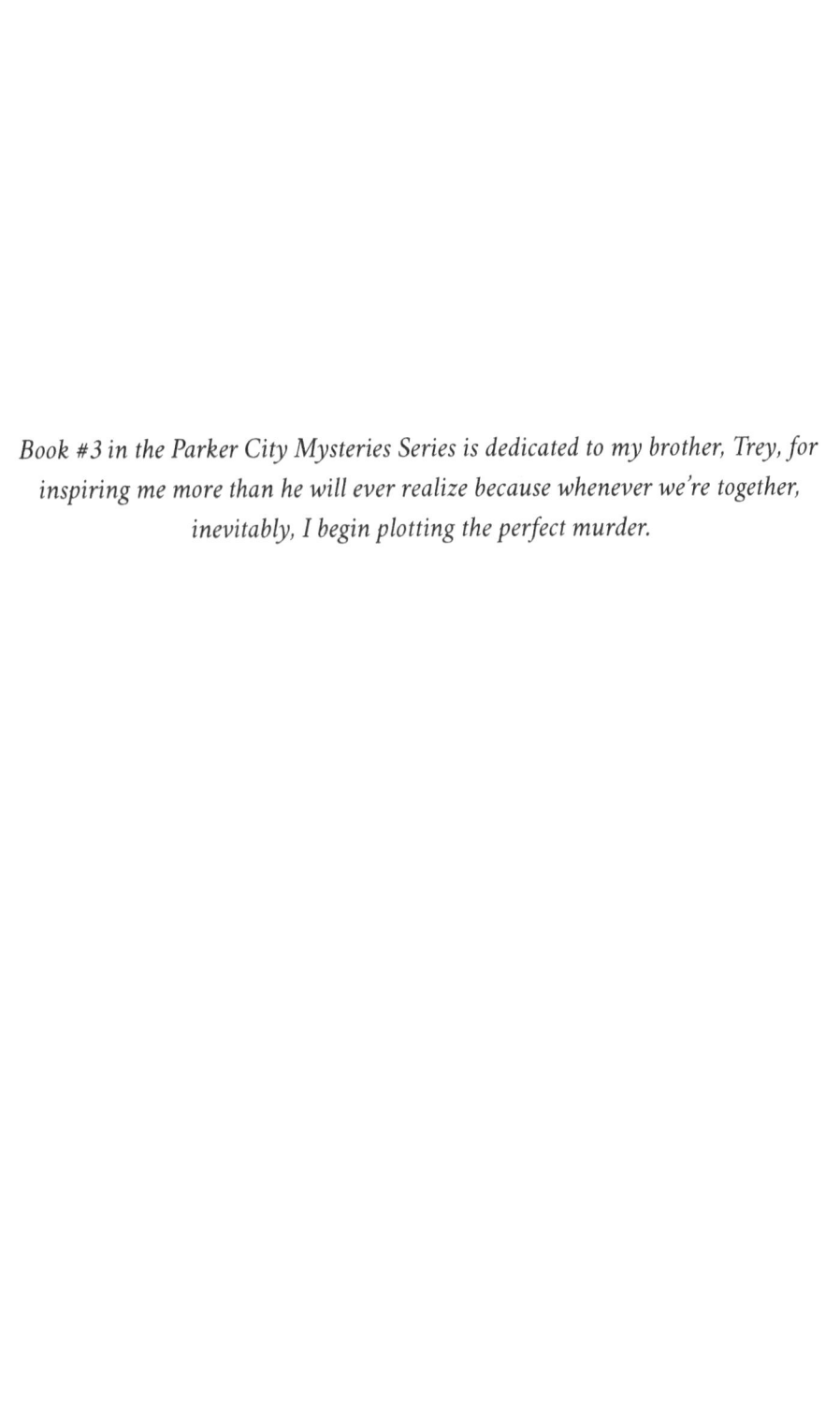

Book #3 in the Parker City Mysteries Series is dedicated to my brother, Trey, for inspiring me more than he will ever realize because whenever we're together, inevitably, I begin plotting the perfect murder.

Prologue

1984...

He could feel the spirits of the past surrounding him. Whispering to him. Telling him he was so close. Voices urging him on. Telling him not to let anything or anyone stand in his way. With each passing day, he was feeling more and more emboldened. He had already made it further than his father. Now he just needed to get his hands on one final piece of the puzzle.

Standing there with the cool autumn breeze playing across his cheeks, he knew there was no need to try and get any closer. He certainly wasn't going to climb the chain link fence like some schoolboy on a dare just to get a better look at the burned-out rubble of the former sanitarium. It wasn't like he was going to find anything that hadn't already been uncovered in what was left of the place. He just wanted to look at it once more. To feel a connection to the past and a time buried by generations.

In its day, anyone who stumbled upon the hospital without knowing its purpose would have been forgiven for mistaking it for the magnificent manor house of a prosperous landowner. It had certainly looked the part. Its columned portico provided a welcoming appeal to the front of the otherwise imposing three-story structure set upon its rolling acres.

Having been built a handful of years before South Carolina led its southern allies in an exodus from the union, creating the greatest internal conflict the nation had ever experienced, only three photos of the original building existed. Two were included in the archives of the Parker County Historical Society, while the third had been published in a local professor's book recounting the history of the area.

Naturally, the horror stories he'd read about mental facilities throughout the years and the treatments used by the doctors and nurses always made his skin crawl. Most of those reports were only from the early part of the 1900s, though. Fifty years before *that*, practices were downright medieval. What must it have been like to be a patient in there, he thought as a strong gust of wind sent a cold chill through his entire body.

The Aspen House Hospital came to a tragic end late one night in the fall of 1862 during the height of the Civil War when it mysteriously burned to the ground. Left behind was nothing more than charred bricks and a partial shell of the building that once was. Not a single patient survived, nor did Dr. Joseph Aspen, the facility's founder. Why the hospital burned and what had started the inferno had always been a bit of a controversy. But accepted history claimed a particularly disturbed patient had managed to bolt the main doors to the hospital before setting the staircase ablaze.

Over a century later, on another cool autumn afternoon, as the sun was beginning to set, the trees cast ghostly shadows over the scorched remains of the asylum. He couldn't help but notice the eeriness surrounding him. Everything was so quiet. Even the wind blowing through the trees didn't elicit the usual rustling of the leaves. It was like watching the opening scene of a horror movie with the volume turned off.

As he turned and walked back down the hill to his car, a strange feeling suddenly came over him. Momentary. Fleeting. But unsettling.

"Don't be ridiculous," he said to his reflection in the window as he unlocked the door.

Shifting into gear, the car jumped to life. He did a quick one-eighty and headed back into the city. Bumping along the dirt path, it wasn't long before he could see the paved road emerging ahead of him, a sense of unexplained relief accompanying it.

If he was forced to admit it, seeing the Aspen House Hospital was slightly unnerving. But what could one expect of the remains of a sanitarium that mysteriously burned down during the Civil War? It didn't matter how old or educated one was. Seeing the blackened ruins like a preserved shrine to some evil demon sitting behind a chain link fence messed with your psyche.

An overactive imagination could do a lot with that image. And right now, his was working in overdrive.

His mother had always told him growing up that his imagination would get him into trouble one day. Warning his father to stop encouraging his flights of fancy. But it was his mother who first told him the myth that set him on his current path. So, as far as he was concerned, she was the one to blame. Even if his father was the one who kept reminding him of the possibilities if he found what they'd both been looking for.

After so long, he believed he was about to do what his father never could. He knew exactly what he needed to do.

Chapter One

Autumn 1862...

T he only light guiding the carriage and its powerful team of horses as it charged north came from the moon overhead and two lanterns on either side of the driver's seat. Its destination, Parker City, at the foot of the Blue Ridge Mountains. Lingering in the wake of the exquisitely appointed coach was a thick cloud of dust tossed into the air by the rhythmic thundering of the colts' hooves striking the ground. All around, ominous shadows lurked, created by the pale glow breaking through the tree cover.

By his side on the velvet seat, Jonathan Tillman had his pistol at the ready in case any of the shadows turned out to be more than simple illusions. He'd been gripped by a suffocating sense of paranoia since the moment they'd crossed the bridge leaving Washington, DC. He wished his employer had waited until the morning, or at least asked for an escort. But under the circumstances, everyone involved thought a clandestine journey in the middle of the night would attract the least attention. Even if Tillman had voiced an objection, it wasn't as though anyone would pay much attention to a simple coachman. His job was to tend to the horses and not ask questions.

Crossing over the ridge, Tillman let out a sigh of relief, seeing the burning lights of Parker City rising in the distance. The trip was almost over. It wouldn't be much longer before they were safely returned to Drake House. Once there, he would stable the horses and say a little prayer that they'd returned without incident. Tucked into his small bed above the stalls in the carriage house, he hoped to forget about the day's unexpected journey to and from the nation's capital.

"How much longer, Tillman?" The raspy voice coming from within the carriage was followed by a sharp series of raps on the roof.

"Very nearly there, sir. Not much longer. City's just now come into view."

"Straight to the Courthouse, remember! Make haste."

Tillman didn't bother to reply. He'd only been reminded of their final destination roughly every quarter of an hour since they crossed into Maryland. Why they were to go to the Courthouse instead of straight home was not something to which he'd been privy, but it was not his place to question his instructions. At this hour, though, who would be there for his employer to see?

Casting a look over his shoulder, Tillman thought he'd seen a light moving between the trees off in the distance. Upon second glance toward the wooded area, he reasoned that his eyes were tired and his nerves were getting the better of him.

The sudden trip to Washington had set his mind alight. As of late, many things were happening around Drake House that piqued his interest and caused him to wonder what his employer, Eustace Drake, was now involved. No doubt, it was something to do with the war.

Situated as it was, Parker City had become a thoroughfare for the armies of both the Potomac and Confederacy as they marched on their campaigns. Parades of soldiers had been passing through town for the last week leading to a clash at the base of South Mountain only a day earlier. And now, word came that troops from both sides were amassing not far west in Sharpsburg for what many feared could be one of the bloodiest battles yet.

The recent troop movements were causing great anxiety amongst the residents in the area. Not that tensions weren't high throughout the rest of the country. But for the time being, Parker City felt like it was at the epicenter of the war between the states.

Just south of the Mason-Dixon Line, Maryland found itself divided in its fidelities. Much like the rest of the state, Parkertons' allegiances were split between the Union and the Confederacy. Families were being torn apart as brother went to war against brother and neighbors turned on one another. Schisms had been torn in the city's community, and no one was sure if the wounds would ever heal.

The dense tree line was beginning to give way to open fields as Tillman cracked his whip, urging the horses on.

The relief of knowing the beastly ride was nearly at an end was short-lived as Tillman, squinting through the darkness, made out the shape of a wagon stopped on the road in front of them. As the coach drew closer, he saw a man in dirty work clothes struggling with the rear wheel of the large cart. Possibly a broken axle, he thought. There was no chance his master would allow him to stop and assist. Whatever their mission was, it could not be interrupted. Though it was in Tillman's nature to want to provide aide, especially at this late hour, he gave the reins a tug to ease the horses around the broken-down wagon.

To his surprise, from under the tarp that covered the wagon's bed, three men sprang up, each aiming a rifle in his direction. The man who'd been so focused on the cart's rear wheel pulled a pistol–from where he did not see–and put himself in the path of the carriage, forcing it to a jerking halt.

Little good his own pistol had done them, Tillman thought as Eustace Drake shouted from inside the carriage, "Why have we stopped, man! There is no time to procrastinate. Haste, Tillman! Haste!"

The coachman watched in horror as the three riflemen slowly spread themselves out around the carriage. With the pistol-brandishing workman and his cart blocking the way forward and armed men now surrounding them, there was nothing he could do. Even if he managed to get a shot off, that left three other men with guns pointed at him. He'd never be able to survive the volley of gunfire that would inevitably follow.

Since the beginning of the war, highway robbery had become more common. The stories Tillman heard from travelers coming from the west and parts of the south were terrifying. But this close to Parker, with the lights of the city in clear view, it was unthinkable. He could only assume that the scoundrels were not from the area. If they had been, they would have easily recognized the carriage of Eustace Drake and not dared ambush a man with such power and influence in the community. Tillman had seen what happened to men who crossed his employer.

If these highwaymen were simple robbers looking to secure a sizeable prize, they were not going to be pleased when they discovered the carriage was carrying no treasure. Which could end up being another reason in itself to worry about their fate.

"Answer me, Tillman! Why have we stopped?" Drake asked, opening the door to the carriage only to come face-to-face with the barrel of a rifle. "What is this? What is the meaning of this?"

"Wha' does it look like, ole man?"

Eustace Drake, who had built his fortune from nothing and never allowed another man to intimidate him, pushed the rifle aside as if it were a mere twig. Stepping defiantly from the carriage, he straightened his jacket and smoothed the front of his silk vest. Glaring at the gunman before him, he asked through gritted teeth, "Do you know who I am?"

Before another word could be said, all eyes turned toward the unmistakable sound of horses' hooves galloping toward them from the direction Tillman thought he'd seen a light some ways back. Both riders carried lanterns which grew brighter the closer they came, the rumbling growing louder as the two giant horses thundered toward them.

The coachman allowed himself a moment of relief, thinking the robbers would flee rather than confront whoever might be riding to their rescue. It was not until they were close enough for Tillman to see the men on horseback were wearing the uniform of the Confederacy that his heart sank once again. Dirty and tattered, neither soldier looked much older than himself, which would put them in their twenties at most. Practically children, something about the twisted sneers on their faces led him to believe they'd lost their innocence long ago.

When the riflemen did not lower their weapons at the sight of the armed soldiers, Tillman realized what was really happening. This was not a simple robbery. It was an ambush.

"Well, well. Looky what we got here," said the first soldier as he handed his lantern to the other so he could dismount. Scratching the dark stubble on his chin, he locked eyes with the old man before him.

"Who do you think you are?" Drake asked, still standing his ground, not willing to give a single inch or show a modicum of fear. It was simply not in him.

Now in his later sixties, Drake still stood ramrod straight with his shoulders back, and chest puffed out. Still physically fit, if it were not for the pure white beard that hung down to his chest, one would not know he was a man advanced in age. With his jaw firmly set, he stared coolly at the young Confederate officer standing in front of him, taking the measurement of the man.

"Who'm I?" the younger man repeated with a heavy southern drawl. "Well, allow me t' introduce myself, Mr. Drake. The name's Anderson. Lieutenant William Anderson. Som' my friends like t' call me Bloody Bill."

Before he was able to ask why, Anderson pulled his revolver and shot Drake square in the stomach.

Chapter Two

C aleb Post watched from the steps of his boarding house as yet another regiment of Union soldiers marched along Commerce Street. Like the others that passed before, it was heading west towards Sharpsburg, where General George McClellan was hoping to bring an end to Robert E. Lee's Maryland Campaign.

Already, hundreds of wounded soldiers from the battles at South Mountain and Harper's Ferry were being brought to Parker for medical attention. The entire city was being turned into one enormous network of makeshift army hospitals. From the Parker Trading Company building on the Center Square, to the fledgling Hammermill College campus on the north side of town, buildings across the city were being commandeered and repurposed to house the casualties of the recent battles. It was obvious to all, regardless of medical training, that most of the men now lying on cots around the city would not recover. And if the clash between the forces of the North and South in Sharpsburg was as bad as many feared, hundreds–if not thousands–more men would be brought to Parker City to convalesce. And worse.

As one of Sheriff Samuel J. Tildon's deputies, Caleb understood he had an important job helping to bring peace and order to a county now at the center of the action. But that didn't stop him from thinking he should be one of those marching toward the coming fight. He, too, wanted to do his duty and serve his country. Which is exactly what he was already doing, the sheriff reminded him on numerous occasions. Just in a different manner.

Sheriff Tildon could be very philosophical when he wanted. Which was especially impressive for a man who never put too much stock into formal education. Ironic, considering he'd received the very best coming from a prominent family. He much preferred the type of education one received outside of the schoolhouse. The county's chief lawman could be called many things, but a fool was not one of them. Which is why he knew he wasn't going to live forever. So as his age was beginning to catch up with him, he had his eye on the future and knew he needed someone at his side upon whom he could rely. Possibly even step in and replace him one day.

Caleb was honored to be that someone. Having lost his own father at an early age, Tildon, a longtime family friend, took the boy under his wing and practically raised him as one of his own. Now, twenty-four, he was proud to put on the shiny silver star every morning. Even though he was the youngest deputy, the sheriff said he had an old soul and the wisdom to match.

After watching the soldiers for a few more moments march off toward their fate, Caleb started for the Courthouse. The wide brim of his Mosby helped to keep the bright morning sun from his eyes as he made his way along Commerce Street. As the shops began to open, he tipped his hat to their proprietors, all of whom he'd formed friendly relationships with and each of whom appreciated the effort he made to keep Parker's streets free of louts and ruffians during the tumultuous time.

One might have thought, with so many soldiers about, incidents of public disturbance would be nonexistent. But in many cases, it was the soldiers themselves getting into brawls with one another that Caleb and the other deputies would have to break up. These occurrences were particularly prevalent near the taverns. Drunken soldiers who knew the next battle could send them to the grave did not care much for inhibition.

"Good morning, Deputy Post," a young lady said from under her lilac-colored bonnet as she and her mother passed Caleb on their way into Short's Milliner Shoppe.

"Good mornin' to you, Miss Clara," Caleb answered with a tip of the hat and a slight blush on his cheeks. "And to you, Mrs. Worthington."

"Deputy Post," Eleanora Worthington said with a stiff nod of her head.

"Come, Clara. We haven't the time to dawdle, and I am sure the deputy has his own work to see to." With that, she pulled her daughter into the hat shop, leaving Caleb to go on his way.

Caleb Post was a sociable gentleman with a job that came with a great deal of responsibility. It made him a very appealing potential suitor in the eyes of many of the young ladies in the county. However, not all of their parents saw him that way. Parker was very much made up of a few wealthy families and everyone else. Even though Caleb was widely known as being Sheriff Tildon's righthand man—the Tildons being one of Parker's powerful founding families—he was still on the lower rungs of the social ladder.

"Good day to you, Mr. Upton," Caleb said as he rounded the corner and found an elderly shopkeeper cleaning his spectacles on his clean white apron. "Have the Carmack boys been givin' you any more trouble?"

"Not since last you talked to 'em, Caleb. Haven't seen hide nor hair of 'em. I think you might have put the fear of God into 'em."

"I won't say that. I just gave them a stern talkin' to. I'm glad to hear that it worked. I'll be stopping in after work today to pick up some shavin' supplies if you're stocked up."

"I'll put together your usual package," Mr. Upton said with a smile as he walked back into the shop and placed an OPEN sign in the front window.

After a few more blocks and a handful more greetings, the Courthouse was just across the street. But before he could cross, Caleb paused as a phalanx of carts trundled down the road carrying the all-to-familiar sight of wounded soldiers. The last wagon was covered with a bloodstained tarp.

Removing his hat and bowing his head, Caleb knew all too well what lay under the filthy rag.

His heart ached every time a wagon like that passed by. Sadly, the sight was becoming more and more common, not to mention more gruesome, he thought to himself as he darted across the street in front of a painfully slow delivery wagon.

"Watch y'ursself, Deputy Post, or I'll run yas down next time," the driver said with a wink as he sluggishly rumbled by.

No sooner had Caleb reached the other side of the street than a buggy pulled up at his side. He recognized it immediately. It was the sheriff's personal rig. But instead of the sheriff at the reins, it was being driven by Oscar Gimble, another deputy.

"Caleb!" Gimble shouted as he eased the mare to a halt. "Caleb! Sheriff Tildon sent me to fetch you."

"What have you, Oscar?"

"He needs you south of town. They found Eustace Drake's carriage and… well…it ain't purdy."

Chapter Three

I f something had happened to Eustace Drake, Caleb understood why the sheriff would have sent his personal buggy to retrieve him from the Courthouse. Not only was Drake a successful manufacturer in the region, through offhand comments Tildon made, Caleb also gathered the businessman was somehow involved with the federal government in Washington. Though he never asked, he just assumed it had to do with the war.

Everything had to do with the war these days, it seemed.

Caleb took the reins from Gimble once he was settled into the rig, as he was more familiar with Dolly and her idiosyncrasies, having driven the sheriff countless times. For his part, Gimble was happy to simply navigate.

Knowing just how hard he could push the Arabian, Caleb got Dolly up to a decent gallop and headed out of town as Gimble directed. Not much was said between the two. Gimble didn't appear eager to provide Caleb with any information. Whether that was because he'd been instructed not to by the sheriff or because he was fifteen years Caleb's senior and had been sent to fetch him like an errand boy, the younger deputy did not know. There was also the possibility that whatever he had seen left Gimble speechless.

Leaving the morning clamor of the city behind, Caleb finally turned to his companion and asked, "Has something happened to Eustace Drake?"

The look on his fellow deputy's face was puzzling. Caleb still could not understand why Gimble was holding his tongue. He couldn't imagine what he was driving toward, which is why he was becoming increasingly uneasy the further from Parker Dolly took them.

"The trouble is, Post, we don't know what's happened to Mr. Drake," Gimble said out of the side of his mouth, not taking his eyes off the path in front of them.

Before Caleb was able to press Gimble further, he saw Sheriff Tildon with a couple of other men up ahead. They were standing around what he easily recognized as Eustace Drake's carriage. He could tell something wasn't right. The men were clustered around the coach which was sitting abandoned in the middle of the road. Noticeably missing were the fine Thoroughbreds that he always saw pulling it through the streets. All of the men's faces looked ashen and bore serious expressions.

Pulling up alongside the group, Caleb handed the reins back to Gimble and quickly stepped down from the driver's seat.

"Sheriff," he said, tipping his head in greeting.

Samuel Tildon was a man with a round face and an even rounder gut. His once dark amber mutton chops and bushy eyebrows had long since turned gray, hinting at his age. As did the wrinkles and sagging jowls, which had become much more pronounced in recent years. But one look into his bright blue eyes showed he was as sharp as ever.

A bit of a flamboyant dresser by Parker City's standards, the sheriff was wearing his brown and gold checked vest and trousers under his dark overcoat and matching bowler hat. A bright red carnation was affixed to the lapel of his jacket, something the sheriff was well known for.

"We've got trouble, Caleb," Tildon said, using his cigar to point to the open carriage door.

The sheriff could be a man of very few words. But usually only when he was deeply concerned. This was clearly one of those times.

Caleb slowly approached the carriage feeling his heart start to beat just a little faster with each step. He felt a bead of sweat streak down his cheek from under his hat, even though it was a cool morning. The young deputy had no idea what to expect when he stuck his head into the passenger compartment. When he did, the site was more than he could believe. Reflexively, he stepped backwards covering his mouth with his closed fist. After taking a moment to collect himself, he once again looked into the carriage and began to examine the carnage in front of him.

Chapter Four

1984 ...

Detective Sergeant Ben Winters sat in the unmarked police cruiser across the street, watching the building's front door. It was late, and he was getting tired, but after days of trying to track down a burglary suspect, he and his partner thought they might finally have the guy cornered.

Ben compared the time on his watch to the clock on the dashboard. They both read 11:32.

Between him, his partner, and a couple of other officers, they'd had their eyes on the rundown apartment building in Downtown Parker City for the last two days straight. It was reported that their suspect had been seen entering the building but since then had not left. They didn't have enough manpower to do a door-to-door search without taking the chance the guy would do a runner and get away. On top of that, they had no idea which apartment he was hiding out in either. So, Ben made the decision that they'd wait him out. He'd have to leave eventually.

The detective looked at his watch again.

11:33.

He was afraid it was going to be another long night.

If something didn't happen soon, he wasn't sure what he was going to do with himself. Worse yet, if they sat on the building for another few days and the suspect never came out, the chief might order them to drop the stakeout altogether.

Ben started to wonder if the sighting of their suspect had been wrong, and he wasn't even in the building, to begin with. That definitely would not go over well, he thought, watching the ragged bum sitting on the sidewalk a few feet from the door to the apartment building.

For all the talk of revitalizing the city's downtown, and the projects that had begun, there was still a long way to go. Ben remembered when Parker's Downtown was a bustling corridor of restaurants and shops. It was a booming city center back in the '50s and '60s. Then the economic downturn of the '70s hit, followed by the Great Flood of 1978, and the heart of the city was left in ruins. Boarded-up buildings, abandoned storefronts, graffitied walls. Even the four magnificent, historic Pre-Civil War buildings that made up the city's Center Square and used to house Parker's oldest companies now sat empty and derelict.

11:34.

Ben looked at the magazine sitting on the seat beside him. He'd already read it cover-to-cover and finished the crossword puzzle in the back. He wasn't sure why tonight seemed so much more difficult than the previous ones. Maybe it was because he was starting to think they'd made a mistake, and all of this was just a waste of time and resources.

Pushing the magazine aside, he picked up the case file sitting under it and started to thumb through the pages. Their suspect was one Roosevelt "Rooster" Jones. Why he had the street name "Rooster," Ben had no idea. And it didn't seem like anyone he talked to knew either. Over the years, he'd been arrested for a half dozen burglaries and a handful of B&Es. He wasn't exactly dangerous, but at thirty, to have already racked up such a list of offenses, he was definitely a "menace" in the loosest sense of the word.

Ben looked once again at the mug shot paperclipped to the inside of the folder.

There was nothing particularly remarkable looking about Jones. He was a young black guy with short hair, big eyes, and a beaklike nose. Maybe that was why he was called Rooster, Ben thought as he tossed the folder back onto the seat.

Jones's latest crime–*allegedly*–was robbing the apartment of one of his grandmother's neighbors. Coming up with a suspect was pretty easy. Not that Jones made it all that difficult. The smartest thing he'd done since committing the burglary was *not* going home. If he'd only been as dumb as so many others and gone straight back to his apartment, they'd have had him in a holding cell the same day. Four days later, however, Ben was sitting in his car, bundled up on a cold October night, hoping they'd found Rooster Jones's hiding place.

Chapter Five

Drumming his fingers on the steering wheel, Ben found his mind wandering from one topic to the next. He couldn't help thinking about the paperwork sitting on his desk that desperately needed his attention or the fact his fiancée was still waiting for him to officially decide who his groomsmen were going to be.

Since the string of police shootings early in the summer, everything had been a blur. Three police officers were gunned down in a span of three days, setting off a city-wide manhunt for the killer. A manhunt Ben was overseeing as the head of the Parker City Police Department's Detective Squad. A squad consisting only of himself and his partner.

The investigation had been intense and attracted quite a bit of attention. Remarkably enough, it was the pair's second big case in their short time as detectives. The first was the Spring Strangler back in '81. Police officers could go their entire careers without being involved in any major cases. Now, having just turned thirty, Ben had already been involved with two cases that had garnered national attention.

If the details of the cases weren't enough to interest the press, the fact Ben and his partner were practically just out of the police academy and already serving as detectives only added to the sensational stories. But three years earlier, when the mayor, who was proving himself time and time again to be a forward-thinking city executive, ordered the then-chief to create a specialized detective squad dedicated to handling the department's criminal investigations, Ben was tapped to head the new team because he was young, innovative, and didn't have the sense to turn down such a fraught position.

At the time, the PCPD was still very much stuck in the past. A small police force doing things the way they'd been done for decades. That wasn't good enough for a mayor trying to revive the city. He knew crime rates needed to be brought under control before his revitalization plans could really have an impact. He wanted the Parker Police to be a modern law enforcement agency. And to do that, they needed a modern investigative unit.

Not that the small city in western Maryland was a hotbed of criminal activity. It was certainly no Baltimore or Washington, DC, both of which were only about an hour away. But Parker had its fair share of criminal offenders. Up until the Spring Strangler struck, though, it had been almost ten years since there'd been an actual homicide in the city.

As far as major cases went, the Detective Squad was two-for-two. But as Parker City continued to grow, which would naturally bring more crime in addition to the prosperity everyone was anticipating, Ben was hoping their luck didn't run out. Only time would tell. For now, though, he was all right dealing with random burglaries and minor crimes.

Just as he remembered he'd tossed a new book he'd heard about by an author named Tom Clancy in the backseat that morning, so he had something to read, he saw two young black men exit the apartment building and light up a pair of cigarettes. The single bulb hanging haphazardly above the building's entrance wasn't very bright, making it difficult for Ben to tell if one of the guys was their suspect. Squinting to try and make an ID, he didn't want to make a move without being certain. Then he saw what he needed to confirm that one of the guys was Rooster Jones. It looked as though *The Hunt for Red October* would have to go on without him for the time being.

Quickly exiting the car, Ben sprinted across the street, one hand resting on the gun on his hip.

"Roosevelt Jones," he said as he approached the men. "I'm Detective Ben Winters with the Par..."

He never had the chance to finish.

Jones turned and took off down the sidewalk.

"Don't run!" Ben shouted after him. Not that he thought that would actually work.

Before the guy could hit his stride, Ben watched as the vagrant who he'd had his eyes on all evening sprang into Jones's path knocking him to the pavement.

Straddling him, the man dug around in the layers of dirty clothing he was wearing and pulled out a badge hanging from a chain around his neck.

"My partner was trying to introduce himself to you, Rooster," the bum said. "So, let's try this again. That is Detective Ben Winters. I'm Detective Tommy Mason. We're with the PCPD, and you, dirtbag, are under arrest."

Chapter Six

It took both Ben and Tommy to get Rooster Jones on his feet, cuffed, and into the car. He didn't make it easy on them. Thankfully, his friend stood by silently smoking his cigarette and did not try to interfere with the arrest. Something else that made Jones angry. With all his yelling, he managed to wake up everyone in the building. By the time Tommy closed the car door, muffling his protests, there were faces peering out every window, watching the action unfold below.

The drive back to the station was filled with creative expletives and shouts from the backseat. Even Tommy found himself shocked by some of the things their collar was spouting. Though he did find himself trying to stifle a laugh every now and then. Rooster had a way with words, and being couped up in hiding for the last several days clearly had caused some build-up of frustration that he needed to let out.

Ben kept his eyes on the road while Tommy absentmindedly flipped through the Clancy novel his partner brought along to read.

"You know, if they ever make a movie of this, I think I could play the Ryan guy," Tommy said, closing the book.

"Did you just read the ending of the book?" Ben asked.

"Yeah. Don't worry. They find the sub."

"What?"

"They find the sub. You know, they're *hunting* for Red October."

"Man, that ain't funny at all," Rooster said from the backseat.

"Hey! Nobody asked you," Tommy said, turning around and giving the wannabe street tough a dirty look. "My humor is an acquired taste."

19

"How many times have I told you not to get into an argument with our suspect over your bad jokes?" Ben asked as he turned into the PCPD's parking lot. "But he isn't wrong. It wasn't one of your better jokes."

"Well, excuse me, but it's late, and I'm tired. Not to mention half frozen after standing around outside all night."

"It was your idea to dress up like a homeless person and wait outside the door for him to come out."

"Yeah. I did it so if he came out of the building, I could ID this schmuck, and we could arrest him. Which he did. And I did. And we did. So...you're welcome."

"There really is no talking to you when you're in this kind of a mood."

Ben Winters and Tommy Mason had been friends since they were children. They'd grown up together, gone to school together, attended the police academy together, and were now partners. At times, they were also like an old married couple.

When they'd been tapped to form the department's Detective Squad, everyone thought it was a suicide mission. But together, they'd shown everyone what a formidable team they were. Three years later, with two major cases under their belts, they were no longer the butt of jokes around the locker room.

Yanking Rooster out of the backseat by his collar, Tommy guided him toward the backdoor of the station where the booking officer would take him into custody and show him to his temporary accommodations in the holding cells.

"I think since I'm the one who had to dress up in these smelly rags, you should have to fill out all the paperwork on this one."

"Again. It was your idea."

"See, you keep dwelling on that part. I thought *you'd* rather do the paperwork. You know how I am with those damn forms. And you like forms. I see the way you try and hide that smile when you're checking off those little boxes."

Ignoring the remark, Ben turned to the desk sergeant on duty. "Evening, Tony. We got him. It took a couple of days, but we got him."

"You just made some of the boys real happy," the officer said with a smirk. "We got a pool going on whether or not he was in the building."

"And you didn't let me in on the action?" Tommy asked incredulously.

"You know very well it wouldn't have been fair if we let you in on it."

"You both know how wrong that is, don't you?" Ben said.

"What?" Tony asked, pulling out the paperwork he was going to need to start processing Rooster Jones. "The fact we're betting on you arresting someone or the fact we're talking about betting on you arresting someone *in front* of the actual perp?"

"I give up," Ben said, rolling his eyes. "Just get this guy behind bars. Please."

Chapter Seven

E ven though it was well after midnight by the time he and Tommy had gotten Jones all squared away, Ben still headed up to the second floor, where the Detective Squad had its small office. A converted storage closet that was just big enough for a couple of desks and pair of filing cabinets, it was cramped, but it had been the detectives' base of operations for the last three years. It wasn't much to brag about, but it kept them from having to work out of the over-crowded, noisy bullpen the patrol officers used on the first floor. If nothing else, they had a door they could close if they wanted some peace and quiet from the constant dull roar created by all the activity throughout the old station house.

Rumor was that the chief had a plan to reorganize the department, which included expanding the Detective Squad. Being as there was no possible way to fit anyone else into the space they now occupied, new accommodations for the team would have to be provided. Even if they were moved into the basement, Ben would take it if it meant they had more room to spread out.

Before he left for the evening, Ben wanted to leave a message for Chief Brent that the stakeout had been a success and Jones was in custody. There was a time when Ben would be in before the chief each morning, so would have been able to tell him himself first thing. But that was back when Edgar Stanley was chief and didn't come in until close to lunchtime. That was in "the old days." With Nicholas Brent now running the department, it was a breath of fresh air to show up at seven in the morning and find that the chief had already arrived and made a fresh pot of coffee.

Ben and Chief Brent worked very well together. Much better than he and Stanley. What could one expect, though, when the former chief was counting on the new detectives to fail? Stanley was the embodiment of everything that was wrong with the department at the time. He'd been chief since God was a child and liked everything to be done the way it always had. He saw no reason to change things. Ben and Tommy had been charged, specifically, with modernizing the way the department investigated crime.

Shuffling a handful of files from one side of his desk to the other, Ben placed the Roosevelt "Rooster" Jones folder on top of the stack. He would finalize all the paperwork in the morning and then send everything over to the State's Attorney's Office. He and Tommy had done their part. It was up to the prosecutors now.

Even though he wanted to continue straightening up his desk, having only slept a few hours over the last several days, exhaustion was beginning to set in. Ben was even thinking he might come in a couple of hours late in the morning. Unheard of for him. The list of open cases he and Tommy were currently working was not long or particularly pressing. Thankfully, there were no major crime waves sweeping the city at the moment.

Chapter Eight

Across town, the silver crosses atop the twin steeples of Saint Paul's Roman Catholic Church glistened in the moonlight. Built some hundred and fifty years earlier, it was one of the oldest churches in Parker and remained the largest Catholic congregation until the 1970s when the city's economy bottomed out. As residents moved out of Parker, Saint Paul's saw its numbers dwindle to a fraction of what they once were.

A stately church with steeples that towered one hundred and thirty feet in the air, Saint Paul's cast a long shadow–literally and figuratively–over the neighborhood surrounding it. Like so many of the buildings found around the city, it had a storied history. From being one of the very first churches in the Archdiocese of Baltimore to serving temporarily as a makeshift headquarters for Stonewall Jackson during the Civil War. One Sunday in the late-'50s, then-Senator John Kennedy even attended mass there.

Parker City was still very much a protestant town, but Saint Paul's had made its mark.

Most recently, the church found itself in the headlines when a new priest was assigned to lead the congregation. A community activist and energetic man of faith, Father Roland Taylor took the reins of the church from the retiring monsignor, making him the first black priest to celebrate mass at the historic twin-towered Saint Paul's.

Father Taylor immediately went to work, introducing himself to the community and letting everyone know he was not there to rock the boat. He was not a radical new-age priest who was going to turn everything on its head. He had ideas about how to strengthen the church's bond with the

24

neighborhood by building on and honoring the hard work of so many at Saint Paul's who had come before him. Taylor quickly became an influential and trusted community leader. Something not easy to do in Parker when you begin as an "outsider," which Taylor was transferring from Ohio.

While there were some in the wider Parker community that frowned on a black man leading one of the city's oldest churches, the majority of residents who took the opportunity to get to know him found Roland Taylor to be a charming and charismatic man full of hope and optimism.

Before he retired to his private apartment above the church offices each evening, Father Taylor always took one last stroll through the chapel to center himself. On nights when there was a clear sky and the moon shone bright, the heavenly images in the stained-glass windows glowed. The first time he'd seen them like that, it took his breath away. Months later, the feeling was still the same.

After a long day, Father Taylor was finally ready to turn in for the night. Passing the corridor leading to his private office, he noticed a dim light shining through the frosted glass window in the door. He would have sworn he turned off all the lights when he packed up for the evening. It was late, and he was tired, so maybe he'd forgotten to turn off his desk lamp. It wouldn't have been the first time, he thought, heading down the hallway to his office.

Fumbling in his pocket for his keys, he thought he heard someone moving around on the other side of the door. Pausing, he couldn't imagine one of the church secretaries had come back to the office this late. Bonnie and Hester were dedicated to Saint Paul's without question. But nothing could have been that important for them to have returned at midnight. Let alone let themself into his office. For that matter, Hester was out of town.

As quietly as possible, Father Taylor unlocked the door and eased it open. Letting out a sigh of relief, feeling a little foolish, he saw that he hadn't turned off the green banker's lamp on his desk. Then he noticed the bookcase behind his desk. All of the books had been pulled from the shelves and tossed on the floor.

"What in the...?" he said, stepping into the office and turning on the overhead lights.

As the fluorescents lit the room, the puzzled priest stopped, standing in stunned silence. His office had been ransacked. The drawers of his desk rummaged through, the contents thrown unceremoniously about, the file cabinets emptied of church documents and official papers.

Greatly disturbed by what he saw, he also felt a modicum of relief that nothing of true value appeared to have been touched. The gilded framed icons still hung on the wall; the antique Byzantine candlesticks sat on the credenza on either side of the glass case displaying the church's original charter signed by Archbishop John Carroll in 1810.

Across the room, the door leading to the outer office sat wide open. Its frosted windowpane shattered. Taylor fought the immediate urge to check the other offices to see if they'd also been vandalized. Instead, he did the responsible thing and went straight to the telephone on his desk to call the police.

His mind was racing as he dialed the operator. Who would have broken into his office? Who would have broken into *a church*? What could they have been looking for? Was it just a prank?

Crunch.

Taylor froze.

The silence was broken by the sound of…what? His grip on the receiver tightened when he realized someone had walked in behind him and stepped on the shattered glass by the door.

The priest turned just in time to see one of the Byzantine candlesticks arching toward him.

Chapter Nine

1862...

He had seen many discomforting sights since the beginning of the war, but the beaten and bloodied body lying on the floor of the otherwise majestic carriage was going to give Caleb nightmares for some time to come. Casting his eyes around the passenger compartment, the young deputy tried to carefully observe the entire picture. From the streaks of blood cascading along the ceiling to the unrecognizable, disfigured face of the deceased, he worked to commit everything he saw to memory. As gruesome as it may be, he didn't want to overlook anything.

Without a word, he examined the scene making mental observations as he went. From the position of the body to the state in which the carriage had been left, he noted each detail. Tuning out the conversation of the men behind him, Caleb was in his own world. His focus was complete and uninterruptable. From examining the most minute tear in the fine leather upholstery to the crusted dirt on the victim's well-worn boots, nothing and no one could distract him.

Sheriff Tildon knew not to interrupt Caleb when he was like this. Some might think he was possessed or under a spell, but the sheriff understood how quickly the gears in his deputy's brain were wheeling away. When he was ready, after he'd taken as much time as needed, Caleb would give his report. Until then, the sheriff and the others would wait.

Deputy Gimble, frustrated by what he viewed as theatrical actions by his junior colleague, paced haphazardly around the sheriff's buggy. With his oversized coat and floppy-brimmed hat, Gimble's boxy frame made him look much more squat than he actually was in reality.

"Oscar," the sheriff said before blowing a thick cloud of blue cigar smoke into the air. "Stop your damnable fidgeting. You're making Dolly nervous. If she takes off with my rig, I'll be riding you back to the Courthouse, mark my words."

"Yes, sir," Gimble grumbled. "It's jus' that...I mean...What's he doing?"

"He's trying to figure out what happened here, is what he's doing."

"I think it's pretty obvious what happened. Highwaymen robbed old man Drake and killed him."

"We don't know with certainty that Eustace Drake is dead," Caleb said, finally turning his attention away from the carriage. "And I'm not ready to agree that this was a simple robbery."

"What?" Gimble asked. "What do you think happened?"

"Well, I'm sure I don't know yet. But what I do know is that that body does not belong to Eustace Drake. The clothing is not of the expensive quality befitting one of Parker's leading citizens. And, though it is hard to make out the features of his face...as badly beaten as it is...he has no facial hair. So, unless Mr. Drake decided after decades of wearing a finely cultivated beard to shave his face clean... And if you still need to be convinced, all you need do is look at his hands."

"Look at his hands? What are you on about, Post?" Gimble didn't like feeling as though he was being lectured.

"If you wipe away the blood, you'll see the hands belong to a younger man. Judging by the placement of some of the calluses on the poor devil's palms, I would venture to guess that body belongs to Eustace Drake's coachman."

"Jonathan Tillman," offered the man standing next to the sheriff. Caleb recognized him as a dairyman he'd seen making deliveries around town. He had the unmistakable complexion of a man who spent most of his time outside in the sun.

"And you are?" Caleb asked.

"Me? I'm Wilkins. Moses Wilkins. It was me what come across this. Me and my boy, that is. I sent him there to get the sheriff straight away. Ghastly sight."

"Did you remain here with the coach while your son went for Sheriff Tildon?"

"I did."

"And everything is exactly as you found it?"

"Is."

Caleb saw that the milkman's horse and wagon were being tended to by Wilkins's boy several yards from the carriage. The younger Wilkins, the deputy judged, was in his late-teen years. Most likely learning the family trade.

Where were the two horses that would have brought the carriage to this point? Could they have been what the coachman was killed for? But then why not simply take the Thoroughbreds? Why beat and kill Tillman? And more importantly, Caleb thought, where was Eustace Drake?

Deputy Gimble cleared his throat, interrupting Caleb's train of thought. "I think the first thing we need to do is go round to Drake House and see about the whereabouts of Mr. Drake. Tillman could have been on an errand for 'em. He may be tucked up snug in his bed right now."

"I doubt that, Oscar," Caleb said, shaking his head. "Though I very much hope I'm wrong. I fear Eustace Drake may have been the target of this attack from the beginning."

"Now, wait just a minute. You said you didn't think…."

"I said I didn't think this was just some robbery by a group of common highwaymen who happened to have the good fortune to come upon one of Parker's wealthiest men. I believe Mr. Drake may very well have been a target all along."

"What makes you think that?" the sheriff asked. He would never doubt his young protégé, but that didn't mean he wasn't going to make inquiries into his line of thinking.

"Well, if you will notice," Caleb said, walking back to the carriage, "there appears to be a bullet hole here on the side panel and blood on the ground in this area."

"That could belong to the coachman," Tildon pointed out.

"Except," Caleb held up a finger, "upon my examination of the body–though brief–I did not find any bullet wounds. That would indicate someone else was shot while standing here. Then most probably fell to the ground after the bullet traveled through them and exited into the side of the coach. Which would account for the large amount of blood here."

"It don't mean it was Drake," Gimble chimed in.

"True," Caleb agreed. "However, this was laying just by the wheel not more than a foot from this large stain of blood." Reaching into his vest pocket, he withdrew a silver pocket watch. Snapping it open, he revealed the etched initials E.A.D. "Eustace Alan Drake. Mr. Drake was most certainly here. And if this expensive timepiece was left behind, along with the equally expensive diamond-studded walking stick I found in the back of the carriage, I very much doubt this had anything to do with robbery. What's more, whoever did this, didn't even try to make it *look* like highway robbery."

"Nicely done, Caleb, my boy," the sheriff said with a smile. His feeling of pride in the young man was dampened by the growing realization that one of the city's most powerful men might have been snatched out of his own carriage for God only knows what reason.

"We do still need to pay a visit to Drake House like Oscar suggests," Caleb concluded. "If for no other reason than to inquire as to the last time anyone saw Mr. Drake."

Tossing the butt of his cigar into the grass and climbing into his buggy, Tildon said, "Then we should get this over with. If something has happened to Eustace Drake, there are going to be a lot of people banging on my door. Gimble, you stay here and watch the body. I'll send Doc Crum to collect it and you. Mr. Wilkins, if we have any further questions, we'll call on you. Thank you for your help here today."

Before Caleb was even seated, the sheriff gave the reins a slap and pointed Dolly back in the direction of the city. Tildon brought the horse up to a near gallop before easing off and leaning back in his seat. There was no time to waste.

As the carriage bounced along the dirt road, Caleb turned to his mentor and said, "I fear I might have frustrated Oscar again."

"Don't think about it. Deputy Gimble is frustrated because he doesn't have the wits that you possess. You are what the Europeans call a wunderkind."

"That's not a term I'm familiar with."

Tildon smiled to himself. Maybe there were a few things he could still teach the boy after all.

Chapter Ten

D rake House was a magnificent manor only a few blocks from the Courthouse. Situated behind an ornate wrought iron fence that encircled the entire property, the red brick façade was accented with stark white Italian marble trim and corbels around each of the windows and doors. Eustace Drake had been very particular regarding its design. Having grown up in a small three-room house with his parents and five brothers and sisters always within arm's reach of one another, it was now important for him to put his wealth and success on display. To him, that meant having a house with an excess number of rooms on a piece of land that covered nearly an entire city block of its own. It was a grand home indeed, Caleb thought, as the sheriff pulled his rig to the curb in front of the estate.

In some towns, a private residence the size of Drake House might stand out as an oddity. However, the mansion was not the only one of its size in Parker City. Grandview Avenue, which ran along the north side of Jefferson Park, was where the city's oldest and wealthiest families lived. The address was sought after by all of Parker's gentry. In fact, each of the five founding families had their homes side-by-side along the street. This included Sheriff Tildon's own boyhood home. Though his older brother, Jonah, was presently master of the house.

Eustace Drake did not inherit his fortune as had most of his neighbors. He was the son of a butcher who, through drive, tenacity, and sheer force of will, built a small textile manufacturing empire from the ground up; and with the advances in tanning made over the last decade, he was quickly becoming the region's largest producer of leather goods.

His position in the city was not just that of a leader of commerce, he was also active in the community. Though Drake could be detached and hard at times, he was the benefactor of a number of Parker's charitable organizations. Most believed it was really his wife who encouraged him to support the various causes, for he might not do so of his own accord.

If something had befallen the man, there would, without a doubt, be an uproar throughout the city. Drake's peers would demand to know what happened to one of their own. In turn, Caleb knew the sheriff would be under extreme pressure to find the culprit, or culprits, behind the crime.

"Let me do the talking," Sheriff Tildon said, stepping down from the driver's seat and tying Dolly to a hitching post. "We don't know for certain anything has happened to Drake. So, we don't want to worry anyone. Tread lightly in there, my boy."

As he jumped down from his seat, Caleb noticed another carriage sitting across the street. It shouldn't have attracted his notice except for the fact a soldier in a finely pressed blue uniform sat in the driver's seat. And another, with a rifle over his shoulder, stood at its rear. The calash itself was not the type he'd become accustomed to seeing used by the army. Instead, it looked like one he would expect to see along Grandview Avenue traveling between the stately houses. It was the soldiers that seemed out of place. Though there were now so many roaming the streets of Parker, why these particular men caught Caleb's attention, he was not sure.

Locking eyes, Caleb and the rifleman quickly sized each other up. In the first half of his twenties, Caleb may have been young, but his appearance and deportment led people to assume he was older. Standing over six feet with broad shoulders, his otherwise thin frame was concealed by the rugged duster he always wore. In a fight, Caleb preferred to rely on his wits rather than brute force…or guns. But if circumstances demanded, he did wear a pistol on each hip.

Looking at the soldier across the street, he thought it must be the exact opposite for him. A decent six inches shorter than himself, there was something in the rifleman's expression that said he was not someone with whom you wanted to brawl. It was something in his eyes–a fierceness barely contained.

Caleb snapped to as Tildon called to him from halfway up the walk. Quickening his step to catch up, he straightened his vest and removed his hat as the sheriff used the large brass doorknocker to announce their arrival. What seemed an eternity later, the door was opened by an older man dressed in traditional butler's livery.

"Good morning," the sheriff said, tipping his hat. "Is the master of the house available?"

"I am afraid not," the man said in a rather shaky voice.

"And the lady of the house?"

"I'm sorry, but Mrs. Drake is otherwise occupied."

"This is official business." Opening his jacket, Tildon revealed the silver star on his vest. "We do need to speak with Mrs. Drake regarding an urgent matter."

"If you will please wait in the parlor, I will let Mrs. Drake know you are here."

The parlor was as Caleb expected. Expensive furniture surrounded by paintings taking up nearly every spare inch of space on the walls. Taking seats opposite one another on a pair of chairs, Caleb could only assume came from Europe because of their distinct design, he asked, "Sheriff, did you notice the Union soldiers across the street? One of them appeared to be paying particular attention to this house."

"The city is teaming with soldiers, Caleb. It would be hard to look anywhere and *not* see a uniform."

That point certainly could not be argued. But at the same time…

Before he could finish his thought, the manservant reappeared in the doorway, a sour expression on his wrinkled face.

"If you gentlemen will follow me, please. Mrs. Drake will see you." With that, he turned on his heels and began shuffling down the hallway. Caleb and the sheriff quickly got to their feet and followed after him.

Drake House was as impressive on the inside as it was on the outside. A rich green velvet wall covering was itself covered with dozens of oil paintings running the length of the main hall, which Caleb felt went on forever. Passing by several rooms whose doors sat open, he could see more European furnishings and paintings, making him wonder if this was what the inside of a French castle looked like. The opulence was a far cry from the sparse furnishings in his room back at the boarding house.

At the end of the hallway, the butler showed them into a conservatory with windows that reached from the floor to the ceiling. The view of the garden outside beyond the windows was exquisite. Even more remarkable, though, was the marble fireplace, which was flanked on either side by two imposing wingback chairs. Seated in one was Margaret Drake, the lady of the house. A sturdy woman, her round shape took up most of the chair. The excessive layers of lace and frills on her dress filled the rest. In the second chair sat General George McClellan, commander of the Army of the Potomac.

Chapter Eleven

"General McClellan?" Sheriff Tildon said when he saw the military commander unexpectedly sitting there. The tone in his voice betrayed his surprise. If it was true that thousands of troops were about to begin another battle any day, it would have been wild to expect to find the Union general this far from the battlefield. But there he sat. Dressed in his full uniform, boots polished and saber glistening.

"Hello, Sheriff," McClellan responded without getting up. His eyes quickly traveled across the two lawmen standing before him; stone-faced, not giving away any emotion.

The men had met not long before when the Army of the Potomac set up a temporary headquarters in Parker City in preparation for the stand against Lee and his troops. But to Tildon's knowledge, the general had departed several days earlier to take up personal command on the battlefield near Sharpsburg.

"What is it that Mrs. Drake can do for you, gentlemen?" McClellan asked, not giving Margaret Drake the chance to speak for herself.

"Well, General, my deputy and I needed to have a word with Mrs. Drake about a private matter. I hate to disturb her but it's official business, you understand?"

As the wife of a successful businessman, Margaret Drake herself was accustomed to being in the presence of powerful men. Which was to say, she understood their egos. Sensing the tension beginning to build in the room, the elderly woman–who Caleb had the distinct impression could handle herself in any situation–cleared her throat and said, "Sheriff, General

McClellan is a trusted friend. Anything you need to speak with me about can surely be discussed in front of him."

Tildon thought for a moment then cast his eyes in Caleb's direction. With a slight nod of his head, he gave him the unspoken signal to proceed. For Caleb's part, he was a little surprised the sheriff felt it was appropriate for him, a simple deputy, to interview someone of Margaret Drake's status. Let alone, in front of George McClellan. Hadn't he said he should be the one to do the talking?

"Good morning, Mrs. Drake. We're sorry to bother you at this hour," Caleb began, quickly trying to establish his footing. "But the sheriff and I needed to know when the last time was you saw your husband."

Watching for the smallest reaction, Caleb saw Mrs. Drake's lips pursed ever so slightly. It was only for the briefest of seconds, but he'd seen it.

"Why, Deputy...I'm sorry. I didn't...I don't believe we've been introduced."

"I beg your pardon, ma'am. Deputy Post. Caleb Post." He realized he was fidgeting with the brim of his hat as he held it in front of him like some sort of shield.

"I don't believe I know any Posts. Is your family from Parker?"

"Margaret," the sheriff gently interrupted. "We're looking for Eustace. When was the last time you saw him?"

With a slight laugh that Caleb thought sounded forced and very unnatural, she answered, "He's in his room presently. Sleeping. He had a very trying evening. He cannot be disturbed." She then immediately turned her eyes toward McClellan.

"We really hate to wake him," Caleb offered, "but it would help us greatly if we could speak with him."

"You heard Mrs. Drake," McClellan's voice boomed like a cannon firing in the sitting room. "Mr. Drake is not to be disturbed. I insist you explain what this is all about."

"Very well, General. This morning, Mr. Drake's carriage was found south of town, abandoned and horseless. His coachman, one Mr. Jonathan Tillman, was found beaten to death inside the carriage. And this was found near a pool of blood on the ground."

Caleb withdrew the pocket watch from his vest pocket and held it out for the two to see. At the sight of the timepiece, Margaret Drake clasped a hand over her mouth and began to cry. McClellan, sitting forward in his chair, reached across the empty space between them and took her free hand in a comforting gesture.

Lowering his voice, the general said, "Sheriff Tildon, Deputy Post, I think we should leave Mrs. Drake and speak outside."

Chapter Twelve

Following the general out onto the back porch of Drake House, Caleb, and the sheriff silently watched as McClellan leaned against the iron railing and lit a cigarette. Neither knew if they should speak or wait for the general to initiate the conversation. This wasn't a situation in which they frequently found themselves.

Breaking the silence, McClellan asked, "Would either of you care for a cigarette?"

"I prefer a good cigar," the sheriff said with a half-smile as he took a silver case from his pocket and began the ritual of lighting the dark brown roll of tobacco.

"Deputy?"

"Thank you, sir. But I never cared much for the tobacco."

"Uh-huh…"

Taking another drag of his cigarette, McClellan turned and looked out over the manicured lawn, his eyes fixing on some point in the distance. Caleb wondered if this was how the man looked when he was surveying the battlefield. Even as the leaves on the trees had begun to brown in some spots and the plants were entering their cold-weather stage, the gardens still looked so much more pleasant than what the soldier had been surrounded by as of late.

At only thirty-five, to hold the position of Commander of the Army of the Potomac, Caleb was somewhat in awe of the general. But the man's fierce, dark eyes seemed to hold the explanation for his success. There was a drive–a fire–burning inside them. As Caleb understood, though, this drive had earned McClellan something of a reputation, which is why he knew they needed to tread lightly. With a major battle expected to break out at any moment, for McClellan to have left the field to return to Parker City unannounced on the same day Eustace Drake turned up missing...something serious was afoot.

"I'm sorry, General, but Mr. Drake is not upstairs in his room, is he?" Caleb's question was met with a chilling silence.

"If something has happened to Eustace, we need to know," the sheriff added.

Without taking his eyes off the horizon, absentmindedly running his finger along his mustache, McClellan asked, "You don't believe this could have been highway robbers? The stories I've heard are very troubling. It's gotten so one can't travel some roads at all without fear of being highjacked...or worse. Especially in the south. But what can you expect of those *seceshes*? A bunch of barbarians."

Still fiddling with the brim of his hat, Caleb said, "I don't know much about that, sir. But we don't believe this was a common highway robbery. We've never had an occurrence of that nature around Parker City. But if it were, why would they've left behind Mr. Drake's pocket watch and an expensive walkin' stick? Surely items like that would have been the first things they snatched."

"There was nothing else found in the carriage? No papers? Documents of any kind?"

"No, sir. I examined it myself. The inside had been torn to pieces as if an animal had had at it." Caleb stopped, realizing the implication of McClellan's question. "Or as if somebody was lookin' for something important that might be hidden."

McClellan, cutting his eyes sideways toward Caleb, flicked his cigarette butt into the lawn without saying a word.

"General?" the sheriff prodded. "What is it you're not telling us?"

Turning on them, McClellan, in a most commanding voice, declared, "Gentlemen, there are forces at work here that you cannot comprehend. I suggest you leave this matter rest."

Before either Tildon or Caleb could offer a protest, the general marched passed them defiantly, as the soldier he was, back into the house.

"What do we do now, Sheriff?"

"Caleb, my boy, you don't need to have horse sense to know that uppity blowhard knows something about what happened to Drake. Obviously, it has something to do with this damnable war. I need to get back to the Courthouse and make some inquiries. General McClellan is unquestionably an important man. But let's not forget, I am not without my own influence and resources."

"What would you like for me to do?"

"Stay here and see if you can get any of the servants to tell you where their master went yesterday. When they saw him last. If he'd had any curious guests here at the house recently."

"How can I do that? If Mrs. Drake won't let anyone talk to me…."

"You are a very charming young man," the sheriff said with a smile. "I'm certain you will figure something out."

Chapter Thirteen

Several miles from the Drake House, and not terribly far from where Eustace Drake's carriage had been discovered, Dr. Joseph Aspen was finishing his morning rounds at the Aspen House Hospital. Purposely built on the outermost edge of town, the wealthy families that controlled the goings-on of the city could not possibly have fathomed a mental asylum being constructed anywhere near their beloved homes in the heart of Parker City. So, a compromise was reached with Dr. Aspen. He could build his facility, but it needed to be as far from Parker's Center Square as possible. It wasn't that these powerful individuals didn't believe a sanitarium was necessary. They just didn't want to have to see or think about the poor unfortunate souls that would be housed within its walls. Even if some of the patients were their very own family members.

A newcomer to Parker City, Joseph Aspen was revered for his medical research. And though his hospital was something upon which no one wanted to draw public attention, he, himself, was always welcomed with open arms to any and all social functions around town. The stories of his research and experiments fascinated party-goers. Quite frequently, it was those of the fairer sex who were most intrigued to learn about the workings of the brain. While the doctor could not discuss all of the experiments he conducted within his asylum, some of the details being far too shocking, he was always happy to regale a gathering with tales of his less gory work.

As of late, he'd become something of a celebrity at the various house parties along Grandview Avenue. Young, handsome, and charismatic, Joseph Aspen had a way of making the ladies blush while not appearing to cross any lines of propriety. Coming from humble means, he was enjoying the benefits of his newfound status, even if he did fully understand both he and his work were considered something of an oddity.

After giving his final lunchtime instructions to the stern matron who oversaw the nurses at the hospital, the doctor disappeared down a rarely used corridor on the first floor behind the surgical theater. At the end of the hall was a large iron door, much like the ones in the asylum's attic, behind which were roomed the more "troubled" patients. Unlocking the two heavy bolts that secured the door, Aspen slipped through the opening into the cool, damp corridor on the other side. Throwing the bolts behind him to prevent anyone from following, he started down the stone staircase. Candle sconces lined the walls lighting his way down to another corridor that ran beneath the hospital.

Underground and surrounded by stone walls, the near-constant shrieks of patients were completely muffled. In the basement rooms, he could escape the noise and think. Here he could plan and study away from his staff and the hospital's residents. This was also where he could perform the experiments that could not be done in view of anyone with a moral or ethical conscience. Aspen was well aware that some of his work would be considered too shocking to allow to proceed if certain authorities learned of his actions. But that was never going to stop him.

Passing doors on either side of the passage, he stopped at the end of the hall. A second iron door, slightly smaller than the one at the top of the stairs, stood between him and the voices on the other side. Stepping into the room, he surveyed the men around the table. Seated on one side, in his usual place, was William McClinton scribbling in his ever-present notebook. Across from him, with their ever-present grim expressions, Silas Moss and Thaddeus Parker. And at the far end, leaning back in his chair with his muddy boots on the table was Bloody Bill Anderson.

Chapter Fourteen

1984...

The best-laid plans, Ben thought to himself as he parked in front of Saint Paul's Roman Catholic Church on Braddock Street. His hope of getting a few extra hours of sleep after spending the last several nights out late on a stakeout was shattered just a little after eight in the morning. The ringing of the telephone entwined seamlessly with his dream of being a concert violinist making his debut at Carnegie Hall. Something he could not in any way understand because he couldn't play any instrument, let alone the violin. It wasn't until the conductor in his dream started to tell him to leave his name and number after the beep that he realized he was hearing his own voice on the message answering machine.

With bleary eyes, he crossed out of the bedroom and into the kitchen, grabbing the telephone just as Shirley, one of the PCPD's dispatchers, was about to hang up.

"Hello. Hello?" he answered, trying to shake away the mental cobwebs.

"Hey, sweetie," Shirley said with her slight southern drawl. "Sorry to wake you."

"I wasn't...I mean, I..."

"It's okay, sugar. I heard you and Tommy were out late. But you got 'em, so it's all good."

"Yeah. We did. What's going on?"

"I'm afraid you're going to have to catch up on your sleep some other time, dumplin'. You need to get over to Saint Paul's. Patrol is reporting a break-in, and Father Taylor was found D.O.A."

That was all Ben needed to hear. The words were like a shot of adrenaline straight to the heart. He showered, skipped shaving–not that anyone would be able to tell with his baby face–and headed out the door. Just as he was stepping out of the car in front of the church, Tommy's Bronco pulled up next to him.

Rolling down the window, from behind a pair of what looked like extra dark sunglasses, Tommy asked, "Please tell me I didn't hear Shirley, right?"

"A break-in and possible homicide?"

"Yeah."

"You heard her right."

"Dammit."

Tommy did a quick U-turn and parked across the street. Getting out of the truck, he fumbled around in the back seat, finally pulling out a rumpled corduroy sport coat. Pulling it on over his wrinkled shirt, he noticed his partner giving him the once-over as he crossed the road to meet him on the sidewalk.

"This is the best you're gonna' get today," Tommy said, pulling his badge out of his pocket and clipping it to the lapel of his jacket. "Hell, you're lucky I put pants on. But I know how much you like me to dress up for crime scenes."

It was true, Ben was always wearing a suit. He thought it helped to project a certain amount of authority while working a case. Considering he only looked like he was barely in his twenties when he was now thirty, it also helped him to look a little older. Truth be told, Ben could be wearing ripped-up jeans and a leather biker's jacket, and he would still look like the boy next door. He was the poster child for what a stand-up Boy Scout should look like.

Tommy, on the other hand, would love to wear a leather jacket and jeans every day. He preferred comfort when it came to his attire. The reverse of Ben was true for Tommy. Even if he would show up wearing an expensive three-piece suit from a fancy store on New York's Fifth Avenue, he'd still come off as a bad boy. The kind of guy all the girls fell for but would never take home to meet their mother. Mostly out of fear that their mothers would also fall for him.

"Any other details?" Tommy asked as he checked his Tom Selleck-style mustache in the side mirror of Ben's car.

"I just got here myself."

"I thought we were going to be able to take it easy after we picked up that dipshit last night. I mean, come on. We can't even get a few hours of sleep!"

"Our burden is heavy," Ben said, wondering if his sarcasm got through.

"The only thing that could make this morning any worse...."

"You mean other than finding the dead body of a popular priest?"

"You know what I mean..." Tommy said, putting his hands up in his defense, "...is if the responding officer is...*dammit.*"

Ben turned to see Officer Buck LuCoco lumber out of the door to the church offices. A very large man, neither Ben nor Tommy understood how LuCoco was still on patrol. The fact he'd been with the department since the '50s and never been promoted beyond a patrol officer didn't surprise either of them. He was one of the PCPD's old guard that did absolutely as little as possible, while doing just enough to not be fired for complete dereliction of duty. Tommy thought he was a lazy slob. Ben couldn't argue. The only thing LuCoco had going for him was his institutional knowledge of the city. He'd been around long enough to know a little about everyone and everything.

"Be nice," Ben said to his partner through gritted teeth as LuCoco waddled his way to them. "Good morning, Buck."

The officer grunted a response as he wiped his face with a handkerchief, finally saying, "It's not a good morning for Father Taylor."

"There was a break-in?" Ben asked.

"Yeah. One of the secretaries got here about seven-forty-five. She found the front door unlocked and thought Taylor already opened up for the day. Then she found the door to the priest's office smashed and him dead. Now, I'm no expert, but I've been around long enough to know what a robbery gone wrong looks like. Whoever broke in here musta gotten caught by

Taylor, then they offed him."

"*Not being an expert*, what makes you think that?" Tommy asked, barely containing the mockery.

"Well, there's a pretty good hole in the priest's head that looks like it coulda been caused by the heavy candlestick with blood on it lying next to him, smartass."

"Alright," Ben said in a tone that let both men know they needed to cool it. "Where's the secretary now?"

"She's in with Thompson."

Ben knew Tommy was thinking the same thing he was. If Thompson had also responded, he'd have secured the scene using the protocols they'd been trying to get all of the patrol officers to use. He was one of the officers in the department who understood the importance of the new techniques being employed at a crime scene, and, therefore the need to preserve a scene's integrity. Unlike LuCoco and the guys who'd complained when Ben and Tommy had been promoted who thought if you couldn't see a clue with your bare eyes, it wasn't there.

"We're going to head in and take a look around. Buck, will you radio in and have them roll the Crime Scene Unit and let the coroner know they have a pick-up?"

"Your wish is my command, *Detective*."

"Hey. That's Detective-*Sergeant*, remember," Tommy corrected. "Remember, he outranks you in this department."

Watching LuCoco head for his squad car, Ben said, "You really don't need to do that."

"What?" Tommy asked innocently.

"Throw my rank around. Sometimes I think you care more about it than I do."

"Well, he needs to respect your stripes," Tommy said in his defense. "And... I just don't like him. I'm always afraid he's going to have a heart attack and drop dead right in front of us. Then we'll have so much paperwork to fill out. Seriously? Do you think he even knows what a salad is?"

Sometimes Ben needed to play the role of a stern father. "Okay. I get it.

You have very strong feelings about him. But that's enough now. If someone really did kill Roland Taylor, we've already got a big problem on our hands. I don't need you starting another one with LuCoco."

"Fine," Tommy said, doing his best impression of a petulant child. "I'll behave myself. Your wish is my command, *Detective-Sergeant.*"

Chapter Fifteen

When Father Roland Taylor had taken over at Saint Paul's, it was big news. Some quarters of the community were shocked by the appointment. No church in Parker City had ever been led by a black pastor. Or one only in his thirties! It was a scandal if one listened to certain individuals. They also feared that the church's congregation may not accept the new priest, and membership would dwindle. Almost a year into his tenure, the initial concerns were completely unfounded, and the opposite occurred.

Saint Paul's had always been a centerpiece of the neighborhood. Its community events welcomed guests from all across the city. But when Father Taylor arrived, the church's outreach programs kicked into high gear. He brought a new perspective to the church's mission. And with the city desperately trying to drag itself out of the economic slump it found itself in, Saint Paul's was there to do its part. Taylor was becoming so popular, the mayor even asked him to join the official efforts to revitalize the city's Downtown.

All of which meant Father Taylor's murder–if that is what it turned out to be–was going to turn into a major story. No doubt, the press would be all over it, Ben was thinking as he entered the small reception area. Other than a few chairs, the walls were lined with event posters and notices about a variety of activities, both past and upcoming. Ben counted nearly a dozen activities scheduled in just the next couple of months.

"It looks like this door *may* have been jimmied open," Tommy said, drawing Ben's attention to the cheap lock. "It's pretty crappy. And there are some scrapes and scratches here. It could be nothing, though."

"It's hard to believe someone would break into the offices of a church. They probably didn't think they needed a better lock," Ben offered, looking around to see if anything appeared out of place.

"Detectives," a voice from the next room called.

It was Officer Thompson.

Walking around the corner, they found the patrolman sitting across from a small woman whose eyes were bright red. It was obvious she'd been crying. Between them, a cluttered desk piled high with papers. A second desk, nowhere near as unorganized, was on the other side of the room. Set in the dark wood paneling on the far wall, an old-fashioned office door with a shattered pane of frosted glass sat partially open. Glass shards dotting the floor.

"Neil. Who do we have here?" Ben asked.

Standing, Officer Thompson introduced one of the church's secretaries, Bonnie Gillespie. A petite woman, Ben put her in her fifties, maybe older. A pile of crumpled tissues sat on the desk in front of her.

"Mrs. Gillespie, my name's Ben Winters. I'm a detective with the Parker City Police Department. This is my partner, Detective Mason. I am so sorry about Father Taylor. I didn't know him personally, but I have heard nothing but good things about him."

"He was such a wonderful man. He had such a good heart. I don't understand how this could have happened," she said, fighting back another surge of tears.

Ben sat down in the seat Thompson had been in and took out his notebook. He needed to ask the secretary some questions while everything was still fresh in her memory, but he didn't want to push too hard. She was visibly shaken, as anyone would be under the circumstances.

"Is it alright if I ask you a few questions?"

Dabbing at her eyes, Bonnie Gillespie nodded.

"Thank you. While I do that, Detective Mason is going to go into Father Taylor's office and have a look around."

Taking his cue, Tommy carefully stepped over the broken glass and into the office.

Ben gave the secretary another moment to wipe her eyes and compose herself before proceeding.

"Why don't we just start by you telling me what happened this morning? When you arrived? What you saw? Anything you can think of. You never know what may end up being helpful."

"I had some paperwork that I needed to get done before lunch today. I normally don't get in until nine. But the diocese needed these reports, so I came in early. When I got here, the front door was open. I assumed Father had gotten an early start. He did that some days.

"I didn't realize anything was wrong until I came in here and saw the door to his office was open and all the broken glass. I went in, and I found him...on the...I'm sorry," she said, beginning to cry again.

"You're doing good. This is all going to help us. What time was it when you got here?"

"About seven-forty-five or so. They'd just done a weather update on the radio when I was getting out of the car. They usually do that every fifteen minutes."

"And then you found the front door open? Was the door open or just unlocked?"

"The door was closed but unlocked. I thought Father Taylor must have unlocked it when he came down this morning. He has an apartment above the offices. If he comes down before one of us gets here, he unlocks it."

"You didn't think it could be your co-worker...Hester?" Ben asked, reading the nameplate on the other desk.

"No. Hester's away this week. She's visiting her daughter and new grandbaby in Pennsylvania. I thought it had to be Father."

"And you didn't find anything disturbed in this office area? Nothing's missing? Out of place?"

"I haven't looked through everything yet. But it all seems like the way I left it yesterday."

"What time did you leave work yesterday?"

"Five o'clock, like normal."

"Did anything strange happen yesterday?"

"How do you mean?"

"Did you or Father Taylor have any strange phone calls, or did anyone come in that wasn't supposed to?"

"No. It was a quiet day. Father had a meeting with the church's ladies' auxiliary committee in the afternoon. Gladys Higgins can be a pain sometimes. Going on and on about how we need more chicken at the summer picnic or how we need to raise the price of our raffle tickets, but other than that..." she ended by shrugging her shoulders.

"When you found Father Taylor, what did you do then?"

"I called the police straight away."

Ben was making notes as she spoke. He'd taught himself how to write without looking down at the paper. It allowed him to never look away from the person to whom he was speaking. That way, he never had to break the connection. Tommy never understood how his notes still turned out so legible. On several occasions, Tommy suggested witchcraft had something to do with it.

"Did you touch anything while you were in Father Taylor's office?"

"No. I...I barely made it through the door before I saw...."

"I just have one more question for right now, Mrs. Gillespie. In the last few days, had the Father been having problems with anyone? I know when he'd first come to Saint Paul's, not everyone was happy about that. Did he seem tense or troubled by anything?"

"Oh, that was all over and done with. Everyone loved Father. He got a letter every once in a while that he'd just throw away and ignore, but nothing recently."

"What did these letters say? Did you ever see them?"

The secretary nodded, then took a deep breath. "They were always very vulgar. Usually said something that had to do with...Father's color." She whispered the last word.

"I don't suppose they were signed."

"No. And I can't say I ever saw any that looked like they came from the same person. It always seemed like if Father Taylor made it onto the front page of the paper, some nasty person would say that he didn't belong here."

"But you can't think of anyone in particular who would want to hurt Father Taylor?"

"No. He was such a saint."

Priest or not, Ben didn't like when people referred to victims as "saints." A description like that made Ben fearful that one's judgment was clouded. By nature, he was a positive individual. But he still had just enough cynicism in him to keep him grounded. Though, from what Bonnie Gillespie had to say, the priest didn't seem to have any trouble with anyone at the moment. However, he would have liked to have seen whatever letters he'd gotten in the past and thrown away. It was possible someone's hatred had taken over, and they finally worked up the nerve to act. Ben would need to keep that in the back of his mind for now.

After explaining what was going to happen next, how the crime scene technicians would be coming in soon, and the coroner's people, Ben told the secretary that they may still have some questions for her in the future, so took down her telephone number and home address. He then asked if there was anyone she wanted to call or if she would like to go freshen up.

As she headed for the ladies' room, Officer Thompson asked, "Do you know her?"

"Hmmm? No. Why?"

"You called her Mrs. Gillespie right away. How did you know she was a missus?"

"Ah. Just an observation. There was a photo of her and a man on her desk with a twenty-fifth wedding anniversary sign behind them. She was also wearing a wedding ring. So, even if she was a widow, I got the feeling she still went by *missus*."

"You got all that in a split second of meeting her?" Thompson sounded genuinely impressed. "Let's see how your powers of observation are in here," he said, motioning toward the door to the priest's office.

Chapter Sixteen

"How's she doing?" Tommy asked as Ben walked in and found his partner kneeling over Roland Taylor's body.

"She's pretty shaken up. As you'd expect. I got the basics from her, but nothing really jumped out." Taking a quick glance around the room, Ben noted the dark paneling from the outer office continued into the priest's private space. It gave the room a warm feel, but also made it seem dark. Even with a lead glass window looking into the church's garden. From the window, his eyes couldn't help but be drawn down to the hideous green shag carpet he was standing on.

"What do we have in here?" Ben asked after his initial survey of the room.

Tommy shifted back, so he was sitting on his haunches and looking up at Ben. "The place has been tossed. Whoever was in here was looking for something. No way it was just a robbery. There's gold stuff all over this place. He didn't take any of it. Assuming it's a *he*. There's a candlestick over there…matches this one here on the floor…some gold frames up on the wall…I'm sure those religious-looking pictures are worth something."

"Notice how none of the objects on the table over there or on the shelves even look like they've been touched. Things that any thief could have just picked up and walked away with. He just went through the desk and file cabinets," Tommy pointed out.

"Maybe he was looking for money," Ben said. "It wouldn't be that easy to pawn a holy icon like those."

"Possible. But why would someone think the padre kept cash in the file cabinet? Whatever they were looking for, though, at some point, Father

Taylor got cracked in the head."

Ben stepped back and looked at the whole room again.

"So...the question becomes," Ben said, trying to envision what had happened, "when was Taylor struck? *Before* or *after* the place was tossed?"

Ben bit his lower lip as he looked back at the door. "If the perp jimmied the lock on the front door, why did he smash the window to open this one?"

"Take a look at that lock," Tommy said. "That door is a solid piece of wood with a heavy-duty bolt lock. My guess is it is an original from when the church was built eight hundred years ago. Back when they actually knew how to make things that lasted. There's no way that bolt could have been jimmied. The only way to unlock it was to break the glass, reach through, and turn the knob."

"Alright then..." Ben was slowly rubbing his hands together.

"Clearly, you have a theory," Tommy said, standing up. "Go ahead. Lay it on me."

"If Father Taylor was in here working, odds are, the doors weren't locked. Which means whoever broke in, would *not* have had to smash the glass to open the door. And if he was in here working, he wouldn't have just sat by and let someone go through his things. Were the lights on or off when you came in?"

"On."

"I think they broke in and searched the office first. Father Taylor came in...maybe he heard something or forgot something...turned on the lights... because no respectable burglar would break in somewhere and turn the lights on for fear of being seen...he sees the mess, maybe even went for the telephone. The perp comes up behind him, Taylor turns, and is struck with the candlestick. You can see the blow was to the front of the head, not the back." Ben said all of this as he took a closer look at the bloody gash on the priest's head. It would be up to the coroner to officially determine the cause of death, but it seemed pretty clear what had killed Taylor.

"I obviously didn't need to get out of bed this morning. You figured the whole thing out by yourself," Tommy said, closing his notebook and sticking it in his pocket as if there was no reason for him to take any more notes.

Ben gave his partner the usual look he did when he was being a wiseass. "Very funny. We still don't know who did it or why?"

"I assumed you knew that too and were saving it for your big finale. You're on a roll. Keep going."

It was their ability to make each other smile, even in the most tense and serious of situations, that kept Ben and Tommy from slipping into the dark place that some police officers did after years of seeing the worst part of humanity. Over their years as partners, they'd found the perfect balance. If nothing else, it kept them sane.

Tommy had always been a smart alec. The first to crack a joke or make a sarcastic remark. He'd also made it his mission in life to help Ben loosen up. Which he felt he'd done since they were kids. Ben, on the other hand, had helped Tommy to realize when *not* to say exactly what was on his mind.

"I don't suppose we got lucky, and there's a bloody fingerprint on the candlestick?" Ben asked, only half joking.

"Not that I can see. But maybe the forensic guys can find something. We do need to think of this as a robbery, right? Even though it doesn't appear to be. I mean, what else would someone break into a church office to find?" Thinking for a moment, Tommy then said, "What if it doesn't have to do with the church at all? Maybe the perp was looking for something they knew...or *thought*...Taylor had. Something personal."

"Information? Maybe about someone or something," Ben suggested, following his partner's train of thought. "Like if he made notes after confession?"

"It would explain why just the files and desk were tossed."

"We need to look upstairs," Ben said as he took one more look around the room. "Taylor has an apartment over the offices. If they were looking for something more personal, he could have kept it there. But we're still going to have to ask Mrs. Gillespie if anything is actually missing from in here."

The detectives stepped back out into the outer office to await the arrival of the forensic team. Thompson had taken Bonnie Gillespie outside for some fresh air.

"I had a bad feeling about this from the start," Tommy said. "No way it was going to be a simple robbery gone wrong. I just knew there was going to be something more to it. With our luck, we're going to find out Father Taylor was a CIA spy or something, and now we're dealing with East German assassins."

Staring at his partner in silence, all Ben had to do was raise an eyebrow.

"Relax," Tommy said with a twinkle in his eye. "You know I'm kidding. Odds are more likely they're Russian assassins."

Chapter Seventeen

The apartment Roland Taylor occupied above the church offices was surprisingly spacious. Filled with antique furniture that belonged to the church for generations, there was a certain regal atmosphere about the rooms. Yet, even with the expensive-looking furnishings, there was still a simplicity to the space. It was a contradiction, Ben thought as he looked around the living room.

After the arrival of the CSU team and additional uniformed officers to assist securing the church, Ben and Tommy made their way up the stairs to the late priest's quarters. Neither was certain what to expect as they climbed the narrow steps. They'd never even known there was an apartment that was part of Saint Paul's.

"You learn something new every day," Tommy said after Bonnie Gillespie explained to them a number of old churches, like Saint Paul's, were built with accommodations for the priests to live.

Other than a couple of photos of Taylor with some people, Ben thought could be family, it didn't seem as though the priest had put his personal touch on the apartment. The living room certainly showed no signs of the priest's own personality. No magazines lying around or knickknacks on display. The only book in the living room, sitting on the coffee table, was a copy of the Bible.

Tommy's inspection of the kitchen produced much the same. Nothing.

"So far," he said, joining Ben in the living room, "other than a bowl in the sink, it doesn't look like anyone even lives here. Taylor'd been the priest here at Saint Paul's for a while now. But it doesn't seem like he ever really moved in."

"It is rather...sparse. Not that I would know what a priest's place should look like."

"But you'd expect some personal items. More than what? Just a few photos," he said, pointing to the pictures on the wall.

"Maybe Father Taylor believed in a simple life," Ben offered. "Material things might not have meant anything to him. Especially if he really was the saint Mrs. Gillespie said."

"Still. You can be completely devoted to God, Buddha, or whoever and have a magazine subscription. Or a blanket on the couch. There isn't even a TV in here. I mean, it feels like a museum."

"There's still the bedroom," Ben said, heading down a short hallway.

At the end of the hall was a bathroom, on either side of which was a bedroom. One of these rooms had been converted into a study with a desk and a couple of bookcases. It was that room in which the detectives became most interested. And judging by the state of it, the intruder as well. It had been searched. All the books had been pulled from the shelves, and the desk draws emptied like they were downstairs.

"Well...at least we know our theory was right. They were definitely looking for something specific," Tommy said, carefully stepping into the room. "On the bright side, though, whoever did this touched a lot of stuff. Maybe CSU will get a print."

"If they do, I bet they won't match anything we have on file because...."

"...they belong to Russian assassins, and they burned their fingerprints off so they couldn't be left behind. I was thinking the same thing," Tommy said.

"*Because* anyone who would be in the system would probably think twice about touching all of this with their bare hands."

"You're giving some of those putzes too much credit. Think about how many idiot criminals there are out there."

"Yeah. But still. If you were going to search a place for something, wouldn't you wear gloves?"

"But I'm not a putz. Although I do agree with you," he said, becoming more serious.

"Take a look and see if you find anything, then go let CSU know they need to come up here. I'm going to take a look in the bedroom."

As Ben stepped across the hall, he noticed that the bedroom had also been rifled through. Not nearly as bad as the study, but the dresser drawers had been opened, and the various pieces of clothing moved around. Next to the bed, the nightstand was open, and several books strewn on the floor. From the little he'd seen, Ben didn't think this was just Father Taylor being sloppy. He got the impression the priest preferred his surroundings to be orderly. Whoever had broken in went through his bedroom as well. Again, confirming that they'd been looking for something more personal. Something the priest might have kept close to him. They just had no idea what it might be.

Looking at the books lying on the ground, for the first time, Ben came across something that told him a little about Roland Taylor. At least, his interests. They were books about the Civil War, including one entitled *Lincoln and His Generals*. Was the Father a Civil War buff, Ben wondered.

"Hey, Ben," Tommy called from the other room. "Come take a look at this."

Crossing back to the study, Ben found Tommy on his knees, staring at a piece of notebook paper lying on the floor.

"You said Taylor got hate mail?" Tommy asked.

"Every once in a while, according to Mrs. Gillespie," Ben confirmed. "But she said he would just throw them away."

"Well, he didn't throw this one away." Tommy pointed to the page he'd been hovering over reading. "And you aren't going to believe this. This George Willis putz even signed it!"

Chapter Eighteen

1862...

C aleb Post found himself standing alone on the back porch of Drake House, wondering how he was going to manage to get any of the household staff to answer his questions without permission from their mistress. He was also troubled by the fact General McClellan, who obviously knew something about what had happened to Eustace Drake, was not willing to share this information. If the general was as dear a friend as Margaret Drake said, why would he not want to help with their inquiry? And if Eustace Drake's disappearance had something to do with the war, well, what did that mean?

Until now, Caleb's service as a deputy had been mostly stepping in and breaking up squabbles in public and dragging the heavily inebriated off to the drunk tank to sleep it off. For the most part, Parker City was a pretty quiet and peaceful town.

The outbreak of the war seemed to change all that. Tensions were running high everywhere. While it hadn't translated into any occurrences of more serious wrongdoings, everyone was looking at each other very differently these days. Caleb hoped the days would soon return when his most difficult chore was running the Carmack boys out of Mr. Upton's General Store after they tried to steal a sweet from the barrel he kept by the counter. For now, though, he was looking for one of the city's richest men, who quite possibly had met an untimely fate.

Letting himself back into the house, he found the hallway was empty, and he was alone. He wondered if McClellan was still in the house somewhere or if he'd headed back to the front to prepare for battle.

The room in which he'd first been introduced to Mrs. Drake and the general was now deserted as well. The large grandfather clock he'd seen in the corner was chiming the half hour. Quietly retracing his steps through the expansive home to the front door, Caleb thought he heard some shuffling sounds coming from behind a door that was now closed, though it had not been when he and the sheriff were first shown to the conservatory.

Gently tapping on the door, he said, "Excuse me. Is someone in there?"

There was a moment before the door was opened by a young housemaid wearing a dark gray dress and white apron. Her blonde curls were pulled back and tucked under a mop cap. Caleb was instantly taken by her shimmering blue eyes.

"Um, pardon me, miss. I'm…uh…Deputy Post. Caleb Post. I was wondering if, um, you knew the whereabouts of Mrs. Drake. I was hoping to speak with her before I left."

"I'm sorry," the girl began, a slight blush rising on her pale cheeks, "I believe the missus has retired to her bedroom."

"Oh. I see." Not that Caleb actually thought Margaret Drake would be willing to speak to him, but he thought he would take the chance. "Might I ask you a question, Miss…?"

"My name is Bridgett."

"Miss Bridgett."

"I think it might be better if I went and fetched Mr. Moxley for you. He's the butler. He'll be able to answer your questions, Sheriff."

"No. No. I'm just a deputy, Miss Bridgett. But I just have a real simple question. I wouldn't want to bother him. I'm sure he's extremely busy runnin' this house for the Drakes."

The maid's eyes wrinkled for a moment as she weighed the consequences of possibly speaking out of turn versus disturbing the cranky head of the household staff.

"Ask it then," she finally said after making her decision.

"When was the last time you saw Mr. Drake?"

She did not need to think very long before answering, "Yesterday afternoon. I remember because a message arrived for him from Washington, and he ordered his carriage brought 'round, and he left shortly after."

"Do you know who the message was from?"

"I couldn't say. I just overheard the soldier at the door who delivered the message."

"A soldier?"

Caleb was quickly sorting through all the new pieces of information in his head. The carriage had been discovered on a road that would have led to Washington. So, that made sense. And if a soldier had been the one to deliver the summons to the capital and General McClellan had shown up after Drake disappeared, that could not be a coincidence. This was all related to the fighting. Which was only going to make it more difficult to figure out what was really going on, Caleb thought.

"Miss Bridgett," Caleb began with a smile. "Did Mr. Drake have a study or a library where he worked here at home and met with important visitors?"

"He did. Yes. But only Mr. Moxley is allowed in there." The maid's cheeks reddened further as she became slightly flustered. No doubt guessing what Caleb's next question would be. "It's not worth my job to show it to you. I'm sorry. I just can't."

Caleb knew it wasn't going to be easy, but he thought if he could just take a quick look and see if Drake had left any papers out or recent correspondence, it might provide a useful clue. Trying to figure how to proceed with Bridgett the maid, he was just about to make his plea when a voice from behind him stopped him cold. He'd only heard it once before, but seeing Bridgett's eyes widen as they did, he knew the haughty tone belonged to Margaret Drake.

Chapter Nineteen

"Bridgett is right to say that she cannot show you my husband's study."

A line of perspiration rose on Caleb's brow. Slowly turning to face the mistress of the house, he felt a wave of guilt rush over him even though he knew he was only trying to do his job. He was also concerned that Bridgett might be punished, or worse–dismissed for having spoken with him.

"You may go now, Bridgett. You have duties to attend to," Margaret Drake said without a hint of anger or recrimination in her husky voice.

With a quick nod and courtesy, Bridgett excused herself, saying, "Yes, Mrs. Drake. Good day, Sheriff...I mean, Deputy."

Margaret Drake's eyes now focused solely on the young man before her. With her hands firmly clenched together in front of her, she studied him. She'd regained her composure from earlier when she had broken down at the sight of her husband's pocket watch.

"You are very young to be a deputy, are you not?"

"I'm young, ma'am, yes. But not all that young. And Sheriff Tildon has trained me well."

"Samuel has always been a good judge of character," she said. "At least in my experience. He must trust you quite a bit."

"I'm honored to have that trust, ma'am. The sheriff has been like a father t' me since my own died."

Reaching into his pocket, Caleb once again withdrew the watch he had taken from outside the carriage. Handing it to Margaret Drake, he said, "I don't think the sheriff would mind if I returned this to you."

Tears began to form in the corners of her eyes, but as the strong woman that she was, she held them back. She needed to remain steadfast for her husband. That's when she said, "It would have been wrong for Bridgett to let you into my husband's study. But not for me. I can only assume you are looking for something to help you find him, Deputy…Post?"

"Yes, ma'am. Anything that might give us an idea what he's been involved with or if there was anyone out to do him harm."

Without saying another word, Margaret Drake turned and started down the hallway. Caleb supposed he was meant to follow. Passing several doors along the long corridor, she finally stopped in front of one and placed her hand on the bronze doorknob. Several seconds passed before she silently turned the knob and stepped into her husband's private study.

Walking into the room, Caleb felt as though he was entering a different world. He'd never seen so many books in one place in his life. One entire wall of the study was floor-to-ceiling bookcases. Each shelf practically overflowing with handsomely bound copies of books ranging from Charles Dickens's *A Tale of Two Cities* to Nathaniel Hawthorne's *The Scarlet Letter*. Caleb noticed several other titles he'd heard of as he scanned the shelves.

"My husband is an avid reader, Deputy Post. These books are some of his most valuable treasures."

"He's read all of these?" Caleb asked, more than a note of amazement in his voice.

"Each one from beginning to end," Margaret Drake confirmed proudly. "He did not enjoy a formal education growing up. So, he has tried to make up for it since."

Caleb had heard stories about Eustace Drake and how he'd made his fortune. And though he wasn't part of one of Parker's founding families, he certainly was counted among the town's influential residents. It was through his philanthropy that Caleb had gotten to know the textile industrialist. There was always talk on the street about a charitable donation Drake had made to one group or another. So, Caleb had respect for the man though he did not know him personally.

It dawned on Caleb that Margaret Drake was still referring to her husband in the present tense. She wasn't willing to believe she might not see him alive again. Just another sign that she was a strong woman who would not be dictated to by circumstances. No matter how dire. Caleb was beginning to wonder if Eustace Drake had become as successful as he did in part because of his wife and her own fortitude.

Looking around the man's study, he could tell that Drake prized order. The bookshelves might have been overflowing, but the books were all arranged in alphabetical order, and each spine sat the exact same distance from the edge of the shelf. The small table next to the window had three stacks of papers perfectly aligned side-by-side with three small ledgers, also perfectly aligned, sitting above them.

Drake's desk, an enormous roll-top with more than a dozen pigeonhole compartments, sat next to a marble fireplace that matched the one Caleb had seen in the conservatory a short time earlier. As with the table, all of the papers were neatly stacked and organized. Three full inkpots sat next to one another with a polished silver pen resting on an equally shiny silver charger. Three stacks of paper, three ledgers, three inkpots…Caleb wondered if that meant something to Drake or if it was merely a coincidence. Regardless, it gave him some insight into the man who was now missing.

Turning to the lady of the house, Caleb asked, "Mrs. Drake, was yesterday the last time you saw your husband? Before he left for Washington?"

"It was," she answered, a tightness in her voice.

"Do you happen to know why he was going to Washington?"

"He didn't discuss matters like that with me." That was the first thing she said that Caleb didn't believe. "He was always coming and going. His business is thriving, and he finds himself very busy."

"Why did General McClellan decide to pay you a visit today? By all accounts, there's t' be a big fight in the next few days. It must'a been pretty important for him to leave the troops to come see you."

"As I told you and the sheriff, General McClellan…George…is a friend."

"You did say that. But beggin' your pardon, ma'am, that doesn't explain why he was here the very mornin' your husband turns up missing."

Silence filled the room as Caleb turned his attention back to the desk that featured so prominently in the study. Everything looked as though it had been meticulously placed. Which is why his eye was drawn to a small drawer that was not fully closed. Sliding it open, Caleb withdrew two pieces of paper. Unfolding the first, he found the note which had been delivered to Eustace Drake the day before summoning him to Washington. Specifically, to the White House! The message was written and signed by Edwin M. Stanton, the Secretary of the War Department. Caleb felt his palms beginning to sweat.

The second piece of paper was a fragment torn from a pamphlet. The piece had been ripped in a fashion as to not have left any full words to read. What Caleb could see, read…

LDEN CIR

SUCCES

FEDERACY

Placing the pieces of paper into his pocket, Caleb wondered what else he might be able to find if he went through the other drawers. But he could also tell by her fidgeting that Mrs. Drake's patience was wearing thin. He didn't want to tempt fate any longer. He knew he'd already been fortunate enough to have not been thrown out of the house.

Turning to the austere-looking woman and putting his hat on, Caleb said, "Thank you for allowing me to look around in here, Mrs. Drake. Sheriff Tildon and I will do everything we can to locate your husband."

Once again, he saw the woman's eyes beginning to fill with tears, but she quickly blinked them away, saying, "Deputy Post, I am certain this is all just a misunderstanding. Eustace is probably just…he's just…."

"Let's hope that's the long and short of it, then. And when he gets home, would you be so kind as to send for me at the Courthouse? Just so's we can clear up a few things with Mr. Drake."

"Of course."

With a tip of his hat, Caleb headed for the front door, wondering if Mrs. Drake was simply in denial or if there was more to her unwillingness to believe something had happened to her husband. General McClellan's visit meant something. A murdered coachman meant something. Caleb needed to find the sheriff. He was beginning to feel as though something much bigger was afoot. And that didn't sit well with him.

Chapter Twenty

Sheriff Tildon was seated behind his desk when Caleb returned to the Courthouse. Through the thick glass window in the door, Caleb could see standing opposite him was a very unhappy looking and agitated William Gladhill, Parker City's esteemed mayor. Usually a calm and collected gentleman, he looked anything but as Caleb took a seat at the table outside the sheriff's office.

The other deputies were out, so Caleb sat quietly, waiting for the sheriff's conversation with the mayor to conclude. He couldn't hear exactly what was being said, but he had a pretty good idea what the two were discussing. News traveled fast around Parker, and he couldn't figure a way that Gladhill hadn't heard about the discovery of Eustace Drake's abandoned carriage outside of town that morning.

To pass the time, Caleb took the pieces of paper he'd found at Drake House out of his pocket and laid them on the table. The message from Secretary Stanton was easily understood. It was the scrap of torn paper that puzzled him. Studying the printing on the paper fragment, he was trying to determine what the missing letters were. Standing up and walking over to a credenza along the wall, Caleb retrieved a clean sheet of writing paper from a tray and a pencil. Copying the letters from the pamphlet scrap onto the center of the blank paper, he began to add his own letters at the beginning and end to come up with complete words.

Working from the bottom up, it took no time to figure FEDERACY was the end of *Confederacy*, a word he'd seen and become all too familiar with over the last couple of years. SUCCES could have been *Success, Successful…*

But thinking about it, in the context of the Confederacy, it more likely was *Succession*. LDEN CIR stumped him. He sat writing several combinations of letters, trying to make as many words as possible, but none fit with the others.

As he was about to try another combination of letters, the doors to the sheriff's office swung open, and Mayor Gladhill stormed out and headed for the hall without saying another word. The mayor was followed by Sheriff Tildon, who stood in his doorway shaking his head and chewing on his cigar.

"To say that the mayor is unhappy would be an understatement," he said, blowing a ring of blue smoke into the air. "I can't hardly blame him. Up until a few hours ago, it seemed as though our biggest concern was keeping all the blue and gray soldiers in our town away from one another."

With his cigar in one hand, he ran the other through his hair and scratched the top of his head, leaving his graying mane standing at disorderly attention. Staring out into the hall, he stood in quiet contemplation for a moment. Caleb didn't want to disturb him but was itching to show him what he'd found in Drake's desk.

"What have you, my boy?" he asked, finally noticing the papers sitting on the table in front of his deputy.

"Mrs. Drake allowed me a chance to inspect Mr. Drake's study. I found these?" Caleb said, indicating the pieces of paper. "Yesterday, this message arrived summoning him to the White House in Washington, DC. It was sent by Edwin Stanton, the head of the War Department, and was delivered by a soldier. Accordin' to one of the housemaids. Both she and Mrs. Drake said that Mr. Drake left shortly after receiving it."

"I see," the sheriff said, holding the message up so he could read it for himself. "I think there can be no doubt—with this personal summons from the secretary of war and the appearance of General McClellan this morning—that Eustace Drake was deeply involved with the Union Army. I do not believe he was simply supplying the soldiers with boots."

"There does indeed seem to be more to his involvement," Caleb agreed.

"After I left you at Drake House, I sent a telegraph message to a friend I have working in the War Department. I was hoping he might have some useful information as to what Drake was up to. If McClellan wouldn't be of any assistance, I thought maybe someone higher on the ladder would."

"Might I ask who your friend is?"

Tildon thought for a moment before answering. "For the moment, it may be better not to share that information, my boy. Let's just leave it at a friend who owes me a favor."

Caleb knew Samuel Tildon was a powerful man in Parker City and its immediate surroundings. He didn't realize that his influence and connections also reached into the federal capital. Though, it shouldn't have surprised him. The sheriff's father had been a high-ranking army officer, which would explain how he could know people in the War Department.

"What else do you have there?" the sheriff asked, eyeing the scrap of paper and the sheet with random assortments of letters.

"I don't exactly know just yet. There's some printin' on here, like it was ripped from a pamphlet or handbill, maybe. I might have figured out two of the words. But I don't know the first one. If Mr. Drake was doing secret work for the government, it might make sense this has something to do with the Confederacy. See. I think those two words are *succession* and *Confederacy*."

Tildon frowned as he studied the first set of letters. He was not afraid to admit that he wasn't as clever at puzzles as his young protégé, so if Caleb had not figured out the letters' meaning yet, he wasn't sure that he would be able to. Even though there was something nagging at him in the back of his brain. And that feeling worried him.

Chapter Twenty-One

That evening, Caleb sat at the dining room table with the sheriff at one end and Elizabeth Tildon at the other. Before them, the cook had prepared more food than the three could possibly eat. But it was the custom at the sheriff's house when Caleb was invited for dinner. Which was quite frequently.

"The meal is delicious as always, Miss Edie," Caleb said between bites of roasted beef.

"You know I can't rightfully take any credit, Caleb. All of the recipes are family secrets of Mrs. May's."

"Even so," he said, wiping up the leftover sauce on his plate with a piece of bread, "you can still take credit for bein' smart enough to hire her."

Edie Tildon laughed as she shook her head. She'd grown quite fond of her husband's deputy. And with their own daughter long married and now living in Philadelphia with her husband, Caleb had filled a void in their home.

"Well, as always, you are too kind."

"I don't think we could get rid of Mrs. May even if we tried," the sheriff added with a smile. "Not that I'd want to, mind you. But she's been with Edie's family for so long. It's almost like I got two brides when I married Elizabeth. They came as a set. Like those candlesticks."

"You stop it, Samuel. Remember what happened the last time Mrs. May heard you making fun? You didn't get any pie."

"How could I forget?" the sheriff asked. "That was the night she made her famous apple pie with the crumble top."

Caleb always enjoyed the time he spent with the Tildons. Though it wasn't a common relationship they shared, he valued it more than he could put into words. The sheriff had always been like a father to him, having been far too young to remember his own father when he died. Then, when his mother passed just a few years earlier, Elizabeth Tildon had taken it upon herself to make sure Caleb was well taken care of as if he were her own son.

It always confounded Caleb that so many of Parker City's oldest and wealthiest families were so stuffy and looked down on so many of their neighbors just because they didn't happen to have the same good fortune. Yet, Samuel and Elizabeth Tildon, both from wealthy families, treated everyone as equals. It didn't matter if you were the fruit seller on the street just trying to make a few pennies to feed your family or the mayor of Parker City. They offered everyone the same amount of respect.

Ringing a small silver bell on the table, Mrs. Tildon alerted the butler to the fact they were finished with the meal and ready to be served dessert. From a side door hidden in the wood-paneled wall, Mr. Percy appeared along with his serving assistant, prepared to remove the finished plates and ready the table for dessert.

From what Caleb understood, Percy, at one time, had been a slave on a plantation in Georgia. Somehow—Caleb had never learned the full story—he had made his way north and was now employed to run the sheriff's household. Mr. Percy was always the first to point out that he may still be in service, but he was free to walk out the *front* door anytime he pleased. But he was quick to say he didn't foresee that happening because of how well he was treated by the Tildons.

"What does Mrs. May have for us for dessert this evening, Mr. Percy?" the sheriff asked, barely containing his excitement. It was no secret Samuel Tildon enjoyed sweet treats.

"Now, Sheriff, you know Mrs. May likes t' present the dessert t' you herself. It's worth more 'en my job to spoil her surprise."

"Not even a hint?"

"Not even a hint," the elder black man said with a big smile. "Would you like for me to serve the coffee in here this evenin', or will you take it in the parlor?"

"What do you say, my dear?" the sheriff asked, looking to his wife.

Before she was able to answer, the bell in the front hall rang.

"Good heavens," Mrs. Tildon said. "Who could be stopping by at this time unannounced?"

"Would you like me to get the door?" Caleb asked, trying to be as helpful as possible.

"Don't you budge an inch Master Caleb, that's what I'm here for," Percy scolded. "Please excuse me."

As the butler headed for the front door, Billy, his assistant—and the Tildon's houseboy—collected the plates and disappeared back through the door to the kitchen. As all of this was happening, Sheriff Tildon exchanged a concerned look with Caleb. No one called this late at night without an appointment unless there was a reason. Both of the lawmen just hoped it had nothing to do with the disappearance of Eustace Drake.

When Percy returned, he looked disturbed. His usual pleasant expression much harder now. "Sheriff, sir. There is a gentleman here to see you."

"Who is it? Who's interrupting my dessert?"

"He wouldn't give a name, sir. But he's quite insistent. Just said to say he was a *'friend from Washington.'* And you'd know what that means."

The sheriff leaned forward in his chair. "And he's *here?*"

"I asked him t' wait in the front sittin' room. Yes."

Tildon cast another look at his deputy and exhaled heavily.

"Is everything alright, Samuel?" Mrs. Tildon asked, worried about the stranger's arrival and what it could mean.

Standing, the sheriff motioned for Caleb to follow and said, "Edie, my dear, it looks like you'll need to enjoy Mrs. May's dessert without us tonight. Caleb and I have some unexpected business to see to."

Chapter Twenty-Two

1984...

"There's no way this is going to be this easy," Tommy said between drags on his Newport.

He and Ben were standing outside Saint Paul's watching as the coroner's guys were loading Father Taylor's body into the back of their van for the trip back to Baltimore, where the official autopsy would be performed. After searching the priest's apartment, Tommy said he needed a cigarette, so the pair stepped outside so they could talk and Tommy could get his nicotine fix.

As always, after lighting his own, he offered the pack to Ben. It was like a ritual with the two. In response, Ben would then say, "We've known each other since we were five, you know I don't smoke."

It's not that Tommy ever forgot. He just played the odds. At some point, Ben was bound to take one. Tommy always said it would help him relax. Ben would just roll his eyes and thank his partner for being willing to share.

Continuing his thought, Tommy said, "I mean, people can be pretty stupid, but do you really think this guy is the one who did in the padre?"

Tommy was referring to the threatening letter they'd found in Taylor's apartment. As threatening letters went, it wasn't the worst they'd ever seen. But it was full of racial slurs and Neanderthalic statements. Most importantly, it was signed.

"It's a starting point," Ben said, writing something in his notebook. "Since we don't have a better lead at the moment, I think we need to pay Mr. George Willis a visit. Is he actually going to be the killer? Maybe we'll get lucky with this one."

"I'm not gonna get my hopes up."

"Do you have a better idea of where we should start looking?" Ben asked, then before Tommy could exhale a puff of smoke and say anything, finished with, "That doesn't involve assassins."

"You're gonna be pissed when it turns out that I'm right. You know that, don't you?"

"If it turns out to be the case, I guess I will just have to live with it," Ben said, tucking his notebook back into his jacket pocket. "I'm going to call in and see if I can get an address for George Willis."

"I'm gonna stand here and smoke for another minute...keep an eye on the door and make sure no one sneaks in."

"You're in a mood today, aren't you?"

"What are you talking about? I've been an absolute peach today. Besides, one of them could be the killer," Tommy said, pointing toward a small group of onlookers who'd gathered to see what all the fuss outside the church was about. "That old lady looks like she could cause some bodily harm."

Ben cast his eyes over the group and instantly picked out the bystander his partner was talking about. A scowl looked like it was permanently affixed to the woman's face. And the cane she was holding could definitely be used as a weapon. But like the others in the small crowd, she was one of the residents who lived on the street and had come out to see why there were police cars sitting in front of their houses this morning.

Along with the elderly woman, there was an older gentleman that looked like her husband, a couple of middle-aged ladies who Ben imagined were the neighborhood gossips, and a teenager who he thought should be in school.

Before he could give the group much more thought, he saw a familiar silver Crown Victoria park across the street where the coroner's van had been.

"The chief's here," Ben motioned with his chin.

76

Nicholas Brent was a bear of a man. Barrel-chested, six-foot-four, a former Naval officer, he was an imposing figure without question. And a good chief. There wasn't one member of the department that did not respect the man. Since taking over as chief after the sudden death of his predecessor, he'd been making big changes. Changes that were making the PCPD a much tougher police force.

Brent had also been one of Ben and Tommy's strongest supporters when they'd made detective. He fully understood the need to have a dedicated investigation team, even when so many others did not. He'd come from the Buffalo Police Department, so was much more familiar with the need for detectives to handle serious criminal investigations. At the moment, he was contemplating expanding the PCPD's Detective Squad and adding additional men. An issue he and Ben had been discussing for some time.

Even though the chief was wearing his usual mirrored sunglasses, Ben could tell he was agitated. He didn't need to see Brent's eyes.

"Chief," Ben said with a nod of his head.

"Detectives."

"Hey, Chief," Tommy said, offering Brent the pack of Newports.

"Thanks," he said, taking the pack and shaking out a cigarette. "I definitely need one of these. I've been on the phone all morning with the mayor, the head of the Parker Religious Coalition, members of the City Council, the mayor again…all while avoiding the calls from the press. The word's out about Father Taylor."

"There was no way we *couldn't* let Taylor's secretary make some calls," Ben explained. "There were some members of the church's board that needed to be informed. And the diocese in Baltimore."

"Oh, I understand," Brent said, lighting the cigarette and taking his first hit of tobacco. "I'm just saying I would have liked to have been here sooner to see things for myself so I actually had something to tell everyone who's been calling me."

"Except the press," Tommy quipped.

"Except the press," the chief agreed. "So, what do we have? Was it a break-in gone wrong?"

"You probably don't want to hear that the answer is yes *and* no," Tommy responded, hoping he didn't sound like a total smartass this time because he wasn't actually trying to be.

"Care to explain?"

Ben rubbed his chin before answering. "There *was* a break-in. But we believe whoever broke in was looking for something specific. Whether they knew Father Taylor was here, we can't tell."

For the next fifteen minutes, the detectives talked the chief through everything that had happened since they arrived and what they'd found when they searched the priest's apartment. Brent didn't say anything. He just listened.

When they'd finished, he asked, "So, where are you going to start?"

"With George Willis," Ben answered.

"Do you think he broke in to get his letter back?" Brent asked, flicking the butt of his second cigarette into the grass.

"I found the letter right on top of a pile on the floor," Tommy said, shaking his head. "If he missed it, then he really is a putz. It was right there."

Brent grumbled in agreement. Then said, "Alright. Find this guy and see what he has to say. Keep me posted. When Taylor's murder hits the papers tomorrow morning, this city is going to go crazy. Everybody loved this guy."

"Well, everybody except George Willis," Tommy corrected. Okay, that time, he was being a smartass.

Chapter Twenty-Three

After walking Chief Brent through the crime scene and showing him everything they'd come across, Ben and Tommy decided to head back to the station. Ben wanted to see what, if anything, he could find out about George Willis before they confronted him with the letter he'd sent to Roland Taylor. It also gave them a chance to grab something to eat since both had skipped breakfast, rushing out to Saint Paul's, and were now starving. So, while Ben was going to search the department's files for anything relating to one Willis, George, Tommy ran across the street to grab a couple of sandwiches.

Thankfully, someone had just made a fresh pot of coffee in the break room. Downing the first cup in just a few gulps, Ben poured another and headed back down the hall to the Detective Squad's small office, wondering how many cups of coffee he actually drank in a day. And maybe more importantly, how many were too many?

Sitting down at his desk, he grabbed the phone book and flipped to the Ws. Scanning down the page, he found one listing for a George Willis on Backstreet Road. He needed to double-check, but he thought that was in one of the smaller neighborhoods heading south out of the city. Not necessarily one of the better neighborhoods either.

Ben scribbled the address down in his notebook just as Betty appeared in the doorway. A stout woman with big hair and a pair of the thickest glasses Ben had ever seen dangling from a chain around her neck, she was the keeper of the PCPD's records. Neither of them knew her age, mostly because they dare not ask, but Tommy always referred to her as a "tough old broad." Ben thought of her as one of the more colorful characters in his life. Literally. Her wardrobe consisted of nothing but brightly colored clothes that were slightly behind the times. On occasion, Ben even thought the color of her hair matched what she was wearing. Though he tended to chalk that up to a trick of the light. What he did know was that her personality was ten times bigger than she was.

"I got the file you called about, hun." She handed him the folder then dropped down in Tommy's empty desk chair.

"You didn't need to bring it up to me. I would have come down to get it," Ben said.

"My doctor said I either need to stop smoking or get more exercise. He's got some real hair-brained ideas. I figure walking up two flights of stairs is enough exercise for the day."

"Maybe you could just cut back on how many cigarettes you smoke every day," Ben offered in his most innocent tone.

"Hun," Betty answered, her heavy Baltimore accent on full display, "my mama smoked every day of her life, and my grandmama smoked every day of *her* life. They also drank whiskey like it was water. They both lived to be ninety-nine years old. Both of them. And I only smoke half as much as they did."

Ben waited to see if she was going to say anything else, but that's where her argument ended. She just sat there giving him a "go ahead, say something else" look. Instead of tapdancing any further into the minefield, Ben turned his attention to the file she'd delivered to him.

"Anything interesting in here?" he asked, flipping the folder open.

"Your boy's got a bit of a record. The IBM pulled up a few arrests for him. They're all in there."

She was right. Willis had been arrested several times for disorderly conduct, once for public indecency and a couple of times for disturbing the peace. Nothing too serious. At least nothing that made Ben think he'd suddenly graduated to murder.

As he was reading about George Willis's most recent run-in with the law, Ben suddenly caught the unmistakable whiff of cigarette smoke. Looking up, he saw Betty leaning back and blowing a cloud of smoke toward the ceiling.

"Betty! You know you're not allowed to smoke in the building."

"I smoke down in the Records Room all the time."

"I know that. But you're not supposed to."

"If no one's allowed to smoke up here, why does your partner keep an ashtray right here in his top desk drawer?" she asked, tapping the edge of her cigarette on the aforementioned small ceramic dish.

"I didn't realize he did," Ben said with a raised eyebrow.

"I didn't know we were going to have company for lunch," Tommy said, stepping into the office with a bag from the deli across the street.

"I think your partner's about to throw me out of here." Betty gave Tommy a big smile.

"He won't dare. But, ah, I have a feeling I know why he would try. We're not allowed to smoke up here on the second floor."

"No one's allowed to smoke *anywhere* in the building," Ben corrected.

Standing up, Betty looked from one detective to the other. "Obviously, there's some disagreement here. So, I'm just gonna head back down to the Records Room where I can smoke without causing a fuss."

"You're not allowed to smoke there either!" Ben tried one last time.

"It's alright. I covered up the NO SMOKING sign years ago." Betty gave Ben a wink and blew out of the office, handing her half-smoked cigarette to Tommy as she went.

"I love her," Tommy said, watching her trot down the hall.

Chapter Twenty-Four

Tommy read through the file for a second time as Ben drove them through town toward the Willis residence. He'd skimmed it back at the office in between bites of his Reuben sandwich, but the details hadn't stuck. All he was able to focus on at the time was the perfectly sliced corn beef. After looking down the list of Willis's previous run-ins with the law, he was wondering if this really could be the person who killed Roland Taylor. None of his previous crimes were violent. Jumping right from a disorderly conduct charge to murder didn't seem all that likely. But that didn't mean it wasn't the case. Tommy needed to keep that in mind. He'd come to learn anything was possible.

The neighborhood in which George Willis lived was just inside the city limits. Which was helpful because if it hadn't been and they discovered they needed to make an arrest, then they'd need to call in the Sheriff's Department or State Troopers because they would technically be outside of their jurisdiction, and it could end up being a real headache. But that wasn't the case today. Tommy hated the inter-jurisdictional hoops they needed to jump through sometimes. He just wanted to do his job.

Turning onto Backstreet Road, the detectives noticed the houses started looking very shabby. Untended lawns and overgrown shrubs lined their path. Houses with broken or missing shutters and stained siding sat on either side of the road.

"Hmmm…" Tommy sighed, watching the scene outside the widow pass by. "I will never understand how people don't take pride in their homes."

"A lot of times, it's a domino effect," Ben pointed out. "It just takes one person to let their house go to hell and then…."

"I can't say that I've heard about too much crime out in this neighborhood, though."

"It's true. It doesn't come up on the crime stat map that often."

"So, what?" Tommy asked. "They won't tolerate crimes being committed on their street, but no one has to mow the lawn?"

"If I truly understood how people think, our jobs would be a lot easier," Ben said, pulling the car up to the curb in front of 704 Backstreet Road, home of George Willis.

Chapter Twenty-Five

A beat-up pickup truck sat in the driveway next to a single-story house with vinyl siding that neither Ben nor Tommy could tell if the color was some odd shade of yellow or if it was just in serious need of cleaning. The lawn and bushes in front of the house, however, were nicely trimmed and appeared well taken care of. A visual dichotomy, Ben thought as he got out of the car and took another look around the neighborhood. He wondered, with some apprehension, what the inside of the house was going to look like.

"Um...Ben," Tommy said, motioning to one of the house's windows.

Following his partner's gesture, Ben turned, his eyes widening. "Oh," he said, seeing the Confederate flag hanging in the window like a curtain.

"The South will rise again," Tommy said under his breath as they started up the driveway.

Walking past the pickup, they were startled to find a pair of legs sticking out from under the front of the truck.

"Can I help you?" came a rough voice that the detectives could only assume belonged to the legs.

"George Willis?" Ben asked, staring down at the steel-toed boots.

Shimmying out from under the chassis, a not-so-big man lay on the ground in front of Ben and Tommy. His work shirt and jeans were covered in grease stains, and lord only knew what else. Ben was surprised by how skinny the man appeared. After reading his rap sheet, he just conjured up an image of a burly tough guy. If this was George Willis, then that image was completely wrong. It didn't look like this guy could hurt a fly.

"That's me. What do you want?" Willis asked, sitting up. His eyes narrowing.

"Mr. Willis, I'm Detective Ben Winters. This is my partner Detective Mason. We have a few questions we need to ask you."

"Uh huh… Questions about what?"

"A letter you sent to Roland Taylor," Tommy answered.

"Who?"

"*Father* Roland Taylor," Tommy repeated.

"You mean that ni…*priest* from Saint Paul's?"

Out of the corner of his eye, Ben saw Tommy's jaw clench. Jumping in, he said, "Yes, Father Roland Taylor was the priest serving at Saint Paul's. Did you know him?"

"No. Why would I? I don't go to church." Willis got to his feet, a wrench in his hand that Tommy didn't take his eyes off.

"You never met Father Taylor?" Ben asked.

"That's what I just said, isn't it? Why would I know him? What's this all about?"

"You don't know Roland Taylor, but you know he's the priest from Saint Paul's? How's that?"

"I didn't *know* the man, but I sure as hell heard about him. It was pretty big news, him coming to town and takin' over at that church. Then him showin' up in the paper all the time talkin' about community this and community that."

"Did that bother you?" Tommy asked, an edge in his voice.

Willis didn't answer.

"Mr. Willis," Ben said, taking a plastic evidence bag out of his jacket pocket and unfolding it. "This morning, Roland Taylor was found murdered in his office. This letter…with your signature on it…was found in his private study. Reading what you wrote here, it certainly sounds like you had a problem with him."

"You wrote some nasty things," Tommy added.

"What the hell are you talkin' about?" Willis snapped. "I didn't know him. Never talked to him. And damn sure never send him no letter. Let me see that." He reached to snatch the evidence bag out of Ben's hand.

As Ben took a step back, Tommy instinctively reached for his gun. "Mr. Willis, I think it would be better if you didn't make any quick moves like that again. You might also want to put the wrench down."

The corner of the man's lips turned up in a sneer. "Sorry, Mr. Poo-leees-man. May I *pleeease* see this letter you say I sent." The wrench clanked on the ground as Willis dropped it at his feet.

Ben held the letter up so he could see it through the clear plastic. The detectives watched as the expression on his face changed as he read the scribbled words on the page. When he'd finished, he let out a grunt.

"It sounds like somethin' I might say. Sure. But I didn't write that letter."

"You signed it, you dumb fu..."

"Mr. Willis," Ben cut Tommy off. "Are you saying that is not your signature?"

"That's exactly what I'm sayin.'"

"Do you know of another George Willis in Parker City?" Ben asked, interested to see how the guy tried to explain away the signature.

"Yeah, I do, as a matter of fact. You see. I'm George Willis, *Senior*. My son is George Willis, *Junior*. That's his handwriting and *his* signature."

Chapter Twenty-Six

Nowhere in the PCPD files that Ben and Tommy had looked at did they see anything about George Willis having a son who was also named George. The lack of this bit of information infuriated Ben. He hated not having all the facts. And he hated getting caught flatfooted in front of a potential suspect.

"How old is George, Junior?" Ben asked, putting the evidence page with the letter back into his jacket pocket.

"Seventeen or eighteen." Willis shrugged.

Ben could hear the frustrated exhale Tommy let out behind him.

The difference between George Willis, Junior being seventeen or eighteen was significant. If he was only seventeen, he was still considered a minor under the law, and they would need parental permission to question him. If he was eighteen, legally speaking, he was an adult, and they didn't have to worry about getting anyone's permission. The difference in age would also mean a difference in the charges if they did find cause to arrest the boy. Details like this mattered.

"Is your son at home, Mr. Willis?" Ben asked, looking toward the house.

"Yeah. I think so. He was in the house last time I saw him. Got home from school a little while ago."

"He goes to school?" Tommy asked, the surprise in his voice evident.

"When he wants to," answered Willis.

"Would it be possible to speak with your son, Mr. Willis?" Ben figured asking this way was the best way to cover their bases and get permission to speak with the younger Willis regardless of age. Sure, Willis may have taken the question as asking to show them into the house to find the boy, but if push came to shove, the state's attorney could argue that the detectives received verbal permission to speak to the minor. If he was, in fact, a minor.

"Come on," Willis said, heading for the house. "He's inside somewhere."

Following Willis toward the house, Ben started counting in his head all the ways things could go wrong from this point on. But if he planned for the worst-case scenarios, then he'd be ready for whatever the outcome. He hoped Tommy was doing the same thing.

When they reached the front door, Ben signaled for Tommy to stay outside. For two reasons. If the boy tried to run, he'd be there to head him off. Hopefully. And two, if something went horribly wrong and Ben was inside, Tommy would be outside, only a quick radio call away for backup.

The inside of the Willis house was much as Ben expected. Cluttered. A half dozen pairs of shoes were scattered around the small linoleumed entry. Coats were piled on stacks of boxes randomly kept next to the front door. The furniture in the living room was worn and served more to hold whatever the family decided to throw on it than for sitting.

"Hey, George!" the elder Willis shouted. "Where are you? Cops are here to see you."

Ben wished his presence hadn't been announced that way.

"George! Where you at?" Willis hollered down the hallway toward what Ben figured to be the bedrooms.

From where he was standing, Ben could see the living room and kitchen were empty. If George Junior was in the house, he must have been in one of the rooms down the hall. Ben didn't like that all the doors were closed.

"Mr. Willis, which room is your son's?" Ben asked, reluctantly placing his hand on the gun on his hip.

"The one at the end of the hall," he pointed. "George, if you're home, get your butt out here, boy!"

As Ben started down the hallway, he motioned for Willis to remain where he was in the living room.

"George," Ben called as he slowly took one step after another. "George, if you're here, I really need you to make yourself known. I'm Detective

88

Winters with the PCPD. My partner and I just have a few quick questions to ask you."

Ben didn't want to have to draw his gun, but George Junior wasn't giving him a choice. Standing outside the closed door to the room, Ben was about to pull his gun so that he could carefully enter the room when the door flew open. The boy charged him, slamming into his chest, knocking Ben against the wall. As Ben regained his balance, he watched the younger Willis run down the hall toward the front door.

"Tommy! He's running!" Ben shouted as he took off after the boy. "Tommy!"

Ben ran out the front door just in time to see the boy running down the driveway, Tommy a few feet behind him. When his partner got to the end of the driveway, Ben watched Tommy stop next to a beat-up metal trash can. Taking the lip off the can, Tommy hurled it at George Junior like a metal frisbee. Ben watched in mild disbelief as the lid spun through the air and collide with the back of the boy's legs, sending him crashing to the pavement.

"What the hell was that?" Ben shouted to Tommy as he jogged down the yard toward his partner.

"I am too tired to run today," Tommy answered, casually walking over to where George Junior was lying, putting a foot on the boy's back as he pulled the handcuffs off his belt.

Chapter Twenty-Seven

1862...

Caleb waited in the library as the sheriff went to retrieve the unexpected guest from the sitting room in which Mr. Percy had left him. The Tildon's library, interestingly enough, did not have many books. A single bookcase stood in the corner of the room near the window, next to a small desk that the sheriff would occasionally use. If it had been up to him, Caleb figured he would have named it the music room for the polished Chickering piano that was the most eye-catching piece of furniture in the room. Elizabeth Tildon frequently suggested she give Caleb lessons, but he would always politely decline. He was never much for fancy music, personally. Not that he had anything against it. It had just never been part of his upbringing. He found that he enjoyed the music he heard in the music halls a bit more. It was more lively. Even though it wasn't his favorite, he did find he enjoyed the evenings when Mrs. Tildon would play for all of them while they sipped their coffee after dinner.

Running his finger over the keys, anxiously biding the time, Caleb paced back and forth in front of the piano. For the sheriff's mysterious friend to have made the journey from Washington and suddenly appeared on his doorstep, it must be of the gravest of natures.

So deep in thought was he, Caleb jumped when the door swung open, and the sheriff barreled into the room. Following close behind was a rather striking-looking gentleman. With an expensive black coat, matching Derby, and leather gloves, the man stood framed in the doorway holding a weighty-looking walking stick. He was a sharp-looking man in many ways, Caleb thought.

The man carefully regarded the young deputy as he removed his hat and gloves. He was methodical in his movements. His eyes quickly scanning the entire room. A brief expression of consternation crossed his face as he discovered his conversation with the sheriff would apparently not be private.

"Samuel, I came here to speak with you about your telegram," the man said as he took a seat in one of the two leather armchairs near the fireplace. "I believe it would be wise for it to be just you and I."

"Balderdash!" the sheriff boomed. "This is my most trusted deputy. If there is something afoot, he needs to know about it just as much as do I."

Weighing his options, he finally conceded. "Very well. If you trust him, Samuel, then I won't object."

Tildon poured himself a drink from the decanter on the side table and offered a glass to his guest. "This is Caleb Post. Don't let his youth distract you. His mind is as sharp as a whip, and he can toe the mark. You need not worry about him or his fidelities. Caleb, this is…."

"No, Sam," the man cut in quickly. "I think it better not to introduce me as I am not, in fact, here this evening. I am still in Washington helping oversee this blasted war."

"I see," the sheriff said as he handed his secretive friend a tumbler of his finest brandy. "For you to make the trip in person and show up on my doorstep under the cover of darkness must mean this is all of the utmost importance."

"You have no idea, Samuel."

"Enlighten us," the sheriff said, easing into the chair opposite his guest.

Caleb remained standing by the piano. He thought it best to remain as unobtrusive as possible. He could tell the gravity of the situation by the look in the other man's eyes. He didn't want to do anything that would in any way cause the sheriff any trouble. Plus, he always felt like he could learn more by simply observing.

"Your message asked about Eustace Drake."

"It did. His carriage was discovered south of town this morning. His coachman dead. Drake missing. Caleb, here, learned that he'd been summoned to Washington yesterday. By none other than your...by Secretary Stanton. Assuming he made that meeting, something happened to him on his way back to Parker City last night. Then this morning, when we paid a visit to Drake House to speak with Mrs. Drake, we come to find George McClellan making a house call."

"I may not have the most sense, but with matters as they are, and two armies pointing guns and cannons at each other just over the mountain a bit, I find it suspicious that the general decides to go visiting. And it's a coincidence that that visit is to a man who just met with Edwin Stanton, *at the White House*, the day prior and is now missing."

"What did McClellan have to say?"

"Oh, he had some humbug for us. Thought it must have been highway robbers."

"And you don't believe that?"

Tildon didn't answer. At least not with words. The expression on his face said everything. He didn't believe McClellan's theory. Especially knowing what they did about where Drake had been.

"Of course, you don't believe that," the man said. After a long pause, as he considered what to say next, he continued. "What I have to say must be held in the strictest of confidences, gentlemen."

"Jonathan!" the sheriff roared in frustration.

"No names, Sam."

"Just get on with it, man! By the time we get to the heart of it, Caleb may be the sheriff, and this war could be over."

"I can confirm that Eustace Drake did arrive in Washington yesterday. I was at the meeting he attended. When he left, he was very much alive and to deliver certain information to one of General McClellan's lieutenants at the Courthouse here in Parker City. It was being used as a meeting point. When he did not arrive at the appointed time, the general became concerned. I wish he had not visited Drake House personally, but McClellan does not always follow orders as well as we would like. That's not much of a secret."

"Might I ask what this information was that Drake was transporting?" The sheriff had finished his brandy and was now running his finger around the rim of the empty glass.

Again, there was a long silence as the man sat, turning over in his head what he could, or should, say. Caleb was forming the impression that this man guarded a number of secrets. And if he was in a private meeting with Secretary Stanton at the White House—and one could only assume the president as well—he must also be someone important within the War Department. But he didn't carry himself like an officer of any rank. And his clothing was certainly too fine for that of a mere soldier. Caleb's curiosity was peaked. Who was the man sitting before him?

When he finally spoke again, his voice sounded strained. As if it went against everything in his nature to be saying what he was about to. Leaning forward, he looked from Tildon to Caleb, then back to the sheriff.

"Gentlemen, have either of you ever heard of the Knights of the Golden Circle?"

Chapter Twenty-Eight

"Hogwash!" the sheriff bellowed, his voice bouncing off the walls around them.

"I thought the Knights of the Golden Circle were just a myth," Caleb said, surprised to hear the words come out of his mouth so forcefully.

"In a sense, they are. And in a sense...they are not," Tildon's guest said as he eased back in his chair.

"Confound it, man!" Tildon's patience was worn thin. Caleb had seen him like this before. Whenever someone was trying to be particularly elusive or evade answering his questions, the sheriff lost his usual jovial demeanor.

"Listen to me," the man said. His voice was so calm. It put Caleb at ease and on edge all at the same moment. "Many of the stories you have heard about the Golden Circle have been completely fabricated. They're fables told to try and scare us into ending the war. But I can assure you, there is an organization out there working against the Union. This group's greatest resource is its secrecy. There are many northerners that would like to see the federal government fall. Many powerful individuals. Some who even outwardly put on a show of supporting the Union."

"What can the Golden Circle have to do with Eustace Drake?" the sheriff questioned.

"Samuel, I suggest you follow the example of your apprentice and allow me to continue without your emotional outbursts. The time for that is long behind us. Especially if they have Drake."

Caleb could not believe anyone had the steel to speak to the sheriff in such a direct and admonishing manner. The last man who tried was quickly laid out on his backside by a swift jab to the jaw. Tildon may have been getting on in years, but he could still land a solid blow when worked into a lather.

Pulling the scrap of paper he'd found in Drake's desk from his pocket, the first set of letters now made sense. The LDEN CIR came from *Golden Circle*. The three words in the center of the pamphlet or whatever the paper had been…

GOLDEN CIRCLE

SUCCESSION

CONFEDERACY

"What have you, boy?" the man asked, spying the paper in his hands.

"I found this in Mr. Drake's desk. It looks like it could be part of a handbill."

Taking the piece of paper from Caleb, he turned it over in his hands several times.

"I believe," he began, "this is part of a recruiting pamphlet. The group has been trying to grow its ranks, and Eustace Drake has been working to uncover the Circle's members here in Parker City. We believe several very powerful men—leaders within the group—reside right here."

"Do you think they found out Mr. Drake was tryin' to unmask them? And they…took him?" Caleb asked.

"Or worse."

"These men, these Knights of the Golden Circle, they are a shadow within the Confederacy. They have been working to amass resources to help bring about the downfall of the United States as we know it for some time."

"A conspiracy?" The sheriff found it difficult to believe. "And you think… you think there are agents of this Golden Circle living here in Parker City? Under our very noses?"

"That is the information Drake was providing to us. He was perfectly placed to infiltrate the group. The men he feared were involved are all a part of the same social set. Possibly his very own friends."

The sheriff's agitation brought him to his feet, and he began pacing before the fireplace. "So, what shall we do?"

"Do? There is nothing for you to do, Samuel."

"Humbug! If these men kidnapped Eustace Drake...*or worse*, then it is my sworn duty to bring them to justice."

"These are not some run-of-the-mill criminals. If they were not deterred by Drake's money or his connections in Washington, do you think they'd fret over you and your men coming after them? You could end up just like Drake."

A silence filled the library, leaving Caleb to wonder what to do next. He understood that the man from Washington was telling them how dangerous this Golden Circle and its members could be. But he also agreed with the sheriff that it was their responsibility to keep the people of Parker City safe.

"Sir, you said that Mr. Drake was to meet one of General McClellan's men at the Courthouse last night. Was he to deliver a message? Or information?" Caleb was working on assembling all the puzzle pieces in his head.

"He was. Yes."

"Might he have been snatched for that information?"

"It is certainly possible."

"Then these men figured out what Drake was up to," Tildon surmised.

"That is also possible," the man agreed.

"What was the information Mr. Drake was to deliver to the general's man?" Caleb asked.

"That, I cannot tell you. Military secrets."

"Which could now be in the hands of this shadow group," the sheriff huffed as he dropped himself back down into his chair.

Chapter Twenty-Nine

Caleb quietly puzzled through everything they'd just been told. Not only was there an actual war being fought to save the Union, there was a secret organization fighting to bring it down as well. These Knights of the Golden Circle.

What little he knew about the Golden Circle was mostly from conversations he'd overheard in the tavern. Tidbits of information he'd picked up from soldiers on both sides. The group's goal was to amass enough wealth and resources to support the Confederacy in defeating the Union. The stories also told how the Golden Circle and its agents had accumulated a vast treasure and hidden it throughout the south to aid in the financing of the war. Caleb never knew if the stories were to be believed. But listening to the sheriff's friend, it did appear that the Golden Circle did actually exist.

"It does seem logical to believe," Caleb said during another lull in the conversation, "that the men Mr. Drake was trying to unmask figured out what he was doin' and set upon him last night so he could not reveal their identities."

"It would not be difficult to believe that," the sheriff's friend agreed.

"Maybe Mr. Drake was the wrong fella to be looking into them," Caleb offered.

Both of the older men had questioning expressions on their faces.

"You said yourself," Caleb continued, "Mr. Drake had power and influence. And that they weren't afraid of him."

"I did."

"He's the sort they may have been expectin.' Someone who could take 'em on. Maybe the person trying to figure who they are should be someone they'd never suspect. Someone who would never try to take on such formidable men. The sort of person that could be underestimated."

"Caleb, I don't like what you're thinking," the sheriff said, shaking his head.

"Sir, they'd know if somebody like Eustace Drake went missing, it would be up to us to look for him. Well, what if we say we're lookin' for him because we believe he was kidnapped by bandits? Go along with General McClellan's story that it was a highway robbery. When in truth, we're really lookin' for the Golden Circle?"

Once again, the sheriff stood and began pacing. His nerves were forcing him to stay in constant motion. Always very animated, tonight his actions were being brought on by sheer unease with the whole situation. The war being on Parker City's front doorstep was bad enough. But secret agents of the Confederacy operating in the city's shadows infuriated him.

For his part, the mysterious visitor from Washington sat silently, staring out the window into the night. Caleb didn't know if he was contemplating what he'd just suggested or if there was more information he'd yet to share. Either way, his silence was unsettling.

"Sam, the boy may be right. I find it difficult to say that. But...subterfuge such as what he's suggesting could give us an advantage."

"I don't care much for this, *Jonathan*. You want to set my boy on finding out who's running this secret organization. An organization out to bring down the government! If your War Department can't bring them down, what makes you think he can?"

"Because we're becoming desperate. I am willing to take a risk if it means saving the Union."

Tildon stood in front of the window, looking out on the street. It was now his turn to lead the uncomfortable silence in the library. After a few painful moments, he quietly grumbled, "Confound it." Then turned and asked, "Where do we begin?"

Chapter Thirty

1984...

George Willis, Junior sat on the curb with his hands cuffed behind him, a look of youthful indignation plastered on his face. Ben, Tommy, and the elder Willis stood over him, staring down at the boy. Junior had put up a bit of a struggle, requiring both the detectives to get him to his feet. The whole time, Senior stood in the front yard yelling at his son.

"Am I under arrest or something?" He spat his words out, his anger barely under control.

"Should you be under arrest for something?" Tommy answered with his own question. His response was so quick and forceful George Junior flinched.

Ben watched as the boy's eyes darted back and forth between his and Tommy's. "Let's take one thing at a time, shall we? Mr. Willis, is this your son, George Willis, Junior?"

"Uh huh."

"George," Ben asked, turning his attention back to the teenager, "how old are you?"

"I don't need to talk to you."

"Oh, for God's sake." Tommy made a quick move toward Junior, causing him to draw back and forcing Ben to put his arm out in front of his partner. It was perfectly choreographed. There was nothing like the *Good Cop/Bad*

Cop Show put on by Detectives Winters and Mason.

"Just tell 'em how old you are, boy," Senior barked.

"Shame you don't know how old your own son is or you could tell 'em!" he shot back.

"Alright. Everyone just take a deep breath. Okay? Now, George, how old are you?"

After biting his lower lip for what seemed like an eternity, he said, "Seventeen. Now don't I get a phone call or something?"

"A phone call?" Tommy looked at him with a puzzled expression. "Who are you gonna call? Your father's standing right here. You are his father, right?"

"Have been for seventeen years, apparently."

"No, I mean to call a lawyer."

"You have a lawyer?" Tommy asked, the sarcasm in his voice deafening.

"I *want* a lawyer, you stupid pig."

"Mr. Willis," Tommy said, turning back to the man. "You're this boy's legal guardian, correct?"

"I'm his father."

"And where's his mother?"

"Hell if I know. We've been divorced almost as long as he's been around."

"Okay, so let's just pretend you're a good father *and* his legal guardian. Since he's seventeen, that means he's a minor, and we need your permission to speak with him. Can we please speak with your son?"

"Sure. Why not?"

"There," Tommy spun back to the boy. "Your father says we can talk to you so you don't get a lawyer."

"Tommy," Ben said. His voice was low and very even. Tommy knew the tone. Something was wrong. He stepped over to his partner, who had moved a few paces away from the Willises.

Ben, never taking his eyes off the boy sitting on the curb just in case he was dumb enough to try and run again, said, "We can't question him."

"What are you talking about? It doesn't matter that he's seventeen. His father gave us permission. You heard me ask him. I'm *actually* following procedure here, and *now* you're telling me we can't talk to him. Why?"

"He asked for a lawyer."

"So? It doesn't matter. He's seventeen, and his father waived the right."

"He can't waive his son's right to an attorney. Especially when the son actually uses the words 'I want a lawyer.'"

"Are you saying we need to waste time getting this little prick a lawyer?"

"If he killed Father Taylor and he ends up getting off on a technicality, you know what will happen," Ben said.

"But he isn't even under arrest. We're just here to ask questions."

"I agree with you. But the wrong judge won't see it that way."

"So, we arrest him for assaulting an officer? You said he ran into you, right? We take him down to the station and wait for his lawyer? Then talk to him about Taylor? When he's all lawyered up?"

Ben kept looking at the boy. His mind was trying to play out the various scenarios, but the technicalities were starting to give him a headache. If this kid was a priest killer and he walked because they screwed up, they'd be handing in their badges, and their careers would be over. But that would pale in comparison to knowing they'd let a murderer get away. If they could just ask the kid a few questions, he might have absolutely nothing to do with the murder and they could move on with the investigation. It was moments like this when Ben always thought how much easier it was to be a police officer on television. The rules in TV Land were much more fluid.

Ben finally took his eyes off George Junior and looked at his partner. "I have an idea. Just follow my lead."

Chapter Thirty-One

Walking back over to the Willises, Ben sighed. "You're right, George. Even though we haven't placed you under arrest for anything. You don't need to talk to us without a lawyer being present. So, my partner—that's Detective Mason, by the way—is going to go radio the station and have them send out a public defender. I assume you don't have your own personal lawyer."

Ben saw a flicker in the teen's eyes. The expression now settling onto his face was that of a victory. "Fine. Send whoever. But I want a lawyer."

"Detective Mason, will you please go radio the station and tell them we need a public defender sent to this address?"

"If I have to." Tommy wasn't sure where this was going, but he knew he needed to keep up the façade of the frustrated cop. If he suddenly became agreeable, the kid might get suspicious. As he walked back to their car and picked up the radio mic, he started wondering what the hell Ben was thinking. They wouldn't actually call in for a lawyer like this. So, for anyone watching, he went through the motions.

A few minutes later, Tommy returned to the group and said, "They're a little busy at the Courthouse, but they said they'd send someone over as soon as they can. Could be an hour or more. Lots going on down there today."

"So? What now? Do I just sit here?" Junior asked.

"I'd say we could spend the time talking," Ben began, "but since you invoked your right to counsel, we can't say anything to you. So, my partner and I are just going to talk about what we're going to do once your lawyer gets here, and we can take you down to the station."

Ben turned ever so slightly away from the Georges, still keeping the teenager in his line of sight, and started talking to Tommy. "We're going to book him for assault on an officer, evading arrest, making threats through the mail…."

"Oh, that's probably FBI territory," Tommy cut in. "Mail's federal."

"Right. Then there's the murder charge. That's a state crime."

"What the hell?! What murder?" the boy shouted as he tried to get to his feet.

"Hey! Shut up," Tommy yelled back. "We can't talk to you without your lawyer. So, we're not talking to you. Mind your business."

"You're talking about charging me with murder. I didn't kill anyone."

"You really screwed yourself up this time. Didn'tcha, boy?" the elder Willis said, shaking his head.

"I didn't kill anyone!"

"I wish we could talk to you about this and clear everything up, George," Ben said, taking a step toward him. "But you asked for a lawyer."

"So, what? If I told you I didn't want a lawyer anymore, then we could talk?"

"We could talk all night long if you wanted," Ben answered.

"Okay. I don't want a lawyer, and I didn't kill anybody."

The boy's entire demeanor changed. The tough teenager was gone. A fragile, somewhat disoriented youth was now in front of them.

"Let's get you up off the street, first of all," Ben began. Helping the boy to his feet, he also uncuffed his hands and walked him to their car. Opening the back door, he had the boy sit down. The only reason he took the cuffs off was because he was going to be sitting in a car and couldn't easily get away. Not with him and Tommy standing right there. But to Junior, it was a sign of goodwill.

"Now, George, why'd you run?"

"Because you're the cops, dude. It's never good when you show up."

Leaning on the doorframe of the cruiser, Tommy asked, "Do you have a reason you need to be running from us? Have you done something?"

"Well, you came lookin' for me, so you think I did something.'"

"Okay, so that could have all gone better," Ben agreed. "But let's forget about it for the moment. Do you know Roland Taylor?"

George, Junior didn't say anything but turned his head and looked away. Whether he realized he was doing it or not, he began picking at his fingernails. Ben didn't need him to say the words. He could tell by his reaction he knew exactly who Taylor was. But did he know what had happened to him?

"George, did you know Father Taylor?" he asked again.

"He's that hot-shot priest. I heard of him."

"Doesn't sound like you liked him very much," Tommy offered.

"I didn't know 'em."

"But you didn't like him?" Ben asked.

"People like *him* shouldn't be priests."

"Exactly what kind of people are you talking about?" Tommy asked, cocking his head to the side.

"You know exactly what kind of people I'm talkin' about. Those darkies."

"He ain't wrong," the boy's father said from behind them.

"Mr. Willis," Tommy growled, spinning around, so they were face-to-face, "I suggest you stay quiet and do not make things worse. Because I am really not in the mood today."

"You have a problem with black people?" Ben asked the boy, trying to keep an even tone, though he felt very much like Tommy did at the moment.

"Don't you?" the boy shot back. "They're ruinin' everything. They should just...."

"Alright," Ben cut him off. "You say you didn't actually know Father Taylor, but you didn't like him because he was black. Is that why you sent him this letter?"

From his jacket pocket, Ben once again pulled the evidence bag with the letter they'd found at Saint Paul's. George, Junior looked at it through the bag and smirked.

"So that's what this is all about. That coon called the police on me."

"No, he didn't," Tommy said. "But I have to give you credit for actually

104

signing that piece of filth. That takes guts. To put your name on something that shouts loud and clear, 'hey, I'm a racist little prick.'"

"Hey! You can't call me that."

"But you did send it?" Ben asked, trying to keep things on track.

"Fine. Yeah. I sent it. He needed to know what people thought of him."

Ben could hear his partner rolling his eyes.

"Well, George, Father Taylor didn't actually call us about this letter. In fact, Father Taylor didn't call us at all. Where were you last night?"

The boy looked at Ben with a puzzled look on his face. "What does it matter where I was?"

"Because last night, someone broke into Saint Paul's and beat Father Taylor to death," Tommy said, staring directly into the boy's eyes.

"I didn't do it. I wasn't anywhere near that church. I was home. Here. No! I was at the arcade for a while with my friends after school. Then I came home for dinner and was here the rest of the night. He was here with me," George Junior said, pointing at his father. "Tell them I was here."

George, Junior was singing like a canary. He went from not wanting to say anything to not wanting to shut up. He kept asking his father to tell them he was home all night. It seemed almost begrudgingly that George Senior did confirm what his son said. He got home for dinner at five-thirty, then was home the rest of the night. The two even watched the late movie together until two in the morning. They'd need to get the exact time of Roland Taylor's death, but the coroner's assistant had estimated the time of death to be around midnight, which would have been when the late movie was just starting.

After talking to the kid, Ben's gut was telling him that George Willis Junior wasn't the person they were looking for. He was a blustery teenage boy with a lot of hate in him. But when the pressure was on, he crumbled pretty fast. Definitely more talk than action. Plus, it looked like he had an alibi. Granted, that alibi was his father. But Ben got the distinct impression that either Willis, Senior or Junior, would sell the other one out at the drop of a hat. And if the younger Willis wasn't the killer, they were back to square one.

Chapter Thirty-Two

Before leaving Backstreet Road, Ben and Tommy knocked on a few doors to see if anyone had seen George Junior the previous evening. Two neighbors said they'd been outside when one of the boy's friends dropped him off in an early-model Camaro. They both clearly remembered because the car was loud—one guessed the kid had "adjusted" the muffler—and bright orange, making it hard to miss. One of the neighbors added that they hadn't seen anyone leave the house the rest of the night. Or at least before 12:30 when Carson ended because his television set was next to the window that faced the Willis's.

It was enough for Ben and Tommy to say George Junior was just a juvenile delinquent and not Roland Taylor's killer. While they were sure they could bring him in on one charge or another, they decided they'd be seeing him again in the future, so why waste the time now. Especially when they were once again faced with not having a suspect for the murder of the popular priest. In a perfect world, Ben would be able to make every arrest, no matter how small or seemingly insignificant the crime. But reality didn't allow for that. The pressure of a big murder case that would be the top headline in the paper the next day didn't allow for the detectives to focus on a kid who had problems. Though if they did, Ben wondered if it would make a difference in the path George Junior continued along.

Turning the unmarked cruiser toward the station, they decided they needed to regroup. The case wasn't even twelve hours old, and they'd already exhausted one theory. They needed to come up with another. Hopefully, they'd come across something in their notes from that morning that would shake an idea loose.

If they needed to, they may even head back to the crime scene at Saint Paul's to take another look around. But that might be a better idea for the next day. Exhaustion was beginning to catch up with Ben and Tommy, and while they wanted to pour what little energy they still had into the case, their bodies were telling them they'd had enough. If they were going to solve this case, they needed to be at the top of their game. Both mentally and physically.

The silence in the car lasted the entire ride. Ben drove as Tommy blew clouds of smoke out the window. The chill on the early evening air was oddly refreshing. If nothing else, it was helping to keep them awake.

Parking the car in the lot behind the PCPD, Ben and Tommy headed into the station through the same door they'd dragged Rooster Jones through the night before. Tony was already at the desk, ready for the night shift.

He looked rested and ready to go. Which didn't help when he said, "Wow. You guys don't look so good."

"It's probably because we haven't slept in the last ten weeks," Tommy snapped. "I'm sorry, Sarge. That's an exaggeration. I think it's actually only been eight weeks."

"Sorry, fellas," Tony said. "You know I didn't mean anything by it. I'm sure you got Brent breathing down your neck over the murder at Saint Paul's. Any leads?"

"We thought we had one," Ben said as he rubbed his eyes with the palms of his hand. "But we knew it was too good to be true."

"Yeah. It couldn't have just been the dumbass, racist kid and made our lives easy," Tommy grumbled.

"It doesn't work like that," Tony agreed. "But you'll get the guy. You two are pretty sharp cookies. Everybody around here knows that."

"That's nice of you to say," Ben said with a weak smile. "But all hell's going to break loose when everyone sees the headline in the paper."

"At this point," Tony began, "I'd be surprised if there is somebody in Parker City who hasn't already heard what happened to Father Taylor. Word travels real fast around our little burg."

"But it's different when it's printed in big letters in black and white," Tommy pointed out.

"And considering recent events, I'm sure some of the TV stations from Baltimore and D.C. will end up picking up the story," Ben added.

"Our little *burg*, as you put it, Tony, ain't all that quiet anymore," Tommy said before letting out a yawn, which immediately caused Ben and the desk sergeant to do the same.

"Well, when you do catch the bastard, I'll be right here waitin' to help you book him," Tony offered as the detectives started down the hall.

Chapter Thirty-Three

With large cups of black coffee in front of them, Ben and Tommy went line by line through their notes from the crime scene that morning. Any detail either one thought might be important was transferred to the chalkboard Ben had squeezed into the office years before. Ben had taken a photo that morning of Father Roland Taylor from one of the church bulletins and taped it to the board. Under it, he began writing the few details they'd been able to put together so far about what happened. Once the coroner concluded the autopsy and the State Police's forensic team issued its report, he would fill in any new information.

For now, he and Tommy were looking for a new angle. Even though he'd been ruled out, George Willis's name was still on the board. He might not have been the killer, but the detectives were fairly certain he wasn't the only person in town that could have hated the priest because of his race. So, it was possible that could still be the motive. They just needed a new suspect.

Ignoring the stack of messages from various reporters looking for comment on the case, Ben was flipping through Taylor's daily schedule to see if anything jumped out at him. Bonnie Gillespie said there hadn't been any recent trouble at the church. But there had been threats in the past. He wished the priest hadn't destroyed the letters. Even though he didn't want to accept his life might be in danger, he should have still kept them just in case, Ben thought.

While he was coming up with nothing of note in Taylor's planner, Tommy was on the phone talking to one of the patrol officers who always seemed to be tapped into the "word on the street." With all of the community clean-up going on around Saint Paul's, maybe some of the dealers were getting uncomfortable and decided to push back. Father Taylor was making a big difference in the fight to revitalize the city's center.

Thinking about that, Ben picked up the phone and dialed the number for Ron Kramer, one of the officers assigned to the department's special Drug Task Force. In fact, he was now the team's senior officer after the task force's original commanding officer had been shot down earlier that year with Kramer only a couple of blocks away. After a second member of the squad was killed a couple days later, Kramer had gone to pieces. But once Ben and Tommy put the killer away and he'd taken some time off, he came back stronger than ever and ready to lead the reorganized task force.

"What can I do for you, Detective?" Kramer asked, his heavy southern drawl seeping through the phone's receiver.

"I assume you've heard about Roland Taylor," Ben began.

"I couldn't believe it when I did. When Woods came in and told me about it, I thought he had to have gotten it wrong. I just saw Father Taylor last week at Saint Paul's Fall Festival. It makes me sick to my stomach."

"So, you knew Father Taylor?"

"To a point. We didn't go out drinkin' or anything like that. But he was helping to clean up the neighborhood. Was really trying to get the young people to take more of an interest in what happened around them. He thought the more invested they felt, the less likely they were to turn to drugs and alcohol."

"Were Taylor's good works rubbing anyone the wrong way?"

"What are you thinking here, Ben? Someone didn't like Taylor cleaning things up?"

"Right now, I'm considering all of the possibilities." Ben was bending a paperclip back and forth as he spoke. As tired as he was, he still had an excess of nervous energy to work out. "Is there a chance one of the dealers around Saint Paul's thought Father Taylor was interfering too much in their business?"

There was a sigh on the other end of the phone before Kramer spoke again. "I don't know of anyone specific who might have had a beef with Taylor.

But then again, these druggies don't always know what they're doing, to begin with. I know that's not the answer you're looking for."

"I guess it would be too easy if some doped-up thug was out there openly threatening the crusading priest," Ben said.

"Wouldn't it be nice if the scumbags always told us what they were going to do like that? Listen. I'll talk to some people and see if anyone's heard anything."

"I'd appreciate that, Ron. Thanks."

Hanging up the phone, Ben looked to Tommy, who was leaning back in his chair rubbing his temples. "Any luck?"

Tommy shook his head. "No one's been talking about a plan they had to kill Taylor. But Jacobson's going to ask around and see if anyone's heard anything since it happened. What about you? Who were you talking to?"

"Ron Kramer. I thought maybe Taylor's push to clean up Downtown might have gotten some of the dealers worked up enough to go after him."

"And?"

"He couldn't think of anyone off the top of his head."

"The criminal element in this town sucks. They don't talk to anyone," Tommy said.

Looking at his watch, Ben said, "Alright. There's nothing else we can do tonight. We're at a standstill. Hopefully, we'll get a preliminary report from the coroner or CSU in the morning, and they will have found something useful. Or we head back to Saint Paul's. Either way, we start fresh."

As they collected their things and closed up the office for the night, neither Ben nor Tommy had ever felt as defeated when it came to an investigation. Even at the height of the Spring Strangler case, as horrifying as that time was, they always felt like there was some forward momentum. But right now, they'd completely hit a wall and were at a loss.

They had nothing.

Chapter Thirty-Four

1862...

By the time Caleb arrived at the Courthouse the next morning, word had already reached the city that the fighting had begun near Sharpsburg. All anyone could do now was wait and prepare for the onslaught of dead and wounded soldiers that would soon be making their way to Parker. It was a terrible feeling. Knowing something so horrendous was happening just over the mountains while everything seemed so normal and people were going about their regular daily routines.

The sheriff and Caleb, along with their unexpected visitor from Washington, had literally been burning the midnight oil. Which is why Caleb was getting to the Courthouse much later than usual. After the events of the previous day, followed by the late-night meeting, he'd overslept, not something he was accustomed to doing. This left him slightly out of sorts as he rushed to dress and prepare for the day.

Cursing himself for his tardiness, Caleb didn't take his usual leisurely stroll from his rooms in the Commerce Street House Hotel to the Court. He double-timed it, only slowing briefly now and again to courteously greet one of the shopkeepers who called his name as he rushed by.

Out of breath, he'd charged into the Courthouse and climbed the stairs two at a time.

Deputies Gimble and Ford were seated at the table outside the sheriff's office playing a card game when he walked in.

Without taking his eyes off his hand, Gimble said, "Not like you to be comin' in late, Post."

"I just figgered he was out looking for Drake with the rest of the boys," Ford said, throwing his cards down on the table. "Everything alright, Caleb?"

"It was a long night," Caleb said, finally taking a moment to catch his breath. "Has anything happened here this morning?"

"Like what?" Gimble asked, eyeing him with a curious look.

Before Caleb could answer, Deputy Ford began to tell him about the news of the battle and how he'd seen a group of city residents heading west to observe the fighting. They all had picnic baskets and looked like they were going for a relaxing afternoon outing. Shaking his head at the idea of people going sightseeing while soldiers were dying, Caleb caught a glimpse of the gathering in the sheriff's office.

Following his eyes, Ford said, "They came in a bit ago all hot under the collar demandin' to know what was being done to find Drake."

Caleb wasn't surprised the men had come seeking answers. It was to be expected. After the mayor's visit yesterday, a couple of Eustace Drake's business associates arrived, offering their assistance in locating the missing industrialist as well.

Judging by the men's rapid and jerking movements on the other side of the glass, Caleb figured these gentlemen were not present to offer their assistance but rather their outrage at the fact something of this nature could happen in Parker City. Both former mayors, they now served on the City Council and had more influence in the running of the city than Mayor Gladhill. After all, in addition to their government service, each was the master of his own business empire and patriarch of his family. Families which founded the city.

Caleb watched as the meeting broke up, and the sheriff escorted his visitors out of the office. With harsh expressions on their faces—something Caleb was used to seeing with these two—Silas Moss and Thaddeus Parker filed out the door, followed by the City Council's chief clerk, William McClinton.

"We won't stand for this, Samuel," Silas Moss, a bulldog of a man—both

113

in look and personality—snarled as he placed the top hat on his head.

It was only that hat that made Moss come close to the same height as his Council colleague. And even then, he was still a few inches shy. Parker, tall and as thin as a crooked stick, loomed over everyone.

"We cannot have highway robbers preying on the people of this city," Parker agreed in his nasally drawl. "We on the City Council want action taken. This does not happen in Parker City. Eustace Drake was a fine upstanding citizen. The scoundrels who did this must face justice."

"I assure you, gentlemen," the sheriff began in his most genial tone, "my deputies are scouring the county for any trace of Mr. Drake and the men who are responsible for his disappearance. As you see, I have men here I was just about to speak with and give directions when you showed up and asked for a word. So, if you will excuse me, I believe the sooner I can talk to my men, the...."

"Just make sure this isn't the beginning of something," Moss interrupted. Turning on his heels, he led the other two men out into the hallway.

Glad to see the trio on their way, the sheriff motioned for Caleb to join him in his office. Before he closed the door, he turned to Gimble and Ford and said, "I want you boys to make your way along the river. Make sure there's no bodies on the shore. That's all we need. To have someone find Drake floating in the Tasker. Hop to."

After watching his deputies clear out, Tildon eased himself into his chair as he lit a brand new cigar from the carved wooden humidor on his desk. Watching the rings of smoke float toward the ceiling, he let the rush of tobacco do its work before he spoke.

"Where do you intend to begin your clandestine investigation?"

"Well, sir, we know who Mr. Drake was lookin' for. So...I thought I would begin by trying to figure out where he was lookin' for 'em. I was going to visit his offices and see if he'd been traveling anywhere unusual or meeting with anyone he didn't normally meet with. And if I can get into his office, maybe he kept something there that might help. He mightn't of wanted to take such dangerous information home with him."

"That's good thinking, my boy," the sheriff said, biting down hard on the cigar. "I just want you to be careful. You have your shooters with you?"

"One on each hip, sir. Jus' like always. But I'm hoping it won't come to anything like that."

"Neither do I. But if anything happens to you, Edie will have my hide. You can count on that."

Chapter Thirty-Five

D rake & Sons Textiles was located on a piece of land on the very edge of town. Owing to the smell of the tanning process that went on in the place, no one wanted to see the tannery built anywhere near homes or retail establishments, so it was constructed next to two small factories, which were already filling the air in that part of Parker with thick, noxious odors.

Caleb was able to smell the foul industrial buildings well before he could see them as he walked from the Courthouse across town. The day was pleasant for the time of year, so the walk didn't bother him. It gave him a chance to stretch his legs and think about the task he'd volunteered to undertake.

In the light of day, he was wondering what he'd been thinking the previous evening when he said he thought he should be the one to try and uncover the agents of the Knights of the Golden Circle in Parker City. How was he going to be able to seek out the leaders of a secret organization aiming to topple the government of the United States? Even if the Parker City contingent was just a small part of a larger whole.

Drake & Sons consisted of a large textile mill and separate tannery building, along with several outbuildings and an administrative building with the firm's offices fronting the property on the street. Standing in front of the three-story brick structure, Caleb pondered the sign on the top of the building. It very clearly announced that this was Drake & Sons Textiles. To his knowledge, Eustace Drake didn't have any sons. Thinking about it, there were a number of businesses in town that were someone "& Son" or "Sons." Caleb wondered if it was all a tactic to appear family oriented. Knowing what he did about Drake, he wouldn't put it past him to use every means at his disposal to build his company. Even if it meant the creation of imaginary children.

Caleb watched as a group of workers came around the back of the building. They were burly men, fitted out in their work clothes. A couple wore leather aprons under their jackets, as others were wiping their hands on handkerchiefs trying to clean them before eating their lunch. Which is where Caleb figured the men were headed. If they'd started work at an early hour, it would make sense for this to be their mealtime.

There were a few taverns right down the road that catered to the workers in this part of town. A little more rough and raucous than the finer eateries closer to the center of Parker, Caleb and some of the other deputies had been forced to break up brawls between the workers several times.

None of the men paid much mind to Caleb as they passed by. They were too busy hollering over one another to notice him as he climbed the couple of steps to the administrative building's entrance. Pushing through the large door, Caleb found himself standing in a long hallway with a series of offices running down its length on either side. He could hear the muffled clicking of typewriters coming from behind one of the doors down the corridor.

The first door he came to sat slightly ajar, so after a light rap of his knuckles, he didn't wait for anyone to invite him in. On the other side, the office was empty. Though two desks sat one in front of the other, both facing the door, there was no one seated at either. Through the wall, coming from the room next door, he could hear voices.

Exiting one door and walking to the next, he found this one sitting wide open. Poking his head in, he saw this office was arranged in an identical fashion to the first. However, here there was a man sitting behind each desk with stacks of what looked to be ledgers in front of them. The clerk at the first desk was calling out numbers to the man sitting behind him. So engrossed were they in their records it took them several moments to notice Caleb standing in the doorway.

"May I help you with something?" the clerk at the desk closest to Caleb inquired from behind a pair of thin wire-framed glasses.

"Sorry to be interrupting, gentlemen." Caleb began, "but I was hoping you might be able to direct me to Mr. Drake's office."

"Mr. Drake?" the clerk responded. "Surely you've heard that Mr. Drake is missing."

"It's all anyone can talk about," added the second clerk with an even greater air of condescension.

Even though the two looked to only be a few years older than himself, Caleb wondered if it was because they were wearing nicely tailored shirts with armbands on their sleeves and polished shoes on their feet that they felt somehow superior to others around them. Not knowing Caleb personally, it couldn't have been anything he'd done to illicit such pomposity, so he could only assume this was how they were towards everyone who crossed their paths.

Which only gave Caleb more pleasure when he pulled aside the lapel of his jacket to reveal the badge on his vest and said, "In fact, I do know Mr. Drake is missin.' That is exactly *why* I'm here. Now, if one of you could tell me where I can find his office, I would be mighty appreciative."

Chapter Thirty-Six

Eustace Drake literally watched over his textile operations from an office on the top floor of the building with windows that looked out directly over the tannery and mill. Once the two clerks on the first floor realized Caleb was not just some rambler walking in from off the street, they'd shown a bit more deference to his position and gladly provided him the way.

Outside Drake's office on the third floor sat two male clerks and a female confidential secretary, as she introduced herself. After only a few words, it was clear Annamarie Wilcox was the one who ran Eustace Drake's office. She was a solid woman in her middle age. A tight bun was pulled up on her head, and she observed everything through a pair of thick glasses perched on the edge of her nose. There were no ruffles or frills of any sort on her dress, letting Caleb know, along with the dull brown color of the garment, this was a woman who did not care much about putting on airs.

Though she'd not been pleased with Caleb's appearance at her desk, asking to be let into Drake's office to look around, she understood it could assist in finding her employer. Her harsh tone did not deter Caleb from seeking answers because when she spoke of Drake, the secretary did seem to have a genuine fondness for him.

Unlocking the door to her employer's office, she said over her shoulder, "I don't know what else you expect to find. Not after the other deputies came through yesterday."

"Other deputies?" Caleb stopped in the doorway. "They were here yesterday? What were their names?"

"They introduced themselves as Daly and Grove. But I don't believe they were actually deputies."

"How so?"

"Their mannerisms and behavior. And their boots," she added offhandedly. "They were soldiers out of uniform. I've encountered enough of their sort around town to know."

That gave Caleb pause. Would General McClellan have sent men to search Drake's office? Caleb wouldn't put it past him. Especially if Drake was secretly working for the government. At the same time, he wondered if it was the sheriff's mysterious friend from Washington who could have sent the men. Or even the agents of the Golden Circle who Drake was investigating. There were too many possibilities. But one thing he knew for certain, Eustace Drake's disappearance had nothing to do with highway robbers.

For a brief moment, thinking about that, something in the back of his brain began nagging at him. Highway robbers? Something about highway robbers...

Putting the thought out of his mind and refocusing his attention on Drake's office, he asked Annamarie Wilcox to step outside so he could have a look around. He said he'd call for her when he was finished. Now, left alone, he stood on the colorful Oriental rug in the center of the office. By first appearances, the office was just as organized as his study at Drake House. Which also surprised Caleb, because if someone had already gone through the office looking for something, they left it in almost perfect condition. One might not even know it had been searched. Except, Caleb noticed as he stepped closer, the three stacks of papers on Drake's desk were not perfectly in line with one another. Someone had riffled through them and not placed them back exactly how they'd found them.

Caleb wondered what there could still be to find if the Army...or federal agents...or the Knights of the Golden Circle had already been through the office. Surely, whoever had been there posing as sheriff's deputies would have found anything incriminating or useful in Drake's search to uncover the Golden Circle members in Parker City.

Unless…Caleb thought, walking around and sitting in the large chair behind Eustace Drake's desk. He slowly cast his eyes over the top of the desk. Other than the papers not being perfectly aligned, everything else looked like the way he would have expected Drake to have left it. A silver pen rested on a charger next to three inkpots. Three wooden baskets sat on the edge of the desk with papers in each. Tapping the top of the desk, he felt the solid mahogany under his fingers. Could there be a secret compartment built into the desk? Would it have already been discovered?

Looking around the room, two stick-back guest chairs sat on the opposite side of the desk. Beyond them was a small table and chairs against one wall and several bookcases against the other. The shelves, very much like the ones in his study, were filled with books. One shelf did not have any books at all. Instead, two vases—Caleb could only surmise how expensive they were—sat on either side of a silver photograph frame.

Taking the frame off the shelf, Caleb looked at the photograph of Margaret Drake. He was still very much in awe of the ability to capture a single moment in time in an image for eternity. He wondered what she'd been thinking at that very instant when the flash ignited, and her likeness was immortalized.

As he was putting the photograph carefully back in its place on the shelf, his finger caught on something on the backside of the frame. Flipping it over in his hands, he noticed a little clasp. Twisting it, the backing of the frame began to slide away. Caleb expected this was how the paper image was placed in the frame. But instead of seeing the back of what should have been Margaret Drake's photograph, he found himself looking at a piece of paper on which was handwritten a list of names, including…

SAMUEL J. TILDON

Chapter Thirty-Seven

1984...

Cold days like this one tended to drive a wedge between the members of the PCPD's Detective Squad. Any time the temperature dropped below seventy degrees, Tommy would start complaining about how cold it was. If he'd had his choice, he'd rather have weather that allowed him to wear a Hawaiian shirt and shorts every day. Which would really make him look like Thomas Magnum from the television show. More than he already did.

Ben, on the other hand, enjoyed the crisp cool fall air that greeted him as he walked to the car. It was refreshing and gave him an extra jolt of energy. Along with the sleep he'd finally been able to catch up on, and the coffee he'd already consumed, he was ready to hit the ground running.

They needed to start over with the investigation into Roland Taylor's murder. Day one of the investigation had not ended well. They'd found themselves right back where they started. At the very beginning, with no suspects. He was hoping that there may be something in either the coroner's report or the forensic team's that might point them towards a lead.

Unfortunately, when he'd arrived at the station, neither of the reports had been delivered. Instead, he found even more messages from local reporters looking for a comment regarding the case. A couple were even trying to get him to do a full interview. It didn't matter what the message was, if the note was marked as being a press call, Ben tossed it into the trashcan without a second thought.

Disappointed that the information he'd been looking for had not arrived, Ben spent a few minutes shuffling papers around on his desk, trying to run through their options. When Tommy got in, he was thinking they should head back to Saint Paul's and take another look around. They could have missed something in their first walk-through. He'd ordered the church offices and the priest's apartment locked down, so everything should be exactly as they left it. Minus Father Taylor's body lying on the floor of his office, of course.

At moments like this, Ben often wondered what the average person would think if they really knew what police work looked like. It wasn't like there was always action and countless clues leading directly to the criminals. There wasn't excitement around every turn. A solitary detective sitting at his desk thinking wasn't what most people thought of.

Not long after he'd rearranged the papers on his desk a second time, he heard Tommy coming down the hallway. He could always tell when his partner had arrived because one thing Tommy was not was quiet. His voice carried over the dull roar of the station. Ringing telephones, clattering typewriters, the loudest mimeograph machine in the city, friendly— and sometimes not-so-friendly—conversations couldn't hold a candle to his powerful baritone.

"I assume you've seen this?" Tommy asked, walking into the office holding up that morning's edition of the *Herald-Dispatch*.

As expected, the headline screamed that Father Roland Taylor had been murdered.

"I've purposely tried to avoid all of the news this morning," Ben answered. "How bad is it?"

"Well," Tommy said as he dropped into his desk chair and kicked his feet up on the desk, "in all honesty, it could be worse. I think the reason the headline was printed so big is because they didn't have much to say in the article."

"What? They didn't speculate that we have a serial killer on the loose?"

Neither Ben nor Tommy were very fond of the press in Parker City. They'd seen how their two biggest cases had created a media frenzy, putting the usually quiet city of Parker in a not-so-good light.

Tossing the paper over to Ben, Tommy continued, "Even Morning Mike got in on it today. He said how he couldn't believe something like this could happen in Parker. And after the shootings in the summer, he thought it might be time for the city to cough up some more money for additional police officers. His words, not mine."

"Let's hope someone at City Hall was listening."

"The chief would sure be happy to put some more guys on the street."

"But I don't think having more police would have prevented Father Taylor's murder," Ben pointed out grimly.

"Let's just keep that between us," Tommy suggested.

Ben quickly read through the article on the front page and had to agree. There wasn't much detail in the piece. He was surprised to see how little information there was actually. With a story like this, the murder of a popular priest, he would have thought the paper would use barrels of ink trying to sensationalize what happened. This article seemed restrained.

Handing the paper back to Tommy, Ben told him that neither of the reports they were waiting for had arrived, so he thought they should head back to Saint Paul's and have another look around.

Fresh eyes might let them see something they missed the day before.

Chapter Thirty-Eight

The trustees on the board of Saint Paul's were not thrilled to learn the church offices would be off-limits for the time being. At least until the Parker City Police Department released it as a crime scene. That final decision would be up to Ben. And with the case only being a little over twenty-four hours old, there was no telling how long the offices and the apartment above them would be locked down.

The church fathers were also not too happy when they learned a uniformed officer would be stationed in a patrol car in front of Saint Paul's as long as the crime scene tape was still up. It was understandable. No one liked the idea of the congregation having to pass by a squad car on their way to Sunday services, but Ben didn't want to take the chance of anyone trying to sneak in for whatever reason they may have.

In his conversation with Saint Paul's president, the chief did point out—as politely as possible—that he could close the entire church down until the investigation was concluded. But he was making a goodwill concession and allowing church services to go on. In reality, even though he would have preferred the entire building locked down, he didn't want to have to deal with the Baltimore Catholic Archdiocese and the headache that would be caused by preventing a church to hold mass. Even if it was to preserve the integrity of a crime scene.

In the end, everyone walked away from the discussion, equally unhappy.

As Ben and Tommy parked their car and headed to the door for the church offices, they gave a nod to the uniform, watching them from his car. Officer Grassman was the unlucky soul assigned to keep an eye on the crime scene that morning. The odds were pretty slim that anyone would try to break in a second time, so he was in for several very long, boring hours sitting in his car with the heater running.

"I can't believe how cold it is," Tommy complained as they walked up the sidewalk, his breath turning into clouds in front of him. "I'm ready for spring."

"It isn't that cold," Ben said, sounding very much like a father correcting his child's over-exaggerated observation.

"Anytime I have to put gloves on, it's cold."

"It's brisk."

"It's cold."

"You're impossible."

"I'm getting old and cranky."

Ben stopped and looked at his partner.

"You're only thirty. *We're* only thirty," Ben said, pointing back and forth between himself and Tommy.

Without saying another word, Tommy turned and carefully removed the yellow crime scene tape from the front of the door leading into the heated offices of Saint Paul's. While he did that, Ben pulled the notebook out of his jacket and made a note of the specific time they were entering the scene so he could add the information to the file once they returned to the station. While there hadn't been much reported about Taylor's murder, Ben knew the story was bound to blow up eventually, so he wanted to make sure every single detail was documented.

Stepping into the small entry with all the posters of recent and upcoming activities, Ben took more time to look at each of the announced events than he did the day before. It wasn't that he thought the answer to all their questions would be magically hanging there on the wall, but he didn't want to take a chance and overlook something that might spark an idea.

Noticing that Ben had stopped, Tommy asked, "Do you think the killer might have touched any of these? Should we get them printed?"

Looking around at the number of posters hanging on the walls, Ben shook his head, saying, "I can't even imagine how many people could have touched these? Even if our guy did, I'm not sure we'd ever be able to tell. But I want to make sure we got prints from the door. It'll be the same problem, but you never know."

"Actually," Tommy paused. "Wait, you mean there's something I know that you don't?"

"What are you talking about?"

"I'm sure it will be in the report, but I heard the CSU guys talking yesterday. The only prints on the door were the secretary's, Bonnie Gillespie's."

"Hers were the *only* prints they found?"

"Yep."

"And the door was unlocked when she got here. That's what she said. She'd thought Father Taylor had already come down and unlocked the door."

"How many people do you think touch that doorknob in a day?" Tommy asked.

"Certainly more than just one."

"So that would lead me to believe…." Tommy began.

"The killer wiped the door down before he left," Ben finished.

"And that tells us what?"

"That he had enough presence of mind to clean up after himself."

"Not just some run-of-the-mill intruder, then? Someone who knows how to not leave a trace of where they've been," Tommy pointed out.

"Please don't say this bolsters your theory that the killer was a ninja."

"I didn't say the killer was a ninja," Tommy said, raising an eyebrow in frustration. "I said he was probably a Russian assassin."

Chapter Thirty-Nine

B efore she had been taken home by Officer Thompson the previous day, Bonnie Gillespie confirmed that nothing in the secretaries' area of the office had been stolen or even looked as though it had been touched, for that matter. Making it clear to both Ben and Tommy that whoever had broken into Saint Paul's was specifically looking for something belonging to, or in the possession of, Roland Taylor.

Once in the priest's office, the detectives started in one corner of the room, and each worked their way around in opposite directions looking at everything. From the pens sitting on his desk to the Bible filled with bookmarks and handwritten notes to the vestments hanging on the rack next to the window, they examined everything.

Ben noted a row of books on the bottom shelf of a larger bookcase that, like the ones he'd found in Taylor's bedroom upstairs the day before, were all about the Civil War. These, interestingly, focused more on the role religion and religious institutions played during the war.

One of the many items that had been thrown on the floor when the office was searched was a small, leather-bound book. It was terribly dirty and worn, so the original color of the leather was impossible to discern. Kneeling down, Ben used his pen to open the front. He quickly realized it was a version of the Bible. It wasn't surprising that a priest would have several copies of the Good Book in his office. But when Ben read the inscription on the front page, he realized just how old this edition was. The inscription read...

STAY SAFE, MY SON, AND MAY GOD GUIDE YOUR WAY.

LOVE YOUR MA AND PA

18 JUNE 1861

"This is a Bible from the Civil War," Ben said, turning to Tommy. "Father Taylor was a bit of a Civil War buff. There's a bunch of books here on the bottom shelf, and I found some up in his bedroom yesterday."

"Does that mean anything to us or the investigation?" asked Tommy, his hand reaching under the priest's desk to see if there was anything hidden beneath it.

Ben thought for a moment, then said, "I don't think so. I just thought it was interesting. This Bible is over a hundred years old."

"I'd think he'd have it in a glass case or something to keep it safe. Where'd you think he got it from?"

"Maybe a gift," Ben said, then paused, noticing something in the trash basket. "Or he bought it at an auction."

From the trash, he pulled an auction brochure. Flipping through the pages, he came across a section with several Civil War-era items.

Holding the catalog out for Tommy to see, he said, "Benson Antiques and Auction House. They had an auction last week. Looks like Taylor may have been there."

"Again, does this help us at all?"

"I'm not sure."

Chapter Forty

"Alright, folks. That's it for me today. This is Morning Mike Moran signing off until tomorrow. Remember, I'm here bright and early every weekday to get you to work and start your day. But for right now, I'm outta here! You're listening to Old Line Radio, FM 87.6."

Flipping the switch to send the live broadcast over to the studio next door for the top-of-the-hour news report, Moran leaned back in his chair and let out a long sigh. It was nine o'clock, and he'd been on the air since five. Just like he was every day. He was the voice of the early morning drive-time in Parker City and beyond and a longtime, popular fixture at the radio station.

Running his hand through his spiked blonde hair, he was trying to decide if he should just plow ahead and record the spots he'd been given by the production manager or take a minute and run down the hall to grab a cup of coffee and a bagel from the breakroom. Looking at the list, he decided to go for a shot of caffeine. He didn't need to be anywhere in the next couple of hours, so he could take his time with the recordings. But he did need to stop in and talk to the station's GM before he headed out for the day.

"Hey, Mike! Loved the Nancy joke this morning. If he wins again, you'll have material for another four years," one of the station's producers said as he walked into the small breakroom.

"I don't know. I've got some good Mondale stuff, too," he said, pouring a cup of coffee into his Baltimore Colts mug. Even though the team had packed up and left the state in the middle of the night the year before, he couldn't bring himself to retire the mug. As much as it hurt to see the team leave the way they did, it was the one he'd been rooting for since college.

With a fresh cup of brew and a bagel slathered with cream cheese, Moran took his morning pick-me-up back to the studio, where he spent the next hour recording spots for the station and some of its advertisers.

Mike Moran was one of Parker's most recognizable figures. Well, his voice was, at any rate. He'd been on the radio for close to two decades, and even if people didn't listen to his morning drive-time show, they still knew who he was because of the public appearances he made, usually MCing one charity event or another. A friendly guy with a wicked sense of humor, everyone liked Morning Mike.

After a quick chat with the station chief about a special election broadcast coming up in November, Moran was ready to call it a day. Working from four in the morning until noon gave him a chance to run around and take care of personal errands in the afternoon when most other people were still at work. But by eight-thirty, when some people were just sitting down to watch television and unwind after a long day, he was already in bed fast asleep. It had been his routine since taking over the morning show.

His only stop between the radio station and his house that afternoon was at the bookstore in the mall. Moran loved reading, especially about history. Being a native of Parker City, the Civil War was a particularly favorite period. And on a cold day like this, he was looking forward to going home, making a nice fire, and spending the rest of his day reading.

How much of a Civil War buff the radio personality was might have surprised people. Not only did he have a vast collection of books on the period, in more recent years, he'd begun attending auctions where Civil War-era memorabilia was being sold. Not that he'd been able to make many purchases because of the ridiculous price some pieces sold for. But he'd been able to acquire some items, including a few sets of letters and books, a Confederate soldier's engraved canteen, and a physician's bloodletting kit—one of the strangest little gadgets he'd ever seen before but knew he needed to own.

After grabbing the latest biography of William Sherman, he picked up a few other non-Civil War books, paid the cashier, and hurried back to his car.

The trip from the mall to his house only took ten minutes. He loved how easy it was getting around in the afternoon when there were hardly any other cars on the road. Especially in his neighborhood, which was an older section of town with brownstones dating back to the early first half of the century. Even with the renovations to modernize the townhouses, they still had a great deal of their historic charm. Which is what Moran loved so much-exposed brick walls, original hardwood floors, and handcrafted crown molding throughout.

Letting himself in through the kitchen door in the back of the house, he laid the bag of books on the counter, hung up his jacket on the hook by the door, and rewound the tape in his answering machine to listen to his messages. When he heard there was nothing he needed to answer right away, he pulled out the Sherman biography, took a Coke out of the refrigerator, and headed for his recliner in the den. This being one of the few days he didn't have to rush off to some appearance or take care of any personal business, he was going to spend the rest of his day relaxing as much as possible.

By the fourth chapter, Moran was beginning to nod off. It wasn't that he hadn't been interested in what he was reading. His body was just taking over and letting him know how tired it was. He kept opening his eyes and reading a few lines, then would fall right back asleep. During these intervals of sleep, his mind would instantly be plunged into a dream state, conjuring up a wide variety of nonsensical images. At one point, when he was half awake and half asleep, he thought he heard glass breaking somewhere in the distance. But he'd also heard cannon fire a moment earlier when his dream landed him on a battlefield. So, what was real and what was imaginary, he couldn't easily discern.

Finally jolted awake by a crash on the second floor, Moran rubbed the sleep from his eyes and looked around groggily. Looking at his watch, he saw he'd only been fading in and out for about an hour. He suddenly realized how hungry he was. The bagel at the station was the last thing he'd eaten.

Making his way into the kitchen, he went right to the refrigerator to see what he could throw together for dinner. He'd been so fixated on finding something to eat he hadn't immediately noticed how cold the kitchen was. It wasn't until he'd pulled some leftover pizza out of the fridge and turned to put it in the oven to heat up that he noticed one of the panes of glass in the backdoor was broken and the lock undone.

Instinctively he reached for one of the long knives in the butcher block on the counter and listened for any sound coming from anywhere in the house. He vaguely recalled hearing a crash—maybe the sound of glass breaking—but he thought it was part of a dream. Could someone have broken in while he was in the den asleep?

Stepping back into the hallway, he continued to listen for any sound at all. Passing by the den, everything was just as he'd left it. The living room in the front of the house also looked as it always did. Starting up the stairs to the second floor, he was beginning to wonder if he was just being paranoid. Then he reminded himself while something may have accidentally broken the glass in the door, neither paranoia nor an errant stone could have unlocked the bolt, which he was certain he'd locked when he got home. It was a force of habit with him. He walked in, closed the door, and locked the lock so he wouldn't forget to do it later.

Moran's heart was beating faster as he reached the top of the stairs. Was he just working himself up? Or was someone in his house?

Going from room to room on the second floor, nothing was out of place. His bedroom appeared just as he'd left it in the wee hours of the morning when he left for work. The guest room was untouched, and the third bedroom, which he'd converted to a small home gym, was also undisturbed.

Back into the hallway, he was beginning to feel a little foolish. But confused as to what could have broken the single pane of glass in the door. Ascending the steps to the third floor, where there were a couple more rooms that he used for nothing but storage at this point, he was beginning to relax and let down his guard.

When he reached the landing of the top floor, everything was quiet. To be a six-foot tall, two-hundred-thirty-pound former college athlete sneaking through his own home made him feel ridiculous. Letting out a sigh and lowering the knife-all he needed now was to end up hurting himself—he turned back toward the steps. That's when he heard the thud all the way downstairs.

Chapter Forty-One

1862...

All of the names on the list Caleb found behind the photograph were ones he instantly recognized. Members of the City Council, the mayor, several prominent businessmen, and the sheriff. What was this list? All of the men were certainly important and influential. But there were a number of other men Caleb could name who were just as well-known and powerful in Parker City and they were not scrawled on the paper in his hand.

There was one name that had been struck through. That of Tobias Featherston, the president of the Parker Trading Company. Caleb wondered what it meant that his name had been crossed through.

Quickly memorizing all of the names on the list, including Featherston's, Caleb asked Annamarie Wilcox to rejoin him in the office. Her annoyance with him going through her employer's office had not diminished in the time he'd been searching the room. She still wore the same scowl as when he'd asked her to wait outside.

"Mrs. Wilcox, by any chance, do the names Silas Moss, Thaddeus Parker, Joseph Best, William Gladhill, Tobias Featherston, Charles Pickney, James Wade, and Samuel Tildon mean anything to you?"

The expression on her face never changed, but Caleb could tell she was trying to understand the meaning of the question. "These names are all familiar to me, as I am sure they are to you, Deputy Post."

"That is true. They are. But can you think of a reason Mr. Drake would have grouped 'em all together?"

"I have no idea what you could possibly mean. They are each a successful and respected member of our community."

"Were they friends of Mr. Drake's?"

"They were his peers."

"But was he friendly with 'em? Did they socialize much outside of working hours?"

"Not that I can say. They were acquaintances and people with whom he needed to work to keep his business running but I cannot say he was particularly close to any of those men."

Caleb thought for a moment, then asked, "Would you be able to recall the last time Mr. Drake met with Tobias Featherston?"

There was a slight easing of the muscles around her lips. It was a more straight forward and simple question. "I believe they met for lunch last week at the Hotel Parker. I would need to check the daily diary to be certain, but I do recall it was mid-week. Mr. Drake was looking to finalize a shipping agreement the two had been discussing for some time."

"Did he seem pleased following his lunch with Mr. Featherston?"

"Pleased?" she asked raising an eyebrow.

"Did Mr. Drake say if he'd reached an agreement with Mr. Featherston? Or were they still hashin' out details?"

"Oh. Well, he said that he believed the shipping agreement should be finalized within a matter of days and that he knew he'd be able to come to a settlement with Mr. Featherston because he'd always been such a fine, upstanding man."

Interesting, Caleb thought. Kind words for the one man whose name was struck from the mysterious list.

With no idea where else to begin, it looked to Caleb as though he would be paying Tobias Featherston a visit at the Parker Trading Company. Maybe he could shed some light on the names he'd found. And why the sheriff's was among them. A detail that was seriously troubling Caleb.

Chapter Forty-Two

Bidding Mrs. Wilcox farewell and thanking her for her assistance, Caleb paused outside the building to make some notes before continuing on. The sheriff always told him to carry a notebook with him so he could write down important information so it wouldn't be forgotten. Other than the list of names he came across, which he'd tucked into his vest pocket, the most interesting thing he'd learned during his visit was that two other men calling themselves sheriff's deputies had already been to Eustace Drake's office. It proved he wasn't the only one looking for clues as to what the businessman had been up to.

But were the pair who'd presented themselves as lawmen friend or foe? And was there a difference at this point?

Caleb began slowly walking back toward the center of town. He found he now had far more questions than answers. He needed to sort through what he knew and what he didn't.

First, he knew Eustace Drake was working with the government to uncover conspirators in Parker City who wanted to harm the Union. That allowed him to conclude that Drake's disappearance was not by accident but rather design. He could also assume, especially if this cabal of nefarious traitors was as powerful as he was led to believe, they *knew* Drake was trying to expose them. Another reason to believe he was taken on purpose.

That all made perfect sense to him. Though, in all honesty, the idea of the Knights of the Golden Circle still seemed downright outlandish. But the sheriff's secret government friend assured him the group existed and meant to do harm.

So, who were these Knights?

If he'd been the one looking to unmask the schemers, Caleb would have started by making a list of those he suspected to be a part of the plot. A list very much like the one he now had in his possession. Each of the men on the list he'd found in Drake's office was powerful, respected, and should be above suspicion of working against the government. Exactly what made each of them a prime candidate to be a member of the secret organization, according to the man Caleb had agreed to assist.

But what about the sheriff? Did Eustace Drake truly believe he might have been a member of the Golden Circle? It was a preposterous notion. Caleb had known Samuel Tildon since he'd been a boy. Surely he would know if the sheriff harbored any ill will toward the U.S., and he was always talking about the treachery of the southern states that had split the country and turned it against itself. He couldn't have been just playacting all this time. Could he?

Wiping a hand across his forehead, the young deputy realized he was covered with perspiration, and his heart was beating a chaotic rhythm. He was suddenly beginning to feel unsteady on his feet.

The thought of his mentor being complicit or a part of this conspiracy was too much for him to fathom. But if the list he'd found in the office was a list of the people Drake suspected, he'd had a reason to include the sheriff.

At the same time, the list could also have nothing to do with Eustace Drake's secret government work, Caleb reminded himself. Trying to reassure himself of Samuel Tildon's respectability.

Before he said anything to the sheriff, he wanted to have a word with Tobias Featherston. Maybe he could explain why Drake had put his name on a list and then crossed through it. Hopefully, the merchant would be willing to speak with him. As head of the Parker Trading Company, he was a busy man. But Caleb hoped the shiny star on his vest would grant him some time with the man so that he could answer some pressing questions.

Chapter Forty-Three

The Parker Trading Company's main offices were one of the four stately yet imposing buildings that made up Parker's Center Square. The largest of the quartet, towering four stories into the air, the massive granite structure with its carved finials and iron trim work looked like it could have been taken directly from a castle somewhere in Europe and set down in the very heart of the city. When the buildings were first going up, Parkertons had no idea what to expect because they'd been told by the architects that these would be like no others in the city. And they were, indeed, correct.

On any given day, the Center Square was always crowded with residents coming and going, stalls with merchants hawking their wares, and those just looking to enjoy a luxurious day in the sun. When the rain was falling, the Center Square was one giant mud puddle. Caleb was thankful that the weather was being friendly today. In fact, if it wouldn't have been for everything he had on his mind, it would be a downright pleasant day to spend lounging on the Square.

There was still the thought of the men over the mountain fighting and losing their lives, though. As Caleb turned the corner, he overheard one of the vendors telling a passerby what one of his customers had been told about the battle over near Antietam. The stories seemed to be relayed as quickly as they were occurring, though Caleb wondered how much of what was being said was accurate after they'd passed so many lips. But from what Caleb could hear, though the Union Army had more soldiers on the field, General Lee's men appeared to be holding their own.

"If they beat back McClellan, they may circle round and take Parker City," the merchant was saying. "Put 'em in a good place to head down the road t' Washington."

"Let's pray that isn't the case," answered the man with whom he'd been speaking.

With tales like that starting to spread, Caleb knew the sheriff was going to have his hands full trying to keep the town calm. He'd need all the deputies ready to keep the peace, which would mean they'd most probably be ordered to abandon the search for Eustace Drake. That thought now weighing on his mind, Caleb knew he needed to speak with Featherston then get back to the Courthouse with as much haste as he could muster.

Climbing the stairs and pushing through the giant wooden doors into the cool lobby of the trading building, Caleb immediately felt a chill as the sweat glistening on his face began to evaporate. The polished marble floors did a good job of keeping the building cool in the summer and cold all through the rest of the year. On some of the hottest days, Caleb might pop in just to try and seek some minor refuge from the heat.

The large open lobby of the building was usually alive with activity as the company's employees went about their business. But today, a large part of the grand entrance was taken up by stacks of cots being laid out in rows, ready to accept the wounded soldiers that would be arriving in short order. The sight put a hitch in Caleb's step. He dreaded to think about what was to come after the smoke settled over the next few days.

Trying to put the uneasy notions out of his head, he spotted the building's security man pacing through the cots which had already been put in place. Caleb had gotten to know the man through his moments of sanctuary from the scorching sun.

A veteran of the war with Mexico some ten-plus years back, Folden Hasbro now spent his days making sure no one caused any trouble in the Parker Trading Company's offices during the day. Not that there'd ever been any trouble. His bulky presence was more for display than necessity, Caleb had learned after talking to the man. But Hasbro was happy for the pay, which put food on the table for his family.

Quickly crossing to the guard, Hasbro could tell by Caleb's demeanor that the young deputy wasn't paying a social visit. He was proved right when Caleb explained he needed to be directed to Tobias Featherston's office.

No surprise, as the head of the firm, Featherston had an office on the top floor. From his perch at the top of the building, he had a view across the entire city straight toward Jefferson Park to the north. For a moment, Caleb was struck by how beautiful the city looked from four stories up.

"A breathtaking sight, isn't it?" Tobias Featherston entered his office through a side door and found Caleb standing by the window. "I can do some of my best pondering while I'm looking out that window."

"It sure is something," Caleb said, allowing his eyes to linger on the horizon just a moment longer.

"I was told the sheriff was here to see me. But I know Sam Tildon and you are not he."

"My name is Caleb Post. I am one of Sheriff Tildon's deputies."

"Post? Caleb...Post... I do believe Sam has mentioned you before." Featherston took his place behind his desk and began fiddling in a drawer, looking for something. "What is it I can do for you, Deputy Post?"

"Thank you for seein' me on such short notice."

"As I said. I was told it was the sheriff who was here to speak with me. It's not wise to keep the sheriff waiting. A deputy, on the other hand...."

Caleb watched as Featherston pulled a pipe from the drawer and began the process of filling and lighting it as he leaned back in his chair.

"But no matter," he continued. "I am always happy to assist when I can. What is it I can do for you?"

Stepping to the edge of the large desk, for he'd not been offered a seat, Caleb looked the man over, trying to get a sense of him. Though he wore fine clothes like the others of his stature, he appeared somehow much more...rough. His callused hands and pockmarked face visible for all to see. The uneven stubble on his chin and cheeks, and a wrinkled collar, gave Caleb the impression that although Featherston belonged to Parker's upper crust, he did not worry much that his appearance be unblemished.

Caleb needed to be cautious in what he said. He didn't want to give too much away while still getting as much information as possible. Especially if Featherston was one of the conspirators Drake was trying to unmask.

"Mr. Featherston, I can only presume you have heard about the disappearance of Eustace Drake."

"Next to what's happening on the other side of that mountain right now, it does seem to be what everyone is talking about today." Featherston watched the rings of smoke from his pipe circle their way toward the ceiling before disappearing.

"All the sheriff's men are out lookin' for Mr. Drake right now, Mr. Featherston."

"So, why are you here in my office, Deputy Post?" Featherston asked, pointing his pipe directly at Caleb. The man's voice was gravelly and deep, making the question sound exceedingly accusatory.

"Well, sir. On the sheriff's orders, I've been takin' a slightly different approach to try to find Mr. Drake. And I understand from Mr. Drake's secretary, Ms. Wilcox, that you and he met last week for lunch sometime. Is that correct?"

"We did."

"And what was it you two gentlemen spoke about during that meal?"

Featherston narrowed his eyes. "That is confidential business, Deputy."

"I understand, but it might help us in locating Mr. Drake."

"I can't see how. Are you suggesting *I* have something to do with Eustace's disappearance?"

"Not at all, sir. I understand you and Mr. Drake were friends."

"As friendly as Eustace was with anyone, I would gather."

"Did he ever discuss the war with you?"

"Of course, it came up in conversation. It has impacted both our businesses. We've been forced to make countless changes to the way we do things. From finding workers to new shipping routes, everything has changed. No one realizes the severe impact this damnable war has had on businesses like mine and Eustace's. And the sooner it ends and we put this country back together and send that traitor Jefferson Davis and all his cronies to the gallows, the better for everyone."

Before Caleb was able to say anything, Featherston continued, emotion filling his voice. "If I was younger and didn't have this damn bad leg, I would be over that mountain fighting along with our boys in blue right now. I'd show that Lee and all his turncoat generals what's what. I fought proudly for these United States of America against those Mexicans back in the forties. Got a bullet in my leg for it. And I'd do it again if I could."

Caleb was beginning to understand why Tobias Featherston's name had been crossed through if he'd, in fact, found a list of individuals Drake considered to be conspirators. The passion with which he spoke could not be questioned. Caleb thought he might even see tears forming in the corner of the man's eyes.

"I know you won't understand, Mr. Featherston, but you've been very helpful, sir. Thank you."

The emotion that had taken hold of the older man's expression was quickly replaced with a look of confusion. Which itself disappeared quickly as he regained his composure.

As Caleb started for the door, he said, "Thank you for your time this afternoon. I appreciate it greatly."

"Deputy Post."

Caleb stopped and turned back. Featherston was now standing, silhouetted by Parker City behind him.

"If you or Sam need assistance in finding Eustace…or if Margaret needs anything…please let me know."

"Thank you, Mr. Featherston."

Chapter Forty-Four

The interaction with Tobias Featherston had been quite unexpected. Not that Caleb had had any idea what to expect walking into the Parker Trading Company, but it wasn't what just happened.

Taking Drake's list from his pocket, he looked over the names again. Politicians, businessmen, and the sheriff. These would most certainly be the type of men with the means to be a part of a shadowy organization set on upending the Union. Or there could be another explanation altogether. How could anyone think Sheriff Tildon was a traitor? If it was a list of conspirators, surely Drake made a mistake. Or had he come across something that made him suspect the sheriff? Tobias Featherston was struck from the list. That proved that Drake only *suspected* these men. Didn't it?

Caleb wanted to tell the sheriff about what he'd found, but if there was any chance he was a part of the Golden Circle... No. It was impossible. Caleb *knew* Samuel Tildon. There was no way he was working against the Union and part of a Confederate conspiracy.

Right then and there, standing on the Center Square in the cool afternoon air, watching the sun quickly make its retreat toward the horizon, Caleb decided he trusted the sheriff completely and would find him and show him the list. He might have been able to gain access to Tobias Featherston's office, but there was no way men like Silas Moss, Thaddeus Parker, and the mayor would agree to see him. But they'd have no choice but to speak with the sheriff.

The Courthouse was just a few blocks from the Square, which didn't take Caleb much time to cover. On his way, he'd come across more residents talking about the battle at Antietam and even saw the first cart bringing wounded soldiers into town. The sight made him sick to his stomach. He could only wonder how many more wagons would be finding their way to Parker in the next few days.

Removing his hat as the cart rumbled by, he watched it turn the corner and disappear along the road running behind the Courthouse. That's when Caleb noticed the sheriff exit the door on the lower level at the back of the building. Even at this distance, it was easy to recognize the sheriff because of the green checked jacket he was wearing. Samuel Tildon's wardrobe always made it easy to pick him out of a crowd.

Where was he headed, Caleb wondered, looking at his pocket watch. It was possible he was heading home for the day, but he was walking in the wrong direction. And the sheriff never walked home. He took his buggy. An uneasy feeling began to form in the pit of Caleb's stomach. He needed to know where the sheriff was going. Which meant he needed to follow him.

"Heaven help me," Caleb said under his breath as he started down the street in the direction the sheriff was heading.

After only a block, Caleb was able to come up with a dozen places the sheriff could be going. All of which were completely legitimate and made perfect sense. And, it was quite possible, if he'd gone into the Courthouse and up to the office, there'd have been a note for him from the sheriff saying where he could be found.

The thoughts provided some comfort to the young deputy as he continued to follow his mentor several more blocks, all the while trying to draw no attention to himself. Luckily, dusk was in full bloom, and everyone he encountered was otherwise occupied with their own plans for the evening and paid him no mind.

It wasn't until the sheriff cut through an alley and emerged onto one of the streets in Parker, where the city's more affluent residents never ventured, that Caleb began to grow nervous again. The sheriff would have no reason to be in that neighborhood. But if he did, and it related in some way to his official duties, he would no doubt have taken a deputy or two with him, for this was not the most savory of neighborhoods.

Just beyond Harlow Street, which itself was fronted on both sides by small, wooden homes with dilapidated roofs and worn siding, was the area of town where most of Parker's negro community settled. At the moment, it looked as though that was where the sheriff was heading.

Caleb watched in disbelief as the sheriff turned down another alley filled with growing shadows and removed something from his pocket. He quickly realized it was a key that granted Tildon access through a door at the back of a rundown tavern.

Watching the sheriff slip through the door and disappear into the back of the questionable roadhouse, Caleb stood in silence, trying to get his wits about him. Before he could think of what to do next, he saw two men coming down the street from the other direction and stopping in front of the tavern. Through the quickening darkness, it took him a moment to realize with horror they were Confederate soldiers. Then he watched them walk into the tavern.

Chapter Forty-Five

1984...

In recent years, the only times Parker City had seen multiple murders over the course of just a few days, Ben and Tommy found themselves in the middle of a shitstorm—to put it mildly. The cop killings earlier in the summer had come three years after the Spring Strangler case. Before that, it had been nearly a decade since there'd been an actual homicide. Now, there was another set of murders in a span of three days. Ben didn't like that the interval between these types of events appeared to be shrinking rapidly.

Before entering a crime scene, Ben was always filled with a mix of emotions. His adrenaline level would ratchet up with every step closer to the crime scene tape. As he tried to remain focused, there were always a hundred competing thoughts running through his head. The anticipation of what he was about to come face-to-face with was always offset by the tragedy of knowing someone had lost their life. No matter who a person was, regardless of whether they'd led a life of vice or a life of virtue, no one deserved to have it taken away from them under any circumstance.

As was his custom upon arriving at a crime scene, Ben clipped his badge to the lapel of his jacket and adjusted the holster on his hip. The holster thing was more of a habit whenever he got out of the car, but at a crime scene, there was something about feeling the weight of his service weapon that helped to focus him and prepare him for whatever he was walking into.

It reminded him of his responsibilities.

He didn't see Tommy's Bronco on the street, which meant his partner hadn't arrived before him. Assuming he'd been at his own home to get the call and not a female companion's, Ben would expect him to be pulling up any time.

The call came in while he was still at home asleep that morning. Natalie, his fiancée, answered the phone in their apartment while she was packing up for work. She was a History teacher at Tasker High School, so wide awake at six o'clock. And when the telephone rang that early, it was always the station looking for Ben. Which meant something had happened that required the attention of the city's lead detective.

When Ben copied down the address that Shirley in Dispatch provided, he'd neglected to ask if the victim had been identified. He was still in a bit of a haze, not yet quite awake. But after a quick shower and shave, he was out the door, and much more coherent. The mug of coffee Nat left on the counter for him had been a great help.

Standing in front of the brownstone, Ben looked up and down the street. This was a nice neighborhood and not an area of the city that was known to have much crime. According to the responding officer, it looked like a burglary gone wrong. Which immediately made the hairs on the back of Ben's neck stand at attention.

Three PCPD cruisers were parked in the street, and to Ben's surprise, the coroner's van was already there. It usually took an hour or more to get them to the scene. He wondered how they'd arrived so quickly. Especially when he'd only gotten the call less than half an hour earlier himself.

Looking at his watch and making a mental note of the time, Ben started across the street. Just as he reached the sidewalk, he caught sight of the chief's Crown Vic gliding down the street with its bubble light swirling away on the roof.

"Why's he here?" Ben asked himself.

Waiting for Brent to park and join him on the sidewalk in front of the townhouse, Ben gave the chief a nod. "Morning, sir. What brings you here?"

The moment the words were out of his mouth, he felt ridiculous. Murders in a town like Parker were extremely uncommon—though growing less so every year apparently—so of course, the chief of police would feel the need to show up at the crime scene. Even more so when the initial report was very similar to the one they'd received just two days earlier.

Brent didn't seem to think too much of the question, answering, "A high profile murder like this, right on the heels of Father Taylor…I'm sure the mayor would be here if I'd called him."

"High profile?" Ben repeated.

"They didn't tell you who the victim is?"

"Honestly, sir, I realize now I never asked. I wrote the address down and wanted to get here as quickly as possible."

"Hmmm…even the great Detective Sergeant Benjamin Winters can make a mistake." The comment was completely meant without malice. Ben could tell by the look on the chief's face. Even though he was wearing his mirrored Aviator sunglasses. He was just surprised because that was the kind of razzing he usually received from his partner.

Heading up the steps that led to the front door, over his shoulder, the chief said, "Victim's Mike Moran."

It only took Ben a moment to register the name. "As in Morning Mike?"

"That's what I've been told," Brent said, giving a half salute to the uniformed officer stationed at the front door, who quickly wrote the chief's name down on the entry log.

"Crap," Ben said as he ran a hand through his hair.

If the press hadn't gone crazy over Father Taylor's murder, they sure were going to over this one. Morning Mike Moran was Parker City's biggest celebrity. He'd been on the radio for years and was always emceeing events throughout the city. He'd even moderated the last mayoral debate that was held at Hammermill College. Everyone knew Moran.

That's when Ben realized that he'd have to break the news to Tommy. His partner had always been a fan of the radio DJ, usually coming in and retelling a couple of his jokes in the morning. Finding out Moran was dead—first thing in the morning, nonetheless—was not going to put him in a good mood.

Ben realized how absurd this train of thought was. A man was dead. Possibly murdered. It didn't matter who he was. Tommy wasn't going to care any more or less about catching the killer just because he'd liked listening to the victim on the radio.

"But cops are people too," Ben said, shaking his head and following the chief into the brownstone.

Chapter Forty-Six

"Tell me it ain't so!" were the first words out of Tommy's mouth when he walked into Mike Moran's den about ten minutes after Ben and Chief Brent. "Not Morning Mike."

"I'm afraid so," Ben confirmed from his position kneeling over the body.

Casting his eyes around the room, Tommy immediately concluded Moran had not gone down without a fight. All the tell-tale signs of a struggle were there. An overturned end table and lamp, pictures hanging crooked on the walls, a splintered coffee table collapsed on the floor. Judging by the visible abrasions on Moran's face, it looked like it had been a brutal tussle.

Willing to pose his own theory as to cause of death without waiting to hear it from the coroner's assistant, Tommy guessed the knife sticking out of the DJ's chest was what finally brought the man down.

"What do we know so far?" Tommy asked, slowly circling the body, taking it in from all angles.

Ben stood and stretched. At only thirty, his back shouldn't be that sore from bending over for a few minutes.

"Moran was supposed to be on the air at five. He never showed. The station tried calling, didn't get an answer. Sent someone over to check on him. They found the back door busted open, came in, and found him like this. Called the police."

"Who found him?" Tommy asked.

"One of the station's interns. College kid from Hammermill. He's out back giving Thompson his statement."

"Yikes. Betcha this isn't what the DJ wannabe signed up for. Was that the

151

chief's car outside?"

"Yeah. He's in the kitchen."

"How long has he been dead…Larry?" Tommy directed the question to the guy looking over Moran's body. He was a heavyset, middle-aged man that Tommy recognized but could not for the life of him remember his name.

Looking up at the detectives from under a pair of eyebrows in serious need of tending, he answered, "It's Dennis. And based on liver temp, the rough temperature in the room…I'd say T.O.D. was sometime yesterday afternoon. I'll be able to narrow that down more once we get him to Baltimore."

"Any chance you can narrow it down a bit now?" Tommy prodded.

Sighing, the guy looked down at his notes and did some mental calculations. "More than twelve hours ago."

"So…no."

"It's not an exact science," Dennis protested.

"Yes, yes, it is," Tommy answered in disbelief. He looked to Ben to see if he'd been wrong about the coroner's job for all these years.

"I mean," Dennis shot back, "making a guess *right now* is not exact. And I would rather not guess, Detective."

"You're killing me, Dennis."

"Great. Just what I need. Another dead body to deal with," he said, standing up and walking out of the room to go retrieve some items from his van.

Waiting until he was gone, Ben turned and said, "You really do have an amazing way with people sometimes."

Chapter Forty-Seven

Ben and Tommy purposely took their time walking through Moran's brownstone after they discovered the DJ's collection of Civil War books and memorabilia. The items were a red flag that instantly made them start drawing parallels to Roland Taylor's crime scene at Saint Paul's.

The den was tossed. Books were scattered about the floor; drawers were wide open. Again, it looked like someone was searching for something. And again, nothing of value had been taken. The television and stereo hadn't been touched. The similarities were beginning to give Ben an uneasy feeling in the pit of his stomach.

When the state's Crime Scene Unit arrived and started its work in the den, Ben and Tommy went in search of the chief, who had stationed himself in the kitchen along with Officer Thompson, the initial responding officer.

"If you look over here, Detectives," Thompson said, drawing their attention to the backdoor, "it looks like this is how the intruder got in. There's a broken windowpane right where the guy could reach through and unlock the deadbolt. I found a decent size rock on the other side of the door sitting on the step. Probably what he used."

"No security system?" Ben asked as he jotted some notes down.

"None that we've seen so far."

There was no question in any of their minds that this was indeed a break-in. But what had the individual broken in *for*? It was the same question they'd asked at the Taylor crime scene. In both cases, someone ended up dead.

"Hey, look it," Tommy said. He walked over to the stove, where a set of kitchen knives stuck out from a decorative butcher block. One space was empty. "These handles look like the one sticking out of Moran's chest. They have the same curve with the silver top. Weapon of opportunity?"

"Just like the candlestick at the church." Ben rubbed his eyes, beginning to accept the fact that the odds were good the two murders were somehow connected.

"What makes you think the two are related," Brent asked, his usual deep voice sounding a bit rough for the early hour.

"The Civil War," Tommy answered.

"Excuse me?"

Ben tried to explain. "It's all the Civil War books and paraphernalia we've found at both crime scenes."

"With all due respect, Detectives, this *is* Parker City. The Civil War is kind of its thing," Brent pointed out. "When I moved down here from Buffalo, all I heard about was the city's war history. Hell, even Lincoln stopped here to give a speech. I've heard that story a hundred times. I'm sure there are a lot of people in this town who have shelves upon shelves of Civil War-related books."

"But have their houses been broken into and searched for something we have no idea about yet?"

"You're not helping your argument, Detective Mason. I'm still not convinced that it's not just a coincidence."

While the chief and Tommy were talking through the similarities of the two crime scenes, Ben was using his pen to look through a stack of mail, at least that's what it looked like. Envelopes, magazines, and an auction brochure.

"We've also got this," Ben interrupted. As all eyes turned to him, he pulled a handkerchief from his pocket and picked up the auction brochure. It was identical to the one they'd found in Roland Taylor's office. "Father Taylor was at this same auction at Benson's. He had the same catalog."

Weighing the new evidence, Brent finally said, "It's still flimsy. But it's enough to *consider* the two cases could be linked. I'll give you that."

"So, we should talk to the people at Benson's and see if anything interesting happened at this auction," Tommy concluded. "See if they remember Taylor and Moran being there. Ask if anyone had a problem with them."

"I'm not sure this auction is going to have been like the ones at Christie's." Ben tried to temper his partner's imagination and enthusiasm. "There probably weren't any bidders trying to beat each other out of a secret treasure or anything like that."

"Did I say anything about that? I'm just trying to think like you. You'd want to know if anything out of the ordinary happened at the auction. Wouldn't you?"

Ben reluctantly shook his head in agreement. "Yes. I would."

"I'm just trying to be a good detective. That's all." The expression on his face told Ben how satisfied his partner was with himself.

"So, you've given up the Russian assassin angle then?"

"Not at all."

Chapter Forty-Eight

"I don't want to get your hopes up, but I think we may have a useable fingerprint on the knife's hilt."

The CSU supervisor who Ben had gotten to know over the last several years, was standing in the den with the blade he'd extracted from Moran's chest carefully sealed in a plastic evidence bag. As he spoke, the wiry lieutenant with the Maryland State Police kept pushing his oversized glasses back in place. He explained that the partial print they'd found was in Moran's blood, which meant it had to have come from the killer. Unless, of course, Moran had grabbed the knife after he'd been stabbed. But judging by its location, it would have pierced the heart and killed him instantly.

"You can figure out how he died, but the medical examiner can't?" Tommy asked in mock exasperation. Then turning to Ben, said, "Even the evidence guy knows how he died."

"In all fairness, Dennis was pretty certain it was the stab wound that killed him. He just didn't want to guess at a *time* of death," Ben gingerly pointed out.

"Why don't you ever take my side? Would it be too much to ask?"

"You two sound like my parents," Lieutenant Clover said after quietly listening to the exchange.

Focusing back on the fingerprint, they had their first solid piece of evidence. Now if they could only match it to someone, they'd have an actual suspect. But until then, they were going to start exactly as Tommy said, at Benson Auctions & Antiques.

Right after, they grabbed something for lunch.

There had been too many days recently that the pair skipped breakfast and lunch because of their presence at a crime scene. So, while Chief Brent went off to inform the mayor about Morning Mike's murder, the detectives drove through McDonald's for some quick burgers on the way to Benson's.

"How can you eat French fries and smoke at the same time?" Ben asked, looking over at his partner in the passenger seat with a greasy fried potato strip in one hand and a Newport in the other.

"I'm multitasking. This way, I won't need a smoke after I finish eating. It all makes perfect sense if you think about it."

Ben just shook his head, keeping his eyes fixed on the road in front of him.

Between bites and his next puff, Tommy said, "You know, ever since you brought up secret treasure back there...."

"Don't even start. These murders don't have to do with secret treasure."

"But isn't there a story that one of the maps over at the Historical Society has a hidden treasure map on the back of it or something? Didn't our teachers tell us that once back in school?"

"That's just an old wives tale. To my knowledge, no one has ever found a hidden map on anything at the Historical Society. Chances are someone there started the rumor themselves just to get people interested in what they have on display."

"Well, it's got me interested."

"It doesn't take much," Ben shot back.

"But wouldn't it be awesome if there was a hidden treasure out there?"

"I'd guess most of the truly hidden treasures from history have been found by now."

"Yeah. You're probably right. It's a shame, though." Tommy sounded like a disappointed little kid. "I'd make a good treasure hunter," he added almost as an afterthought.

"That is something I won't argue with. It would definitely take someone with your imagination to be a treasure hunter."

Pretending to choke up because he was so moved, Tommy looked over at Ben and said, "That is the nicest thing you have ever said to me."

"Finish your fries. We're here. And while we're inside, don't touch any of the antiques."

"Yes, Dad."

Chapter Forty-Nine

1862...

As the streetlamps began to be lit—the few that were in this part of town—Caleb kept to the shadows. Keeping one eye on the front door to the tavern and another on his pocket watch, he was just able to make out that the Confederate soldiers were only inside for about a quarter of an hour. When they left, they headed back in the direction from which they'd come. Could they have just gone in for a quick drink? Or were they there to meet someone?

Caleb still couldn't believe that the sheriff might somehow be involved with the Golden Circle. But secretly disappearing to a strange part of town and then seeing Confederate soldiers appear only made Caleb's imagination conjure up images of deceit and betrayal.

Waiting five minutes after the soldiers staggered off down the street, Caleb decided he needed to see if there was any way for him to figure out what the sheriff was up to.

Crossing the street and into the alley beside the clapboard building was easy to do without being noticed. There weren't too many folks on the street at the moment, and the ones that were all seemed to be minding their own business. It was a rough part of town, and people tended to keep to themselves.

The alley was filled with ghostly silhouettes. Only a slender glow from the streetlamp around the front of the building made its way into the cramped space between the tavern and the small brick house next to it, allowing everything in its path to cast ominous specters along the walls. With no idea what to expect, Caleb unholstered one of his Colts and held it at his side.

There were no windows on the alley side of the tavern, so his only choice to get a peek inside was to go in through the same door as the sheriff. As he reached for the doorknob, his heart was thumping against his chest so hard he thought for sure it was going to burst. He was no doctor, but it stood to reason with as fast as it was beating. Even with the cold fall air swirling around him, his palm was slick with sweat. Slowly turning the knob, he wasn't sure if he was pleased or disappointed the sheriff had not relocked the door behind him. Surprisingly, the door made no sound as he eased it open.

Cautiously stepping into the gloom before him, Caleb found himself in a small, square room. If he reached his arms out to his sides, he could touch both walls at the same time. On the wall that would have been facing toward the front of the tavern, there was a door with a number of heavy bolts holding it firmly closed. Clearly, it could only be opened from this side. Across from it was another door. This one sat open just a few inches. Enough for Caleb to see light flitting in the room.

For one door to be locked with three bolts and the other two—one leading to the outside—to be left unlocked and open didn't sit well with Caleb. There must have been a reason the tiny enclosure was so carefully secured from the tavern. But then why not from the street? Or had something happened to the sheriff when he walked through the door, making it impossible for him to throw the bolt behind him?

Sneaking a look through the opened door, Caleb saw there was a staircase on the other side leading down into a large cellar. A stone foundation with wooden support beams outlined the basement. Which, at the very center, is where Caleb spied Sheriff Tildon, sitting at a rickety wooden table across from two negro men. One was large, bearded, and shabbily dressed in a stained apron only covering half his oversized frame. The other was skinny and wearing a simple suit. Caleb knew straight away he did not

160

know the bigger man. His was certainly a physique one would remember crossing paths with. But the other man, with only a few candles barely providing enough light for the room, he couldn't be certain if he recognized him. Though there was something about the way he was gesturing with his hands that Caleb felt was somehow familiar.

"If it's true and President Lincoln issues his proclamation," Caleb could hear the sheriff saying, "it will be a masterstroke and free countless numbers of your brothers."

"If President Lincoln issues his proclamation," the thin man shot back, "it will do nothin'. He intends to only free the slaves in the Confederate states! The states he has no control ova' right now. Why doesn't the president free *all* enslaved people? In the north and in the south!"

"It will all take time. You just have to trust he's doing what he believes is right."

"And while he takes his time, more and more of my brothers are being tortured, killed, ripped from their families."

"Joseph, that is why we are trying to help as many as we can. But we have limited resources at the moment."

Joseph? Caleb thought for a moment. Joseph Washington. That's who the man in the suit was. He was a negro pastor who had moved to Parker from New York City. He'd met him once before when he showed up at the sheriff's office. That was the only time he'd ever seen him in person, but on occasion, he'd overhear Deputy Gimble grumbling about him when they learned of some community activity planned in the neighborhood.

"It's not enough, Samuel," Washington was saying. "What's worse, it's gonna be a death sentence. D'you think any of those monsters down south are just gonna let their slaves walk out of the fields because *President Lincoln* says they're free? Hogwash! And any man or woman who tries... I don't even wanna think what'll happen to them."

"I agree with you, Joseph. What the president is thinking about doing isn't perfect. But at least he's doing *something*."

After sitting quietly through the exchange, the larger man finally spoke. "What eveah's gonna happen in Washington is gonna happen. There ain't nothin' weez gonna be able to do 'bout it. That's not why weez here, boys."

The pastor sighed and laid his hands flat on the table. "My apologies. You're right, Lucius. With so many Confederate soldiers in the area, we need to find a new route of transportin' the cargo."

Cargo? What *was* the sheriff involved with?

Chapter Fifty

Before Caleb was able to get his answer, there was a loud thud outside in the alley. He wasn't the only one who heard it. The three men sitting around the table in the cellar also jerked their heads toward the noise. The one named Lucius quickly jumped to his feet, and Caleb watched as he drew a revolver from somewhere under his apron.

If they came up the steps and found him snooping, he had no idea what might happen to him. But if he tried to make his escape and there was someone outside in the alley—namely those two Confederate soldiers—that could be even worse. Caleb needed to make a quick decision because Lucius was starting for the stairs.

Heart thumping, Caleb threw open the door to the alleyway and prepared himself for whatever he might find. To his relief, the alley was empty. At least, he thought it was. The darkness, if somehow possible, was blacker than he'd ever seen. Throwing himself into the cool night, he dashed out of the alley and across the street.

Had he remembered to close the door behind him? He couldn't remember.

Standing across the street from the tavern, he took a moment to catch his breath and see if Lucius would come out of the alley after him. When no one emerged from the dark opening between the two buildings, Caleb allowed himself a sigh of relief. Even though he wasn't certain of what he'd just witnessed, he'd gotten out without being seen.

It was time for this covert trip to come to an end, Caleb decided, turning in the direction that would take him back to the Courthouse then on to his boarding house. Once he'd returned to his room, he'd be able to think and try to make sense of everything he'd learned today.

Only a block away from the tavern, as he was getting ready to cross the street, he thought he saw the two soldiers from earlier. They were a couple more blocks down the road, but they were standing under a streetlamp, so he could make out their uniforms in the spray of light being cast down upon them.

Why were they still hanging around? Were they waiting for someone? Looking for something?

Seeing soldiers, in Parker, either Union or Confederate, wasn't something that should attract Caleb's attention. They'd been in and out and around the city since the war broke out. But with everything going on and the thought of a conspiracy fresh in his mind, he couldn't help but think they may be a part of it all.

Telling himself he was being a silly mule, Caleb was just passing under a streetlamp himself when he would have sworn on the Bible he saw the soldiers look his way, and one of them point in his direction. Thinking he was just letting his mind play tricks on him, he shook off the idea. Until a few steps later, he glanced over his shoulder and saw the soldiers had begun following him.

As his feet moved more quickly along the cobblestone street, he was thinking about what the secretary had said. Annamarie Wilcox claimed two men saying they were sheriff's deputies showed up to search Eustace Drake's office. She said she had a feeling they weren't real deputies, and Caleb knew for a fact they weren't, as he'd never heard of either of them. Could the two Confederate soldiers behind him be the two mystery men? Were they part of the Golden Circle? Had they been watching Drake's office to see if anyone else showed up there? If they were part of this secret organization set on bringing down the government, wouldn't it have made more sense *not* to attract attention to themselves by going around in uniform?

The questions were coming faster and faster until Caleb took another look over his shoulder and saw that there was no one behind him. He'd been quick stepping it for nothing. A feeling of embarrassment washed over him as he turned to see the street behind him was empty. Feeling the fool, Caleb took a deep breath and was just about to turn and continue on his way—at a much more leisurely pace—when a large hand clamped down on his shoulder.

Chapter Fifty-One

Spinning around and instinctively reaching for his revolver, he found himself standing face-to-face with a grimacing Sheriff Samuel Tildon. For almost a full minute, neither man said a word. They just stood, stone-faced, staring into each other's eyes. Each trying to decipher what the other was thinking. While Tildon held a lit cigar at his side, Caleb's hand never left the hilt of his revolver.

When the sheriff finally spoke, breaking the interminable silence, his voice did not have its usual jovial bounce to it. It was calm and very flat.

"Caleb. What brings you to this part of town this evening?"

"I..."

Caleb wasn't entirely sure what he should say. Should he be honest and tell his mentor, the man who'd been like a father to him, that he'd followed him because a man who disappeared was trying to unmask the men in Parker City who were working against the government thought he might be one of them? Or should he make up an excuse why he was this far from his usual stomping grounds? An excuse the sheriff would no doubt see directly through.

"I found something at Eustace Drake's office today and wanted to show it to you."

"Wouldn't it have made more sense to wait for me at the Courthouse?"

"That's where I was headin' when...."

"When what?"

"I saw you duckin' out."

"Uh huh." The sheriff raised his cigar and bit down hard on the end.

"Caleb. You and I should probably have a talk."

"I think that would make a heap of sense, sir."

"Good. Back to my house. I'll have Mrs. May throw something together for us to eat."

"I don't know if your place's the best idea, Sheriff."

From behind him, Caleb heard the whinny of a horse he instantly recognized. It was followed by the clip-clop of hooves and buggy wheels bouncing over the cobblestones. A second later, Mr. Percy pulled up alongside them, driving the sheriff's rig.

"Caleb, my boy," the sheriff said, a little of the warmth returning to his voice, "I am famished. And I told Mr. Percy to pick me up at this spot at this time, and here he is. Get in the buggy so I can explain everything."

Chapter Fifty-Two

If it hadn't been for Mr. Percy relaying the conversations he'd heard around town about the battle near Sharpsburg as he ran his errands, the ride from the corner of Jackson and Quincy Streets to the Tildon's house would have been in complete silence. The only thing Caleb was able to remember from the butler's monologue, for his mind was somewhere else entirely, was that General McClellan and his men seemed to have stopped Robert E. Lee in his tracks. But by all accounts, the number of dead and wounded was staggering.

"You gents seem awfully quiet tonight," Percy pointed out as the sheriff's house came into view down the street. "Still workin' on findin' Mr. Drake?"

"That we are, Percy. That we are," the sheriff said, his eyes focused on the burning embers at the tip of his cigar which he held in front of him.

As always Edie Tildon was happy to see Caleb, but could tell instantly by his face something was troubling him. When she saw a similar look on her husband's she became positively concerned.

"Has something happened, Sam? What's wrong? Caleb?"

"Nothing to fret over, my dear. Caleb and I have just had a long day, and we still have a great deal to discuss this evening. There's no rest for the weary. You know that. If you could have Mrs. May send in some coffee and sandwiches to the library. We could both use something to fill our stomachs."

"Of course. I'll see if she has any cake left over from last night too."

"You're wonderful, dear," the sheriff said, giving his still-concerned wife a quick kiss on the cheek before heading down the hall to the library.

Caleb quietly followed behind him, still very apprehensive. He'd discounted Eustace Drake's suspicions that the sheriff was somehow involved with the Golden Circle straight away. But then to find him sneaking off and having a secret meeting...he had no idea what to think anymore. Even if Samuel Tildon wasn't one of the conspiratorial Knights his friend from Washington was so concerned about, he was no doubt involved in something he shouldn't be.

Taking one of the large chairs next to the fireplace, Caleb made certain he would still be able to quickly reach for one of his Colts if the need arose. Even just the thought of having to pull a gun on his mentor made him sick to his stomach.

Only twenty-four hours ago, the two were in this very room devising a plan to find Eustace Drake and the men who'd taken him. Now Caleb had to wonder if the sheriff was in some way involved.

Pouring two glasses of brandy, one for himself and one for Caleb, the sheriff offered the tumbler to his young deputy. "You're going to need this, I'm sure, my boy.

"I can only imagine you have a whole heap of questions for me, Caleb. And I'm not going to hide anything from you. I will tell you everything. I just hope when we're through here, you won't think any less of me."

Caleb wasn't sure where to begin. Was he supposed to say something or wait for the sheriff to continue? When Tildon didn't say anything else, Caleb withdrew the handwritten list of names he'd found hidden in Eustace Drake's office and handed it to the sheriff.

"I found this at Drake and Sons. It was hidden behind a photograph in Drake's office. Judging by the names on the list, I believe those are some of the people he thought were part of the Golden Circle."

The sheriff took the list and ran his eyes down the names. When he reached the bottom, his lips twisted precariously. "Why is it you believe that?"

"The names on that list would be the sort who would have the power to...."

"...be agents of a secret organization out to bring down the government," the sheriff finished.

"Well, yeah. At least to be part of it here in Parker City."

"And this list includes me?"

"It does."

"I'll admit, I didn't know Eustace well. But I never thought he'd think I was a part of something like that."

"But you are a part of something," Caleb said. Even he was surprised by the accusatory tone in his voice. "Mr. Drake obviously had reason to suspect you of something, and here I come across you sneakin' through town and having a meetin' in the cellar of a tavern."

"But did you take notice of *who* I was meeting with, my boy? Joseph Washington. Do you think a negro pastor is going to be colluding with the Knights of the Golden Circle? Or anyone who supports the Confederacy, for that matter?"

In all the confusion and emotional upheaval he'd been feeling, Caleb, in fact, *hadn't* thought about that. But now that the sheriff pointed it out so plainly, it did make him question his suspicions.

"That does make some amount of sense," Caleb agreed. "But you are clearly still hidin' something."

An uneasy silence filled the room as the sheriff drained his glass, then set it on a small table beside his chair.

"Caleb, I swear to you on Edie's life, I am not a part of the Golden Circle here in Parker City. Or anywhere else, for that matter. I love the United States and would never do anything to harm it. I have done everything I can to keep peace here in Parker, whether I've had to work with Union or Confederate troops, that is true. But it's been for the good of the city. But make no mistake where my allegiance rests."

"So then what were you doin' this evening?"

Again, Tildon fell silent as he thought about what to say next. Caleb hadn't touched his brandy but took this opportunity to take a sip, certain he would need the fortitude for whatever the sheriff was about to share with him.

"The Knights of the Golden Circle is not the only secret organization working under the cover of this blasted war. There is another that is helping to get slaves out of the south and to safety in the north. It's called…."

"…the Underground Railroad," Caleb interrupted, his words coming out as a whisper.

"I'm part of a network that helps move the poor souls from the hell they've been enduring to a better life. That's why Joseph Washington came to Parker in the first place. He was looking to find a route that would allow the negros to go through Parker City. And who better to help than the sheriff?"

"But it's illegal, Sam!" Caleb couldn't think of a time he'd ever used the sheriff's first name. But in that moment, it just came out. "Do you realize what would happen to you if anyone found out? Do you know what would happen to Miss Edie? Does she *know*?"

"My boy, you know I keep no secrets from my wife."

"But you're a *lawman*. *We're* lawmen! We're supposed to uphold the law."

"I am upholding God's law, my boy. I am doing what's right and helping people in need. With my help, we've been able to bring countless slaves through Parker. We've given so many negros the chance at a better life in the north. Where it's safe." Pausing to look at the young man who was like a son to him, Tildon finally asked, "Are you angry that I'm helping negros escape slavery?"

"No. What's happening to them is terrible. I don't have…I…they…"

"Then it's the fact I'm breaking the law by helping them escape."

"We're lawmen, Sam."

Chapter Fifty-Three

1984...

Benson Auctions & Antiques was a unique business only a few doors down from the city's Civil War Museum. Ben thought it made perfect sense. Anyone interested in history would visit the museum, then walk down the street and shop for antiques—possibly from the same era. A sign in the window let everyone know Benson's specialized in Civil War memorabilia.

A two-story brick building, it wasn't terribly much to look at on the outside. Unlike so many of the buildings in this part of the city, it wasn't very old. Making it something of an oddity. While the façade had similar details to its neighbors, it really was just that-a *façade*. The craftsmanship was an imitation using modern tools and techniques. They may have looked like the handcrafted features on the surrounding structures, but an architectural historian would be able to spot and point out the differences immediately.

The first floor of the building was set up as a shop. Antique furniture and rugs were in the back, forcing visitors to pass through the rows of glass display cases with the trinkets and bobbles the average antique hunter would be likely to purchase as they browsed through the store. The smaller second floor was where the live auctions were held. That's where the expensive and one-of-a-kind items were bid on by true collectors and aficionados.

As they entered, a little brass bell over the door jingled. The announcement was followed by the appearance of a small, aging man in a vest and bow tie from an office toward the back of the showroom. A wide grin spread across his round face as he approached the detectives, no doubt thinking they were potential customers.

"Welcome to Benson's. How may I be of service to you, gentlemen?"

The man's neatly trimmed beard and rosy cheeks gave him a slight resemblance to Kris Kringle, Ben thought. Though he didn't think Santa would ever wear a bright purple tie like the one around this man's neck, which he couldn't take his eyes off.

"We had some questions we were hoping you might be able to answer for us," Ben began.

"If you're looking to talk antiques, you've come to the right place. Benson's has been in the business here in Parker City for some forty years now. We used to be over on…."

Before he could go any further—and Ben had the distinct feeling this was a man who could talk for a good hour when answering a simple yes or no question—he politely interrupted and introduced himself. "Actually, sir, I'm Detective Ben Winters with the PCPD. This is my partner, Detective Mason. We have a few questions about this."

Ben held out the copy of the auction catalog he'd bagged and taken from Moran's house.

"Well, if you're here to discuss our recent auction, then you'll actually want to talk to my daughter. She handles all of the *upstairs* business, as we call it. I should really say she handles all of the business since I retired. But I come in every once in a while when she needs help in the shop. Plus, my wife thinks it's good for me to get out of the house now and again. And I do miss it. I've always been more of an antiques dealer than an auctioneer. It was my daughter's idea to expand the auction business. When she…"

"Is your daughter here today?" Tommy asked, hoping to catch him between breaths but missing by a couple of words.

"Ellen? Yes. She's upstairs right now. Should I have her come down?"

"That's alright," Tommy answered with a smile. "We'll head upstairs so we don't interrupt your work down here. Thank you for your help, Mr. Benson."

"Oh. I'm not a Benson. I'm an Osbourne. Daniel Osbourne."

"I'm sorry. I just assumed…."

"Common mistake. My *mother* was a Benson. She married my father, John Osbourne and they had me and my two brothers. I was the only one who ended up getting into the family business. David and Dennis were always more interested in…"

"I'm sorry to cut you off, Mr. Osbourne, but we do need to speak with your daughter. It's a matter of some urgency." Tommy was afraid if he didn't stop the monologue, Ben would be too nice and just let the guy go on until he wore himself out.

"Of course. Of course. I'm sorry. She's right upstairs. When you get to the top of the steps, just turn left."

At first, neither spoke as they ascended the staircase. Both thinking the same thing. If it was Daniel Osbourne they needed to question, they would have been there all afternoon.

As they came to the landing on the second floor, Ben said, "I really hope his daughter didn't inherit his loquaciousness."

"His what? Why do you need to use a word like *loquaciousness*? Who are you trying to impress, man? I mean seriously."

"It's a good word," Ben protested.

"For the S.A.T.s! No one actually talks like that in real life. How did you not get beat up more in school? There's her office. Do you want to do the talking or should I do it so we can keep this short because I'm not going to be using any of your fourteen-syllable words?"

"It wasn't fourteen-syllables."

Tommy narrowed his eyes and walked down the short hall toward the open door, leaving Ben standing alone at the top of the stairs.

Chapter Fifty-Four

Reading the name plate on the wall next to the door, Tommy asked, "Miss Osbourne?" as he stepped into the office.

She was seated behind a desk that was a little too large for the size of the room. But judging by the elaborate carvings around the edges and the intricate inlaid pattern on its surface, the piece must have been an antique. Possibly even an heirloom if the Bensons/Osbournes had been in the business for so many years. Several filing cabinets ran along the wall to one side of the office while a half dozen large framed paintings rested on the floor against the opposite wall.

Ellen Osbourne was a striking woman in her forties, early fifties at most. A hairdo to rival any female newscaster and a pair of what must have been extra-large shoulder pads in her teal jacket made her look like a woman in command of her surroundings or an army on the move. For a moment, Tommy even felt slightly intimidated as she looked up from her paperwork and focused her dark blue eyes on him. He had the uncanny feeling as though they were piercing his soul.

"Yes?" It was not an answer. In that one word, she'd responded with her own—*what is it you want, and why are you bothering me?*

"Sorry to disturb you, but your father said we'd find you up here. I'm Detective Mason with the Parker City Police. My partner and I were hoping we could speak with you about an auction Benson's held recently."

"Is there a problem?" she asked, leaning back in her chair, crossing her arms in front of her, looking like she was ready for a fight.

"I guess that depends on how you look at it," Tommy said with his thousand-watt smile.

"Have a seat." She motioned to the guest chairs across from her desk. "You say there was a problem with our last auction?"

"Not exactly." It was Ben's turn. "We were wondering if anything out of the ordinary happened at the auction. This one specifically."

Showing her the cover of the catalog, Ben laid it on the desk in front of her.

"Do you happen to have a list of the individuals who were here for that auction?"

Ellen Osbourne leaned forward and rested her hands on the top of her desk. Thinking carefully before she spoke, she finally said, "We do ask everyone in attendance to sign in when they arrive. Yes."

"Would we be able to see a copy of that sign-in sheet?" Ben asked, hoping she wasn't going to put up any resistance. If she tried to claim some kind of privilege or demanded they get a warrant, it would just complicate matters and slow down the investigation. Which was already plodding along as it was.

Again, there was a pause before she responded. "Can I know what...or who you are looking for on that list?"

It was Ben's turn to weigh how much information should be shared. "Have you heard that two days ago, Father Roland Taylor was the victim of a break-in at Saint Paul's?"

"A break-in? I thought he was murdered."

"Yes. He was. We believe he was at this auction. Do you remember seeing him?"

"You think his death...his *murder* had something to do with our auction? I can't imagine. I...I mean..."

For the first time, there was a crack in the woman's tough exterior. Both detectives thought she was genuinely surprised by what she'd heard.

"I know Father Taylor. I mean...*knew* Father Taylor. I didn't go to his church, but I knew him because of his interest in history. He stopped in on occasion to browse but...yes, he was at this auction." She stopped and opened one of her desk drawers, pulling out a leather portfolio. Opening it up, she began flipping through pages. When she came to the information she was looking for, she said, "He bid on a particular lot that evening. A box of old books."

"Did he bid on any other auction items?" Tommy asked, tagging in for the Q&A.

"No. It was just that one. He was very interested in the Civil War. That particular lot was a collection of books, some of which were thought to be from the period. It was a last-minute addition."

"Did anyone else bid on the books?" Ben was making notes as she spoke, finally feeling like they may be making some headway.

"According to what I have here, there were a few others. Mike Moran, the morning radio guy, he's always looking for Civil War-era items. And Henry McClinton. He's a professor at Hammermill College. In the History Department. Benson's has consulted with him several times."

"So, just those three were bidding on the books?" Tommy clarified.

"No. There was also a representative here from the Historical Society. In the end, Father Taylor had the winning bid. But after the auction, I saw him, Mr. Moran, and Walter Tully—from the Historical Society—looking through the books together."

"Did anyone else show an interest in these books that night?"

Ellen shook her head.

"Were any of the other three bidders angry that Taylor outbid them?"

Again, she shook her head, then thought for a moment. "Well, Professor McClinton seemed a little...out of sorts. He really wanted to have a look through the books. I don't know if he and Father Taylor ever spoke. He disappeared pretty quickly after the auction ended."

"Do you have a list of the books?"

"I'm sorry?" Ellen Osbourne wrinkled her brow.

"The books that these men were bidding on. You just said it was a box of books that might have been from the 1800s...the Civil War."

She stood and walked over to one of the file cabinets. Flipping through the file folders, she quickly found the one she was looking for. It was a complete accounting of all the items that had been auctioned off that evening with their full details and descriptions.

Sitting back down at her desk, she started copying the descriptions of the books. "Like I said, the books were a last-minute addition. I didn't have a chance to look through them thoroughly. But they were very much like other books we've sold. Which is why we put them together in a single lot.

"You can't be thinking what happened to Father Taylor had anything to do with these books? Why would you even think that? Unless… Has something happened to one of the other men? Is that why you asked for the list of people at the auction?"

Not wanting to alarm her anymore, happy that her hard demeanor had softened, Tommy gently said, "We do believe what went on at the auction may shed some light on our current investigation. I can't say much more than that at the moment but what you've told us has been very helpful."

"Yes, thank you, Miss Osbourne," Ben said. "If we have any more questions, we'll be in touch."

Chapter Fifty-Five

L ingering outside Benson Auctions & Antiques, the detectives braced themselves against the late afternoon chill. As they'd been inside talking to Ellen Osbourne, the day had turned dark and gray. A cold breeze rustled the dried leaves scattered along the sidewalk. It was actually feeling a lot more like winter than an autumn afternoon.

Tommy paced beside their car as he lit up a cigarette and blew a stream of smoke into the air. Watching the gray wisps disappearing around him, he gestured to the pack to see if Ben wanted one, as he said, "Two of the four people who bid on this box of books have been killed."

"And their places searched," Ben added, shaking his head at the offer.

"Do you think this is enough to get the chief to admit the two murders are probably related?"

"I'm not sure. It seems reasonable to make that assumption. But I also understand why he wouldn't want the two cases to be connected. Think of what it means. Two of the city's most public figures being murdered days apart... The press will go crazy. I can just imagine how many telephone message slips I'll have sitting on my desk. Not to mention the fleet of television news trucks in front of the station. It'll be just like this summer all over again."

"Yeah. But I'd rather only have one killer out there with a single motive than two killers with two separate motives that we need to figure out," Tommy reasoned.

"You think we've got a motive?" Ben rubbed his hands together to get the circulation moving.

Tommy shrugged. "I'm not exactly sure what the motive is yet, but I'm pretty damn sure it's in that box of books."

Ben looked at the handwritten list the dealer provided them. Some history books, a couple household ledgers, a journal, a collection of newspaper articles from the 1930—not the Civil War. The items had been bought at an estate sale. Someone was cleaning out their late grandmother's attic and sold everything to Benson's.

"I don't remember seeing any of these items at Saint Paul's," he said, running his finger down the list. "Maybe the history books. I can't remember the exact titles that were in Taylor's bedroom. We'll have to check on that. But I didn't see any newspaper clippings or ledgers of any kind."

Flicking the butt of his cigarette into the street and rolling his eyes when Ben gave him a dirty look, Tommy recapped what they knew. "Four men came to an auction here at Benson Auctions & Antiques, and all bid on the same thing. A box of books. The man who won the bidding for the books is murdered, and his office and apartment are tossed as if the killer was looking for something. A couple days later, a second man is killed, and *his* home was searched. This second man also bid on these books."

"If there was something in the box the killer was after, it makes sense he went after Taylor first. He's the one who had the winning bid," Ben offered.

"Then why did he go after Moran?" Tommy puzzled.

Ben's best guess was, "Because he didn't find what he was looking for at Saint Paul's."

"So, he thinks maybe Moran has what he's looking for and goes after him," Tommy said, playing along.

"But since we don't know exactly *what* he was looking for, we don't know if he found it. And if he didn't find this mystery item…."

"Then Walter Tully and Henry McClinton could be in danger."

Chapter Fifty-Six

1862 ...

D r. Joseph Aspen stood over the pale figure of Eustace Drake, looking at his pocket watch. It had been just over two days since Bloody Bill dragged Drake's bloody body into the basement of the Aspen House Hospital for the doctor to tend to. At this point, Aspen was surprised the old man was still alive. Though he wouldn't be for much longer. But he considered it a testament to his skill as a surgeon that Drake was still breathing. Even if those breaths were extraordinarily shallow and labored.

"If you'd'a just given us the information weez was lookin' fer, maybe things woulda went a little different yesterday and General Lee wouldn't'a had t'a retreat," Bloody Bill was saying to the half-conscious man lying on a cot in one of the basement's secret rooms.

"There's really no point talking to him," Aspen pointed out. "He's too far gone to understand anything you have to say. I don't understand why he's even still here. You didn't get what you needed. Why not just get rid of him?"

"Because we ain't done with him yet. As long as everybody's out lookin' fer this bag of bones, they ain't gonna be watchin' fer us."

"I see."

Aspen couldn't stand the young, arrogant lieutenant. But he and his men were the ones sent to carry out the operations in Parker City for the time being, so he was forced to deal with them. He would have much preferred more gentlemanly agents of the Circle, but anyone willing to do what Bloody Bill was willing to do for the cause was certainly no gentleman.

Even though Lieutenant Anderson had a short fuse and a penchant for overreacting, Silas Moss and Thaddeus Parker had been able to keep him under control and focused on the task at hand. But they were all still awaiting further instructions on what was to come next. When those orders would arrive, none of them knew for certain. But there were shadowy figures throughout the country working on much bigger plans. So, for now, they would all do their parts. And wait.

By eliminating Eustace Drake, they'd already taken a big step in keeping their group's identity concealed. Parker City, being so close to the nation's capital, was a strategic location for the Golden Circle to have agents. Though they hadn't been able to obtain the information from Drake that might have turned the tide at Antietam, they'd still been able to provide a safe route for their own information to flow from the south to points in the north.

A wheezing sound coming from Drake's dry, nearly white lips drew Aspen's attention. He knew it wouldn't be too much longer. Then, when Drake was expired, he'd insist the body be removed from the hospital post haste. He couldn't take the chance that somehow someone might stumble upon it. Not that anyone working at the hospital dared venture beyond the steel door leading into the basement. But he couldn't take the risk.

The hospital provided the perfect location for their headquarters. No respectable member of Parker's society would ever venture to the asylum of their own accord, so there was very little chance of anyone important seeing either Moss or Parker entering the hospital to meet with their fellow cohorts. But to make sure the law never came calling, Aspen needed to make certain the hospital appeared above reproach. At least just enough for the sheriff not to care what went on within the sanitarium's walls. So many in Parker deemed the Aspen House Hospital so unacceptable, even with the hundreds of wounded soldiers being transported to the city, it was never asked to house any of the men. And Dr. Aspen himself never asked to attend to any of them. Though he would have liked very much to study how some of the soldiers were dealing with the traumas they'd endured.

Wiping his hands on a rag and throwing it back onto the table next to the door, Aspen said, "He'll be dead within the day. Once he is, he'll need to be removed from the premises straight away. Do you understand?"

"Don't worry so much, Doc. Everythin' will be taken care of."

Chapter Fifty-Seven

Caleb's conversation with Sheriff Tildon dragged long into the night. So late in fact, the sheriff suggested he spend the night in one of the guest rooms instead of walking back to his room at the boarding house. But after everything Caleb had just learned, not only did he need the fresh air to help clear his head, he just needed to get away from Tildon for a little while to sort through everything.

Lying in his bed and staring up at the ceiling, Caleb kept running through the conversation again and again. He couldn't believe Samuel J. Tildon, the man he respected more than all others, was actively breaking the law by helping negro slaves escape from the south. The trouble was, Caleb understood why he was doing it. He knew in his heart it was the right thing to do and, in a sense, admired the sheriff for what he was doing. But he couldn't reconcile the fact it was still a crime. And their purpose was to prevent crime and uphold the law.

To do the right thing, was it sometimes acceptable to break the law? But then, who was to decide what the *right* thing was? And which laws were acceptable to ignore?

For hours Caleb tossed and turned until exhaustion finally carried him away into a fitful sleep. He vaguely recalled waking up now and again just to roll over and be drawn back into the darkness.

By the time he awoke, he'd found he was covered in a layer of perspiration and sweated through his sleep shirt. But once he threw the blankets off of himself and the cold morning air wrapped around him, he quickly began to shiver.

Sitting on the edge of his bed, Caleb wondered if he should go to the Courthouse and check in as he did every morning, or if he should continue with his investigation into the Knights of the Golden Circle. One thing he did know, he could cross the sheriff's name off Eustace Drake's list of possible conspirators. That left Councilmen Silas Moss and Thaddeus Parker at the top of the list.

Silas Moss and Thaddeus Parker?

Something about the two was nagging at the back of Caleb's mind. It was the same feel he'd gotten earlier after seeing the two men with the sheriff the day after Eustace Drake went missing. Something one of them had said. About Drake having been the victim of highway robbers. At that point, neither he nor the sheriff thought it was a random act that Drake's carriage had been laid upon. Did Moss and Parker come to that conclusion themselves? Did someone tell them that was what happened? Or were they the ones trying to make that the official version of events?

Surely neither of them would have abducted Drake themselves. The two men never did anything themselves. They just gave the order, and others did the work.

A clattering outside the window from the street below forced Caleb to his feet. Padding across the room, he drew back the curtain and saw a line of wagons making their way down Commerce Street. The first two carts were carrying soldiers with bloody makeshift bandages wrapped around various parts of their bodies. Caleb saw both blue and gray uniforms in the mix. Once you had a bullet in you, it apparently didn't matter what side you were on, he thought with a great deal of sadness. The rest of the wagons, another four in total, had large tarps covering their beds. Under which would be the bodies of the dead.

"This damn war," Caleb said to his own reflection in the window.

Chapter Fifty-Eight

Even though he'd been in a hurry to get on his way, Caleb's landlady, Mrs. Whitmore, refused to allow him to leave without eating something for breakfast. Not wanting to upset her—for she was truly a kind and sometimes irascible woman—he quickly ate a small bowl of beans with molasses and took a slice of cornbread for his walk.

Where was he walking to, though, he thought, standing on the front steps looking up and down Commerce Street. His thoughts from the night before were still plaguing him, and he wasn't certain if he could yet face the sheriff at the Courthouse. Not until he'd come to terms with what he now knew.

But before he was able to make up his mind on his direction, it was made for him.

He heard a loud whistle followed by the sheriff's booming voice. It could have been a cannon blast the way it echoed off the buildings. As Caleb did, the people passing along the street all turned to see the sheriff's buggy thundering toward them. Coming to a halt in front of the boarding house, Tildon's expression told Caleb what he needed to know. Something bad had happened.

No time to ponder his actions or feelings any longer. He knew there was a job to do. His duty to the town came first. Without saying a word, he jumped into the seat next to the sheriff and grabbed hold of his hat so it wouldn't go flying when the rig took off. Which it did with a quick snap of the reins.

Over the thumping of Dolly's hooves on the cobblestone, the sheriff said, "I was hoping I would be able to find you here. A messenger from the

Courthouse caught me as I was saying goodbye to Edie. Gimble says they've found Eustace Drake."

By the tone in the sheriff's voice, Caleb already knew the answer, but he still asked, "Is he...?"

"I'm afraid so. Gimble and a couple boys are heading there now."

"Where?"

"Edge of the river. Just outside of town."

Some of the deputies who'd been walking the riverbank must have found him, Caleb thought as the buggy took a sharp turn. The wheels bounced along, spinning away as Dolly was being diligently kept under a gallop. As much as he could tell the sheriff wanted to get there as quickly as possible, Caleb also knew the sheriff was not going to put any foot travelers in danger by allowing his powerful Arabian to careen through the streets.

"I have a feelin' I may know who's behind this. I have no proof, sir. But I was thinkin' about it last night, and some ideas popped into my head."

Tildon listened to Caleb's theory about Silas Moss and Thaddeus Parker being the agents of the Knights of the Golden Circle in Parker City as he guided Dolly toward their destination. It was all speculation, but it made a great deal of sense. The Moss and Parker families had a lot of business dealings in the south that he knew had been lost once the war broke out. And there'd been more than one occasion when the men expressed their displeasure with the policies and ideas of the current administration in Washington. But would they go as far as committing acts of treason? That was the rub as far as Tildon was concerned.

"You started thinking about Silas and Thaddeus because they were on the list you found? The one Eustace came up with?"

"The list did help me narrow my focus," Caleb admitted.

"But my name was also on the list. As was Tobias Featherston's before it was struck off. Do you still think I'm part of this blasted Golden Circle?"

"No, sir. I don't."

"Then what that tells me is Eustace got two names wrong. What's to say he didn't get the others wrong as well?" While he was actually inclined to agree with Caleb that Moss and Parker were viable suspects in this mess, he wanted to make sure Caleb was able to back up his theories. Or at least had an idea of how to go about determining if the two City Councilmen were conspirators.

"Respectfully, sir," Caleb began, fiddling with a button on his duster, "those names were of men Mr. Drake thought, for whatever reason, were up to somethin' that might not be on the up-and-up. All I know is Mr. Featherston is not an enemy of the Union. Which clears him in my investigation. Maybe there's somethin' else he's hidin' but that Mr. Drake got a whiff of." He paused. "Like with you."

The sheriff smiled. "That does make sense when you put it that way."

Caleb stared at Tildon for a moment, a thought occurring to him.

"Sir, is Mr. Featherston a part of your...organization?"

The sheriff didn't answer. He didn't have to. The smile said it all.

Chapter Fifty-Nine

Deputies Gimble and Ford were standing over what looked like a heap of rags when Caleb and Sheriff Tildon pulled up beside them. A third man, not one of the sheriff's but an employee at the Courthouse who on occasion would assist the deputies, was tramping around at the water's edge. Their horses clustered together, grazing on the tall grass near the river. As Caleb dismounted and walked closer, he could see the rags were actually a sheet wrapped around the body.

"What have you?" he asked no one in particular.

Gimble spread the sheet open to reveal a soaked Eustace Drake. His skin was beyond pale, his long white beard plastered to his chest. He'd been stripped of his overcoat and vest. His once-white shirt, trousers, and stockings were all that remained.

Caleb's eyes were instantly drawn to the large crimson stain near Drake's stomach. Without a word, he stepped past both Gimble and Ford and knelt to examine the area. As expected—and he suggested two days ago—he discovered a bullet wound. Carefully rolling the body to one side, Caleb found another hole in Drake's back where the bullet exited. A larger red stain around it.

"Shot as you expected?" the sheriff asked.

"Indeed," Caleb confirmed.

"And nearly stripped to his britches," Gimble offered an obvious observation.

"What's Lewis doing?" the sheriff asked, pointing to the man trudging through the high grass and weeds leading into the Tasker River.

"He's lookin' to see if any of Drake's other clothing is in there," Ford said.

"Or the gun what shot him," Gimble added.

Shaking his head, Caleb said, "I doubt that'll be there."

"Oscar, I thought you two searched along the river yesterday," the sheriff said, lighting a fresh cigar and tossing the match into the water.

"We did, Sheriff. And he weren't here yesterday. We went a good half a mile further along here just to make sure. Didn't see anything."

After examining the bullet wound, Caleb stood and walked toward the river. Off in the distance, he could see the Drake & Sons mill. Was it a coincidence this is where the body had been discovered? In sight of his textile factory. Or was it a message? Or a clue?

"How did you know where to find him this morning?" Caleb asked over his shoulder, still staring at Drake & Sons.

"A boy came into the Courthouse," Ford said. "He was lookin' for you, sir. Said he was told to tell you where to find the body."

"He was *told* where it was," Tildon said.

"And then sent to tell you," Caleb included, rejoining the men near the body.

"Did you keep the boy at the Courthouse?" the sheriff asked.

"No, sir. But we asked where he lives. I figured you'd want a word with him," Gimble said with a confident air, very pleased with himself.

"I most certainly do. But for now, Gimble, go fetch Doc Crum and his cart.

"Hmmm." Caleb had once again been looking at the wound on Drake's stomach while they were standing there.

"What is it, my boy?"

Kneeling next to the body a second time, Caleb pulled Drake's shirt all the way open. Then, slowly lifting the waistband of his trousers only a couple of inches, he turned and said, "He's not wearin' any undergarments. And," he paused to reexamine the entrance and exit wounds again, "it looks as though someone tried to patch him up. Sort of."

"What do you mean?" the sheriff asked, now kneeling himself.

"Look here. Someone fixed these holes up a bit."

"You're right. And it looks like they might have had some know-how."

"Like a doctor," Caleb suggested.

Chapter Sixty

C aleb spent the next hour walking the area around the body down to the river and back. He was careful in the pattern he walked, looking for anything at all that was out of place or might suggest who left Drake there to be found. The sheet wrapped around the body was plain white with no discernable marks or details that would lead to where it had come from, though one edge was worn and a little ragged. From that, Caleb could only guess it was not new.

From the state of the body itself, missing its undergarments, someone had obviously stripped Drake at some point. Which made sense if they then performed any sort of surgery on him to stem the bleeding from the gunshot. But just looking at the size and placement of the wound, it was hard to imagine Drake surviving. But someone tried to keep him alive. At least for a little while.

Why?

Could they have been trying to get information from him?

When Caleb and the sheriff spoke with George McClellan the day Drake went missing, even though the general didn't confirm it, he gave the impression the industrialist was carrying a message or information from Washington. Was that what his abductors were after? Had they gotten what they were looking for?

Every moment that passed brought more questions.

Caleb was walking along the edge of the river using a rod from the back of the sheriff's buggy to poke through the tall grass and weeds to see if there was anything Lewis missed. So far, he hadn't found anything. And Lewis was now several feet out into the Tasker itself, the water knee high, walking back and forth.

Doc Crum had arrived not too long before and, with the help of the deputies, was loading Eustace Drake's lifeless body into the back of his wagon.

"Yer lucky I was able to get away," the doctor was saying. "With all the soldiers coming into town today. It's been damn busy. I should be havin' my lunch right now."

Shaking his head, Tildon put his old friend in his place. "These are extraordinary circumstances, Robert. We all need to do our part. And I think Viola would agree with me when I say you can go with skipping a lunch every now and again," he said, pointing at the doctor's gut with the tip of his cigar.

That gave the sheriff's men a good chuckle.

"I'd be careful, Sam," Doc Crum quickly shot back. "You and I could wear the same waistcoat!"

The response elicited more laughter from the men.

Caleb was trying to pay them no mind as he worked his way along the riverbed, turning over everything that had happened in the last couple of days in his head. With every step, he became more and more frustrated.

Eustace Drake was dead, and the only suspects they had as to who was behind his death were shadow figures. People he and the sheriff had been told were out to do great harm to the government. It all seemed like horse feathers to him now as he was sloshing around in the muddy water.

"What are you thinking, my boy?" The sheriff had snuck up on him while he was lost in his thoughts.

"Sorry, sir. You startled me."

"I could tell you were having one of those conversations in your head again."

"Somethin' like that." Caleb took a few steps to get out of the weeds and back on dry land. "I'm just tryin' to make sense of it all."

The sheriff lowered his voice. "My friend from Washington has never steered me wrong in the past. If he says this has to do with the blasted

Golden Circle, then sure as shootin' he's right on the mark."

"So, this was all about gettin' rid of the person who was gettin' close to figuring out who they were?"

"It very well could be."

"What do we do now?" Caleb asked. "Do we keep looking for them?"

"I think we need to be very careful. Maybe we..."

"Sheriff! Sheriff!"

All of the men gathered along the bank of the Tasker turned to see a messenger from the Courthouse galloping toward them.

"Confound it! Now what?" Tildon asked as he flicked the end of his cigar into the river.

"Sir," the rider gasped as he reined in his horse. He was breathing as though he'd been the one doing the galloping. "You got a message delivered to the Courthouse by a soldier from Washington. He instructed us to find you and deliver it immediately."

Taking the sealed envelope and tearing it open, Tildon unfolded the piece of paper inside and read:

URGENT.

PRESIDENT TO MEET WITH MCCLELLAN IN PARKER CITY.

J.

Chapter Sixty-One

1984...

By the time they'd parked their car in the lot and climbed the stairs to their office, Ben and Tommy were feeling pretty tired. Late night stakeouts and early morning crime scenes were taking their toll. Neither wanted to complain because they knew it was all part of the job. But that didn't stop them from groaning just a little as they dropped their weary bones into their chairs. Tommy immediately kicked back and put his feet up on his desk as Ben began massaging his temples.

Staring straight up at the ceiling, Tommy said, "We need to track down Walter Tully and Professor McDonald."

"McClinton."

"What?"

"Professor McClinton. Not McDonald."

"I said McDonald?"

"Yes."

"Are you sure?"

"Don't make me shoot you."

"Hey! That's my go-to solution, buddy," Tommy said, closing his eyes. "So, we need to find Tully and McDonald."

Ben sighed.

"All kidding aside," he continued, "these guys could be in danger."

"If our killer didn't find what he was looking for at Moran's, then he could move on to one of them."

"Exactly."

Ben reached for the telephone and punched in the number for Dispatch. Speaking with the supervisor, Ben asked for patrol cars to be sent around to both Tully and McClinton's homes to check on them and report back to him. The call lasted only a few minutes, but in the time Ben was on the telephone, Tommy had fallen asleep.

A sudden knock on the open office door jarred Tommy out of his light slumber and made Ben, who'd been deep in thought, jump.

"You two look terrible," Natalie said, casting her eyes over the two rumpled detectives seated at their desks.

Standing up and stretching, Tommy said, "Well, they'll just let anyone wander around a police station these days, won't they." Then he threw his arms around Nat and gave her a bear hug lifting her feet off the ground.

"Being the chief detective's fiancée comes with some benefits." She smiled and gave Tommy a kiss on the cheek. "I had a late parent-teacher conference and thought I'd stop by to see if you were going to be home tonight. I heard on the radio that Mike Moran was found dead in his house. Was that the call you got this morning?"

"Afraid so," Ben said, nodding his head. "It was on the radio?"

"Yeah. I heard it on my way over."

Ben looked at his watch. It had only been twelve hours since he'd gotten the call that morning. The plan had been for the chief to brief the mayor, then put out a statement in the morning about Moran's death. Clearly, someone in the know jumped the gun and leaked the story. Being as it was one of the radio station's interns who'd found Moran, Ben should have figured they wouldn't be able to keep it quiet for too long.

"Is this connected to Father Taylor's death?"

"That is the million dollar question, Miss Fitzpatrick," Tommy said, offering his chair for her to have a seat. "We believe it is. There is a loose connection to an auction that both men attended."

"Should you be telling me this?"

"You asked," Tommy pointed out. "And if you tell anyone or somehow obstruct our investigation, I'll just arrest you."

"Actually," Ben interrupted. "You might be able to help us with something. We need to talk to a History professor from Hammermill."

"And you think just because I'm a History teacher, I know all the History teachers and professors in the county? Like we all belong to a club or something?"

"I was just wondering if you knew Henry McClinton by any chance and if you could tell us anything about him."

"Ah. Henry McClinton? Actually...okay, you're going to find this funny...I do know him."

Ben didn't have to say anything. He just smiled. It was Tommy who did a little dance behind Natalie's back.

"Professor McClinton has spoken to a few of my classes before. He specializes in the Civil War. He seems nice. Maybe a little quirky."

"Quirky, how?" Ben asked.

"I guess I would say his interest in the Civil War goes beyond that of a normal history buff."

"Well, if he's a professor who specializes in the subject...." Tommy shrugged.

"Yeah. But he *really* gets into it. I've heard him talk about some pretty obscure theories about the *true* cause of the war."

"He's a conspiracy theorist?" Ben jotted a note on his pad next to the professor's name.

"Okay, I wouldn't go that far. But he has some interesting ideas."

"Natalie," Tommy said with all sincerity, "I love you, and I love that you make my best friend so happy. But you really suck as a character witness."

Chapter Sixty-Two

For the second time in half an hour, Ben hung up the telephone after speaking with the Dispatch supervisor, another sergeant in the department who was always very eager to please when the detectives came to him with a request. He informed Ben that the patrol officers who'd been sent to the homes of Walter Tully and Henry McClinton both reported in. As he relayed the information, Ben took notes so he'd be able to update the case file later.

The call came in just as he'd gotten back to his desk after walking Natalie to her car and telling her not to wait up for him since he had no idea when he was going to be home. There were so many reasons he loved her and was looking forward to spending the rest of his life with her. One of which was the fact she never hounded him about his long, irregular hours. She understood how important his job was to him. How his service was more than a job to him. It was a calling.

Skimming the notes he'd just scribbled down, he looked up at his partner and said, "Do you ever get the feeling Randy is a little too happy sometimes?"

"Randy? You mean Sergeant Randolph James Wesley Hirsh of Dispatch?"

"Yeah. Wait. Wesley?"

"He's a character, alright. I swear I have never seen him *not* smiling. So, what did Sergeant Randy have to say?"

Ben leaned back in his chair and rubbed his eyes. "He sent patrol cars to both Tully's and McClinton's. Walter Tully is out of town on business and has been since the end of last week. That's according to his wife. She supplied his travel and hotel information. We're going to need to check that.

McClinton was not home because he teaches a late class on Thursday nights. That comes from McClinton's neighbor. The class lets out at seven-fifteen. Again, this is according to the friendly neighbor. However, the professor...I know this may come as a surprise after what Nat said...is married."

"You don't say? I guess there really is somebody for everyone." Tommy shook his head and looked at his watch. "The class ends at seven-fifteen? We can head over and catch him after class."

"That's what I was thinking, too," Ben said, standing up and grabbing his jacket off the back of the chair. "If we leave now, we can grab something to eat on the way."

As Tommy began to do the same, he said, "Okay. If Tully has been out of town, we know at least that means he isn't the killer."

"As long as we can confirm that he's actually been out of town."

"Right. But I'm just going to assume the wife's telling the truth. He may not be the killer, but he could still be a target."

Ben shook his head in agreement and allowed Tommy to continue. "Professor McClinton could be either our suspect or another target."

Reaching for the telephone, Ben said, "I'm going to see if I can have a squad car sit on both of their houses tonight just in case our guy didn't find what he was looking for at Moran's and tries again."

"Maybe we get lucky and catch one of them trying to break into the other's house."

"Assuming this actually has anything to do with those damn books," Ben pointed out.

Tommy went to heat up the car while Ben finished making arrangements with the duty sergeant. While Sergeant Randy would no doubt have been more than happy to send patrols to watch the houses, Ben knew he needed to get a supervisor to sign off on the use of patrol resources for something like this. After all, he was requesting that two officers be taken off their usual beats for the night. But he felt confident if the night shift's patrol supervisor didn't agree to his request, the chief would surely back him up and give the order. Luckily he didn't need to call on the chief because word had already spread throughout the station that because of the two high-profile murders they had on their hands, anything the Detective Squad needed to solve the case, they got.

After making the call, as Ben trotted down the stairs toward the door leading to the parking lot, he tried to figure out what could possibly have been in the lot of books that would cause someone to kill to get their hands on them. Neither he nor Tommy had come up with an answer to that question. Which is why he was wondering if they were on the right track. Regardless, the auction was the only thing that connected their two victims. And they had no other working theories at the moment, so talking to McClinton was as good an idea as any at the moment.

Chapter Sixty-Three

Hammermill College was a small, private university started—like so many things in Parker City—just prior to the Civil War. Begun as an educational institution for women, the college was founded by a group of the country's most progressive and philanthropic ladies looking to advance the women's rights movement even before the issue had taken hold in other parts of the nation. The school remained a female-only university until 1975 when the Board of Trustees changed the nearly eighty-year-old policy and began admitting male students. The female population of the student body still vastly outpaced that of the men, however.

When Hammermill College opened, its purpose was to help advance the city and transform it into a modern center of culture and education sitting at the edge of the Blue Ridge Mountains. That was according to Clementine Baker, the school's first headmistress and one of its trustees. A number of the men in town had different thoughts on the school, however. Seeing it as unnecessary and a direct challenge to their authority. No one could argue a college like Hammermill was unheard of at the time for such a rural community. But with the backing of some of the city's most powerful families, the idea became a reality.

While the college as a whole had never landed on the list of the nation's top universities, the History, and Social Sciences Departments succeeded in making a name for themselves. Because of Hammermill's location, the Civil War naturally had a place in the curriculum. And a growing number of respected Civil War historians had joined the History Department's faculty in the last decade bringing with them their scholarly works and notoriety.

From what Ben and Tommy were able to quickly learn about Professor Henry McClinton, he was not a nationally renowned Civil War historian, but he had a solid reputation in the field. But as Natalie explained, his interest could occasionally border on the fanatical.

The campus looked exactly like a college campus should look, Ben thought as they parked the car and walked toward Baker Hall, where the History Department was housed. Classic-looking brick buildings all organized around grassy quads where the students could gather to study or hang out between classes. As he and Tommy cut across one of the green spaces, they didn't find many students out and about. The afternoon had been chilly enough, but once the sun set, the temperature plummeted, and the wind began picking up. Ben kept his hands stuffed deep in his pockets as he jogged toward the tall Colonial-style-looking building with its white shutters and gabled roof ahead of them.

Pulling the door open, the detectives felt a welcome blast of warm air surge toward them. Tommy was rubbing his hands together and blowing into them to try and get some feeling back in his fingers.

"It would have been nice if the parking lot wasn't two miles from the building," he complained, stamping his feet to get the circulation moving.

"You're such a drama queen," Ben said, pulling the collar of his coat down from around his neck.

"I'm not a drama queen. I'm just cold, cranky, and tired. You don't think there's any chance McClinton will just break down and confess when we show our badges, do you?"

"Has that ever happened for us before?"

"There's got to be a first time," Tommy said over his shoulder as he scanned the building directory so he could figure out where they were headed. "McClinton...office four-thirteen. This building better have an elevator. I'm getting too old to do stairs."

"You're thirty!"

Tommy shrugged. "I have an old soul."

Chapter Sixty-Four

Ben could only assume a janitor had just gone through and cleaned the floors because his shoes squeaked with each step as he and Tommy walked down the hall toward office 413. The hallway, other than the sound of his shoes on the slick linoleum, was silent. Not much of a surprise considering the hour. There weren't many classes held in the evening. At least in the History Department, it seemed.

"There's McClinton's office," Tommy said, pointing to a door on their right. "How do you want to play this? Are we treating him as a suspect? A possible witness? Another target?"

Ben thought for a moment. They had no evidence to think the professor was the killer. The only thing tying him to any of the murders was the fact he'd been at the same auction as the victims and been interested in the same items.

"We're trying to find out what could be so special about the books. This is just a fact-finding mission. Let's not alarm him. Just play nice."

"But keep our eyes open for anything that could shout, 'I'm a murderer.'"

Ben smiled and was about to knock on the door when he noticed it wasn't actually closed. Listening, he could hear some movement on the other side. He didn't want to simply barge into the office, so he knocked on the doorframe and waited for an answer.

There was no response. But he could still hear someone moving around inside. He gave Tommy a quick look. Placing a hand on his gun, just in case he needed to draw it quickly, he slowly eased the door open enough for him to look inside.

For a moment, Ben thought they were too late, and the office might have already been ransacked. There were books and files scattered around the office. What he could only assume was McClinton's desk was buried under mounds of papers and blue exam books. The floor was littered with textbooks and random stacks of boxes. Ben was so focused on the mess he didn't notice the young man in the corner. His back was to them, and at first, he thought the boy was taking papers out of a filing cabinet. It took him a second to realize he was actually putting files *into* the cabinet.

"Excuse me," Ben said, hand still resting on his gun.

The boy didn't respond. Just continued filing papers.

"Hey! PCPD," Ben tried again.

Still nothing.

Ben stepped forward and tapped him on his shoulder. It was then that he saw the headphones covering his ears, connecting to the Walkman clipped to the kid's belt.

"Wow! You scared the crap out of me." The boy recoiled slightly when he saw Ben and Tommy standing in the office. His eyes grew even larger when he saw the guns on their hips. "What's going on?"

Ben motioned for him to remove the headphones.

"We're with the Parker City Police Department. We're here to speak with Professor McClinton."

"Oh...ah...he's in class. It should be over any minute. Is something wrong?"

"What's your name?" Tommy asked, looking around, taking in the complete disaster in front of them. "And is this how the office always looks?"

"Ummm...sorry...I'm Teddy. I mean Edward Nestor. I go by Teddy. It might look chaotic, but the professor knows where everything is. He gets mad if I try to clean anything up. Once the janitor moved all of the textbooks on the floor so he could vacuum, and you would think he'd killed the professor's cat or something."

"Why are you in Professor McClinton's office going through his files?" Ben asked, thinking the kid looked somehow familiar but not sure why.

"I'm not going through his files," Nestor protested. "I'm the professor's teaching assistant. I was filing papers."

"Do you usually work this late?" Tommy asked.

"Just on Thursdays when Professor McClinton has his late class."

Ben gave the student a quick once-over. He was clean-cut, skinny. Pretty average looking preppy with his sweater, collared shirt, and khakis.

"I'm sorry, but I didn't get your names," Nestor said, laying the stack of papers he was holding down on top of the file cabinet. "I should let the professor know you're here."

"Does he usually leave right from his class?" Tommy asked, looking back out into the hallway.

"Well, no. But I thought I should go meet him and tell him you're looking for him."

"There's nothing to worry about, Teddy," Ben said with a smile. "We just needed to ask Professor McClinton about an auction he attended at Benson Auction and Antiques. We were hoping he could tell us about one of the sets of items that was sold."

"Supposedly Civil War-era items," Tommy offered.

"Oh, if it's the Civil War you're talking about, then you've come to the right place. Professor McClinton is the foremost expert at Hammermill."

"By any chance," Tommy began, trying to sound as nonchalant as possible, "do you happen to know what the professor's schedule was yesterday afternoon?"

Ben gave Tommy a knowing look, but also, with a slight raise of an eyebrow, silently told him to tread carefully.

The teaching assistant wrinkled his forehead for a moment. "He had his usual class schedule. And office hours."

Before either of the detectives could follow up and try to nail down exactly where the professor was and when, they were interrupted by the arrival of their subject.

"Can I help you, gentlemen?" he asked from the doorway.

"Professor McClinton? I'm Detective Ben Winters. This is my partner, Tommy Mason. We were hoping we could ask you a few questions."

Chapter Sixty-Five

Henry McClinton looked like an academic straight out of a satiric movie skewering institutes of higher education. He looked like the kind of guy who was never very popular in school himself but decided to follow a path that would force students of all stripes to treat him with a certain amount of respect because he was the one who now had the upper hand. It was his decision if a student passed or failed. And the look he was giving Ben and Tommy was undoubtedly one he'd used on his students before. It was a combination of apprehension and annoyance. It was, in fact, a look the detectives had become accustomed to seeing when they showed up to speak with someone unexpectedly.

Ben's initial first impressions were usually spot-on when it came to people. It was just another one of the talents that made him a great detective. Unlike his partner, he didn't have a naturally cynical view of everyone and everything. He wanted to give people the benefit of the doubt. But when he did meet someone who gave off a negative vibe—like Professor Henry McClinton was doing right now—he trusted his gut.

McClinton, standing there wearing the ubiquitous corduroy jacket with patches on the sleeves and a pair of glasses on the edge of his nose, appraised the two police detectives in his office. Ben wasn't the only one who could read people, it seemed.

"Teddy, if you will excuse us. That will be all for the night. Thank you. We can discuss next week's exam tomorrow."

As his teaching assistant collected his bag and excused himself, awkwardly exiting the office, McClinton maneuvered around the detectives and took his place behind his desk. Laying a large binder down, he then moved some spiral notebooks from one corner of the desk to the other. Ben watched with amusement. In the professor's mind, the rearranging must have made some sort of sense. To him, it seemed like a futile effort at best.

"Have a seat, Detectives. What can I help you with? You have questions about something?"

"Thank you, Professor McClinton," Ben began, carefully pulling one of the guest chairs closer to the desk without disturbing any of the arranged piles on the floor. "We were hoping you would be able to answer some questions about an auction you recently attended at Benson Auction and Antiques."

Ben had once again brought the auction catalog with him, and he carefully laid the evidence bag containing the brochure on the professor's desk. McClinton eyed the catalog but made no attempt to touch it. He didn't move at all.

"Yes. I was at that auction. But you must already know that."

"We spoke with Ellen Osbourne. She said that you, Father Roland Taylor, Mike Moran, and Walter Tully were all bidding on a set of books that evening," Tommy said, trying to hide the fact he was getting a not-so-good feeling from the guy.

"I can confirm that that is true. Yes."

"We were hoping you might be able to tell us what was so special about these books. Ms. Osbourne's description of them didn't strike us as anything particularly interesting."

"Interesting? I guess that depends on your definition, Detective. Interest, like beauty, is in the eye of the beholder. I'm sure you've heard that saying before." The professor paused, seemingly for effect. "I believed that I had finally tracked down a journal that belonged to my great-great-great grandfather, William McClinton. He was the clerk for Parker's City Council during the Civil War. There has always been a story in my family that he kept a journal that contained information that any historian like myself would kill to get their hands on."

Ben felt his jaw literally drop.

"I'm sorry, Detective. Did I say something wrong?"

Tommy didn't miss a beat. "Exactly what sort of information would you be willing to kill for, Professor?"

Leaning back in his chair and steepling his fingers in front of him, through an overconfident smirk, McClinton said, "I, of course, was speaking metaphorically, Detective.

"In my studies and research, I have come across information that leads me to believe there was an incident here in Parker City that history may have forgotten. Or, more likely, was *purposely* rewritten.

"You see, William McClinton, my great-great-great grandfather, was known for his record keeping. I have a number of his journals that were passed down through the generations. They provide so much insight into life in Parker during his lifetime. But in a couple of his later journals, he would make reference to something that happened during the Civil War, something that was...very troubling and if the truth about events was known, it could do damage to a great many people."

Finding himself beginning to get carried away by the professor's story, Tommy asked, "Do you have any idea what he was talking about?"

McClinton smiled a wry smile. "I believe I have been able to piece together some details through other sources, but I thought that journal at Benson's may be the key to tying everything together. Especially if it was anything like William's other journals. The details he recorded...have been a treasure-trove of information."

Ben was starting to get a headache. He felt as though McClinton was purposely trying to distract them with what was beginning to sound like a treasure hunt for a secret journal. Tommy would be completely on board with a theory involving some historical secrets trying to be kept hidden, but he needed to keep a clear head and stay focused.

"Professor," Ben said when McClinton paused for a moment, "this journal and the information you believe could be in it...do you think someone would be willing to kill to get their hands on it?"

That gave the professor pause. He slowly leaned back in his chair and crossed his arms in front of him. Ben wasn't sure if he was thinking about how to answer that question or if some other thought was passing through his mind.

"Detective...Winters? I believe individuals are capable of killing for any number of reasons. Some make sense, while others make us all wonder."

"But in this particular case? I mean, what do you believe was so important in this journal? What history do you think was rewritten?"

Leaning back in his chair with a smug look on his face, McClinton asked, "Have either of you ever heard of the Knights of the Golden Circle?"

Chapter Sixty-Six

1862...

Caleb reread the message Sheriff Tildon had pressed into his hands only moments earlier. It was the fourth time he'd done so, knowing that he was not to share what was in the message with anyone else standing around on the edge of the Tasker River. While he found it difficult to believe either Deputy Gimble or Ford were part of the Golden Circle conspiracy in Parker City, there was no way to be certain at the present. He could tell by the way the sheriff passed him the folded paper it was to be kept between themselves. Though it was clear Zachary Ford was curious about the message by the way he eyed Caleb as he put the paper into his pocket after reading it for the fifth time.

"Doc, do you have everything here in hand?" the sheriff asked as he watched his deputies securing the wrapped body of Eustace Drake in the back of Doc Crum's wagon for transport back into town. "Deputy Post and I have some business to attend to. We need to pay Mrs. Drake a visit to let her know...well...."

"All good here, Sam. After I have a chance to take a look at the body, I'll let you know if I come across anything. But I can't say it will be any time soon. Not with all the soldiers floodin' in right now. I've got my hands full," the elder doctor said with a shrug of his sagging shoulders.

"Quite alright," Tildon boomed, heaving himself onto the driver's seat and taking up the reins. "You take good care of our boys, you hear?"

With a tip of his hat, the sheriff gave Dolly the signal to go, and they were off. Neither said anything until they knew they were out of earshot of the group. Even then, the silence continued.

"Are we truly going to Drake House?" Caleb finally asked, "or were you just sayin' that so we could get away?"

"We're truly going, my boy," the sheriff answered with a sad tone in his voice. "We need to let Margaret know. But then you and I need to do some thinking about what the president coming to Parker could mean."

"He could be in grave danger, comin' here with a group of Golden Circle agents at work."

"Precisely," Tildon agreed. "Which is why I don't understand why Jon...my friend from Washington, would allow Lincoln to make the trip. Surely he knows it could be putting the president's life in jeopardy."

"He will be meeting with General McClellan. They'll have bodyguards around 'em," Caleb tried. "Or it could be a secret meeting that no one knows about. And Jonathan just wanted to let you know so you could be on the lookout."

"No names, my boy," the sheriff chided. "That could be a possibility."

The two fell into silence once more as the sheriff guided the buggy toward Drake House.

As the large home came into view at the end of the street, the sheriff shifted in his seat and said, "Once we're done here, we'll head back to the Courthouse. We'll see if there are any other messages or if there's chatter that *something* may be happening. A visit from the president is sure to create some excitement. Even if no one's supposed to know about it."

Chapter Sixty-Seven

When they'd left Drake House, Caleb wasn't sure if he would ever be able to erase the look on Margaret Drake's face from his mind. When the sheriff told her that Eustace's body was discovered, the woman, who Caleb thought was so strong and steadfast, crumbled before his very eyes. She became almost inconsolable. It was heartbreaking to witness. She withered before them and had to be helped up the large staircase to her room by the housemaid Caleb spoke with on his last visit.

"Once she's had some time, I'll send word to the butler about how to go about claiming the body so they can arrange a funeral," Sheriff Tildon said, slowly walking back to the buggy, his hat still in his hand. Placing a foot on the step to heave himself into the rig, the sheriff stopped. Putting his foot down, he leaned against the side. His usual full, fleshy face looked drawn and pale.

"Sheriff?" Caleb eyed Tildon carefully from the opposite side of the buggy.

"This damnable war. It's torn the entire country apart, and now there are even darker forces at work right here in *my* town. And I am completely powerless to do anything about it. If I can't even protect the residents of Parker, how am I going to see the president safely through his visit?"

"Sir…" Caleb trailed off because he wasn't even sure where to begin.

He knew the sheriff was right on all counts. The war was at the root of everything that was wrong at the present. The division between the north and the south had spawned this treacherous Knights of the Golden Circle, which seemingly corrupted otherwise decent men. Men like Silas Moss and

Thaddeus Parker, who Caleb knew would give their lives for Parker City. But if they were agents of the Golden Circle, they were now responsible for the killing of one of the city's most prominent figures. A man who himself had done so much for the city. If they learned of Lincoln's trip to Parker, could they be capable of planning an attempt on the life of the president?

The gravity of the situation was crushing, which is why Caleb understood how his mentor was feeling. In a sense, Sheriff Samuel J. Tildon was a symbol of Parker City. And if his city was being corrupted, what did that mean for him? A man with such a steadfast commitment to doing what was right. To protecting everything. To seeing justice served. To upholding the rule of law.

But then Caleb once again found himself tripping over the sheriff's illegal involvement with the Underground Railroad. He knew that it was going to take some time to reconcile his feelings. He wished he had the time to do so now and come to some sort of understanding and accept the two sides of Sheriff Tildon, but he did not have that particular luxury. He just needed to do his job. He knew the rest would all end as it was supposed to in time.

"Sir," Caleb repeated in a firm tone, "we need to see if we can learn any more about President Lincoln's plans."

The sheriff saw the look in Caleb's eyes—confidence, sympathy, and downright stubborn determination. It was exactly what he needed to see at that moment. As the corners of his mouth slowly turned up into a smile, he climbed into the buggy, patted Caleb's arm, and gave Dolly the signal that it was time to head back to the Courthouse.

Chapter Sixty-Eight

Arriving at the Courthouse, Caleb noticed everyone seemed to be acting a little peculiar. Maybe that wasn't the right word. But there was something going on that had everyone in a state. A group of court clerks was off in the corner whispering as he and the sheriff passed through the building's larger front doors into the grand foyer. On the staircase leading up to the sheriff's office, some lawyers that Caleb recognized were also huddled together, talking in hushed tones.

It wasn't until they arrived on the second floor and came to the door leading into the Sheriff's Department that they understood what all the fuss was about. Three Union soldiers were standing in the hallway, fully armed and at attention.

"So much for keepin' the meeting a secret," Caleb said just loud enough for the sheriff to hear.

"Gentlemen," Sheriff Tildon said, tipping his hat to them and letting himself into the office. None of the soldiers made a move but followed him and Caleb with their eyes.

Once inside, it became even more apparent what had everyone in the building talking. Two more soldiers stood guard on either side of the door while General George McClellan and another pair of officers—judging by the insignias on their shoulders-sat at the large table in the center of the room.

"Sheriff Tildon," McClellan said without standing. "I hope you don't mind that we've made ourselves comfortable while we were waiting for you. Your man at the front desk there said it was alright."

The sheriff's clerk, who greeted all guests visiting the office, gave a shrug.

"Of course, General," the Tildon said, a tone of gentility forcing its way into his voice. "Had I known you'd be paying a visit, I would have been here to greet you. But we had some unfortunate business to take care of on the other side of town."

"I'm sorry to hear that. There's been quite a bit of unpleasantness goin' on lately."

Giving a half-nod in agreement, the sheriff informed McClellan, "We discovered the body of Eustace Drake. He washed up on the bank of the Tasker River. In eyesight of his own factory, in fact. And nowhere near where he went missing, and we found his carriage."

McClellan sat stone-faced. Not even a twitch of the eyes. He just stared at the sheriff.

"I'm sorry for your loss," Tildon continued.

McClellan cocked his head questioningly.

"You said you and Eustace were good friends. Did you not?"

"Ahh. We were. I shall have to pay my respects to Mrs. Drake in due time. When my business here is concluded, and she's had some time to recover."

"May I ask what business it is that you have here, sir? And I must congratulate you on what I understand to be your victory at Sharpsburg."

McClellan smiled. He relished having his ego stroked. "We sent the rebels runnin' for certain."

"I would think you would be hot on their trail, General. Chasing them back to Richmond. Not sitting here in my office."

If the sheriff had intended the comment as an insult, it hit the mark. McClellan visibly tensed but did not immediately respond. He finished his cigarette before saying, "I have my orders, Sheriff."

"That's what brings you here today?"

"It is. There is to be a very important meeting held here in Parker City and, even though my men will be providing the security, we thought it best to inform you. After all, you know the locals better than we do and can help us make sure we know of anyone who may cause trouble."

Sheriff Tildon took a seat at the table across from McClellan. "Do we get to know who will be a part of this meeting? Or where it will be held?"

The general leaned forward and ran a finger along his mustache. "Sheriff, I think it might be best if you and I step into your office and speak privately."

With a slight nod of his head, the sheriff showed the general into his office. Neither Caleb nor the two other officers made an attempt to follow. Though Caleb sorely wanted to hear exactly what the general was about to say.

Instead, the young deputy took a seat at the table and patiently waited as they all watched the sheriff and George McClellan through the window in the door to Tildon's office. After a few moments of awkward silence, the main door to the office flew open, and Deputy Gimble strode in.

"What in tarnation is goin' on in here?" he asked, looking from Caleb to the officers back to Caleb, then to the soldiers he found himself standing between.

"Oscar," Caleb said, pulling out the chair next to him, "why don't you grab your playin' cards and have a seat? We may be here a spell."

Chapter Sixty-Nine

George McClellan and Samuel Tildon, two giants among men, remained behind the closed door for near half an hour. Enough time for the others to play a game of Whist. On only a few occasions could raised voices be heard. Even as the men played their cards, they all kept one eye on the men in the other room.

When the door suddenly opened, and the general marched out of the office and into the hall without saying a word, the other soldiers quickly followed. The sound of all their boots hammered on the floor as they made their retreat from the Courthouse. Where they were now heading, Caleb did not have a clue.

"Gimble!" the sheriff's voice rang from inside his office. "I need you to take this message to the telegraph office."

When Deputy Gimble had left, Tildon motioned for Caleb to join him. Which he quickly did. After closing the door so they could have a private conversation, he took a seat in the same chair McClellan used.

"That was a coded message to our friend in Washington," the sheriff said, plucking a fresh cigar from the humidor in front of him. Caleb was surprised that he'd said *our* friend from Washington. "It will be meaningless to anyone else. But Jonathan will understand."

"Remember, Sheriff, no names," Caleb said lightly. Then went on, asking, "What did General McClellan have to say?"

"The man is a pompous blowhard. I can't believe he's leading our army. But my opinion on that matter isn't worth horse spit. McClellan admitted the president was planning on traveling to Parker City to meet with him and his other generals. It's to discuss the military strategy going forward. Frankly, I believe it will be a security nightmare. But the decision has been made, and the president is coming."

"Did the general say anything about the Golden Circle?" Even though they were alone, Caleb still lowered his voice.

"No. And he never once asked about Eustace Drake or anything we've learned about his disappearance."

"Surely you don't believe *he's* involved?"

"I don't. But if he wasn't willing to share information with us—information that could have headed us in the right direction with our investigation—then who knows what else he is hiding from us?"

Pausing, the sheriff began his regular routine of lighting his cigar. Caleb watched silently. Waiting for the sheriff to clear his head. He knew that was part of the reason Tildon smoked the thick rolls of tobacco. They helped him think. And if someone asked him a question he didn't want to answer right away, he could take a few puffs to delay his response.

After the sheriff had blown several clouds of smoke into the air, he finally said, "We have just two days to figure out who killed Eustace Drake. If we can catch them, then I would feel a lot better about the president's visit."

"I was thinkin' about that. What we observed on Mr. Drake's body. The patch job that was done on the bullet wound. Whoever did that had to have some sort of medical trainin.' So I'm wonderin' if there's a doctor involved."

Leaning back in his chair, the sheriff pondered the idea for a moment. "I'm sure there are some doctors in Parker City that don't have much like of the government right now. But none of them have been making too much of a fuss. I don't know how we figure out who it could be."

"I could always ask Doc Crum. There isn't a medical man around he doesn't know. Even if he's not certain, he might have an idea or two about who might have more than just strong negative feelings about the government."

"Just be careful what you let on, my boy. I like old Doc Crum, but he isn't known for being able to keep his big trap shut."

Caleb smiled. "That, sir, is exactly what I'm counting on."

Chapter Seventy

1984...

L istening to Professor McClinton tell them about the Knights of
the Golden Circle and how he believed there was a branch of the
shadowy group that existed in Parker City made Ben and Tommy
think they were hearing the plot of a movie filled with conspiracy theories
and thrills. Then when McClinton told them that members of some of
Parker's most prominent families were a part of the organization, it left the
detectives at a loss. It all sounded so fanciful that they didn't know if the
professor was crazy or if he'd just given them a whole new list of suspects.

If he was right and some of Parker's most important men had been a
part of a group trying to overthrow the government, it was possible to
believe that maybe some of their descendants wouldn't want that kind of
information coming out. Ben and Tommy had seen first-hand what the
city's founding families were still like and what they were willing to do to
protect their names and reputations. But at the same point, it just sounded
silly. To think a priest and a radio DJ were killed so someone could hide
the fact their great-great-great-whatever sided with the south during the
Civil War was hard to believe.

Though, when Ben offered that assumption, McClinton went off on a
tangent about how some of the members of the Golden Circle didn't just side
with the Confederacy, they wanted to see the Union completely destroyed
and a whole new government put in place. The damage being associated

with a plan like that could be irreparable. Even if it was over a hundred years ago.

Ben was still finding it a little hard to swallow. Like there was still something more the professor wasn't telling them. Something that would actually make sense and point them in a direction based on a rational theory. Ben should have realized that would be when his partner was going to jump in with his own unbelievable idea that could only come from his childlike imagination.

"Professor," Tommy began, Ben instantly recognizing the tone in his voice, "I'm the first to say I wasn't a very good student. And History sure wasn't my favorite subject in school. But I feel like at some point, I heard or read about this Golden Circle group and how there's supposed to be a Confederate treasure buried out there somewhere. Is that true? Do you think this journal could have anything to do with that?"

The incredulous look on McClinton's face told Ben all he needed. But when the academic finally spoke, he was very even-toned. "Well, Detective. Over the years, yes, there have been those who believe the Knights of the Golden Circle accumulated a vast treasure which the Confederacy was going to use to defeat the north. Obviously, that is not what happened, as the south lost. But some believe this *treasure*, as you said, is *buried out there* somewhere, just waiting to be discovered with the right clues."

"And the journal?"

"Has nothing to do with it," McClinton said, bursting Tommy's bubble. "I am not one who believes there is a hidden treasure. I think that is just a myth. So if you are implying someone has killed to get their hands on this journal because, in some way, it will point them toward great riches, then I would suggest you write that all down and submit it to a publisher as an adventure novel. Or maybe it could be part of the next Indiana Jones movie. I understand they've done well, and the general public seems to find those types of stories amusing."

There was one glaring question that McClinton had yet to answer.

"Professor," Ben asked, "did you actually have a chance to look at the journal you believe belonged to your great...great grandfather?"

"Three greats, Detective. My great-great-great grandfather. And no. I was running late and could not see it beforehand and needed to leave before the auction was even concluded, so I did not have a chance to ask Father Taylor to see it afterward. I was hoping to speak with him about it later."

"And you never did?"

"I never had the chance."

The professor had been very cool until this point, but Ben could see they were now wearing out their welcome. McClinton had begun fidgeting in his seat and then reached into his desk drawer and pulled out a nearly empty pack of cigarettes. Without asking either Ben or Tommy if they minded if he smoked, he pulled one from the pack and lit up.

"Thank you for your time, Professor McClinton," Ben said as he stood up. "If we have any further questions, we will be in touch. Um... I don't suppose I could ask you for a cigarette? It's been a long day, and I could really use one before I head home. My fiancée doesn't allow me to smoke in our apartment."

"Umm... Alright. There's only a couple in there. You can keep the pack."

Ben had pulled a handkerchief from his pocket to wipe his nose as the professor offered the pack of Camels to him. Taking them, Ben thanked the professor again for his time and headed into the hallway with Tommy on his heels.

"What the hell was that?" Tommy said from behind him.

"Wait until we're outside," Ben answered over his shoulder.

"I have been asking...."

"Outside."

When they were finally standing in front of Baker Hall, Ben turned to his partner and waited.

"What the hell? Since when do you smoke? Since when does Nat not allow you to smoke? I have offered you a million cigarettes over the years, and never have you accepted one, let alone *asked* for one out of the clear blue."

Smiling, Ben asked, "Are you done?"

"Yes."

"Good." Ben pulled his hand out of his coat, opening it to show Tommy the pack of cigarettes wrapped in the handkerchief.

Tommy looked at it, then up at Ben, and in unison, they said, "Fingerprints."

Chapter Seventy-One

"I thought you'd lost your mind or something," Tommy said from behind the wheel. The pair were on their way across town to the State Police Barracks, where they intended to deliver the cigarette package for fingerprint testing. "Maybe we get lucky and grab a print that matches the one from Moran's house, and we can close this thing."

"That would sure be nice," Ben said, looking out the passenger window, watching the buildings pass by.

"It would also be nice if the PCPD had our own forensics guys, and we didn't have to rely on the state."

"That would be useful," Ben agreed.

"Well, I'm glad you brought it up because…."

"I didn't bring it up. You did."

"You and your details. But I hear that part of the chief's plan to retool the department includes adding a forensics unit."

"Where are you getting all this information?" Ben asked, raising an eyebrow.

"I'm a good detective. I find shit out."

"I don't know if I should be glad we could be getting our own CSU or depressed."

"Depressed? We won't have to work off the state boys' timeline anymore. It will speed things up for us."

"I know that. And realistically, it's a good thing. But it's depressing that we *need* our own team."

"Parker City is growing, man. You always tell me that. We gotta take the good with the bad."

Ben sat quietly, thinking about that for a few minutes. Parker *was* changing. In just the last few years, they'd all seen it. But changes meant growing pains. Those growing pains, Ben feared, were going to end up causing some problems.

But for the moment, that wasn't something he could think about...or do anything about, for that matter. He needed to stay focused on the current case.

"What do you think about the professor?" Ben asked, turning to his partner.

"Oh, I didn't like him."

"Neither did I. But what do you think about his story? The whole Golden Circle conspiracy thing?"

"You know I like a good conspiracy theory as much as the next guy. And like I said back there, I know I've heard about this whole Confederate treasure. But could someone actually kill for a journal that *might* be a treasure map? I don't know."

"Even McClinton doesn't believe in the treasure. So why would someone still want the journal?"

"He could be lying," Tommy pointed out.

"True. He could actually have the journal for all we know."

"Or..."

Ben sighed. "Or...there's something in the journal someone doesn't want known."

"You're talking about one of *the families* trying to cover up the fact one of their grandpappies was trying to overthrow the government?"

Ben smiled. "Something like that."

"Sounds a little far-fetched. Don't you think?"

"Absolutely. But it doesn't mean it isn't true. We've seen what their family names mean to them and how far they'll go."

"But to kill a priest...man, that's cold."

"Okay," Ben said, "here's the plan. We drop this off and ask nicely if they could expedite the test. Then we call it a night and sleep on all of it. There are patrol cars outside Tully's house and McClinton's. So, there's eyes on them. Maybe something'll come to one of us in a dream tonight."

Chapter Seventy-Two

Ben was overjoyed to be awoken by his alarm clock and not a telephone call sending him to another crime scene. When he walked into the apartment last night at a reasonable hour, Natalie was thrilled to see him. After stopping by the station, she just assumed it was going to be another late night for him, leaving her to grade papers and watch television.

A good night's sleep put a bit of a spring in Ben's step. He was ready to take a fresh look at the events of the last two days and see if anything jumped out at him. If there was anything, he and Tommy missed during the first go-through as everything was happening.

He was even beginning to feel a little positive until he sat down with a cup of coffee to read the paper before heading to the station. The headline in the *Herald-Dispatch* announcing the murder of Morning Mike Moran and the subsequent article questioning whether it was related to Father Roland Taylor's murder felt like a bucket of ice water being thrown in his face. Parker City had another series of murders on its hands, and Ben was once again at the center of the investigation.

At that moment, as if on cue, the telephone rang.

Ben looked at the receiver before picking it up. He quickly downed what was left in his cup, nearly scalding his throat as it went down, and answered.

"Hello." Then knowing at this hour, it was bound to be work-related, said, "This is Detective Winters."

"Morning, Ben," the chief's voice sounded extra gravelly. "Glad I caught you at home. The mayor wants to see us in his office in half an hour. Can you be there?"

"Of course. How much does he already know?"

"I've tried to keep him up to speed. But he has questions he wants to ask you himself."

"I'll be there. Thirty minutes."

Ben hung up the telephone and quickly made himself some toast for breakfast before heading out the door.

He spent the drive in running through the case.

Their victims were both public figures. But the theory they were working off of had nothing to do with that. The two men were connected, as far as the investigation was concerned, by the fact they both attended an auction and were interested in the same item. Taylor was the winning bid and walked out with the lot of books. But if, as they were positing, he'd given—or sold—the McClinton journal to someone else, the killer didn't find it at Saint Paul's, so went looking for it with one of the other people who'd bid on it. Mike Moran. For the killer to know who was interested in the auction lot, he—another assumption they were making—must have been at the auction. That left two other bidders from that evening. Henry McClinton and Walter Tully.

McClinton and Tully could either be their perpetrator or potential victims. Tully was out of town, and McClinton was an arrogant academic. Ben would have been more than happy for McClinton to be their guy and slap the cuffs on him. The problem was, there was no evidence to back up an arrest. Yet. There were fingerprints currently with the State Police that could break the case wide open. If the professor's fingerprints were on the knife found at Moran's crime scene, then the case was over. If not...they had to start over.

Ben was having no difficulty tracking the potential suspects and fitting them into the working theory. What he was having some trouble with was the motive. Sure, it seemed that these books were what the killer was looking for. Out of the list of books they'd been given by Ellen Osbourne, only the journal seemed like it could even remotely be something important. That, according to Professor McClinton. But it was his idea that this journal shed some light on a conspiracy in Parker back during the Civil War. A conspiracy that some of the city's leading citizens were part of an organization set on toppling the government. But then there was also Tommy's only half-kidding assertion that the journal may contain secrets to a hidden treasure.

The whole thing just sounded so far-fetched. Yet, it also seemed so simplistic. When you boiled it all down, if the journal was, in fact, at the heart of all this, someone was either trying to cover up their ancestor's involvement in a major act of treason, or they were trying to find a treasure.

"This *cannot* be all about a treasure hunt," Ben said to his reflection in the rearview mirror.

As Ben pulled into the PCPD's parking lot, he caught a glimpse of Tommy standing outside the back door to the building, having a cigarette. Tommy was pretty good about getting to work early if he needed to be somewhere. But it was rare for him to arrive *before* Ben.

"You're here early," Ben said when he reached his partner.

"I wanted to look at something. I compared the list of books Benson's said was in that auction lot with the list that was made at Saint Paul's. Between the notes we made and what was in the CSU log... Their report was delivered last evening while we were with McClinton, by the way... I was able to match up all the books but one."

"We found all the books but one at Saint Paul's?"

"Yes. Proving Father Taylor bought the books at the auction and took them back to the church."

"And which book is it that wasn't found at the church?"

"Do you really have to ask?" Tommy said, dropping the butt of his cigarette onto the asphalt and crushing it with his foot.

Chapter Seventy-Three

"This is all about someone worrying about their family's reputation?" Charlie Oland asked from behind his desk, a look of utter disbelief on his face.

As mayor, he'd been the man responsible for the creation of the PCPD's Detective Squad. Since its formation, he'd never once waivered in his support. He knew the importance of a modern police force. He'd just never thought in its short existence, it would have been faced with three major investigations that attracted so much press attention. Oland was Parker City's biggest cheerleader when it came to development. Unfortunately, this wasn't the kind of growth he was hoping for.

On their way to the mayor's office, Ben was able to quickly catch Chief Brent up on the investigation. He'd explained how they'd spoken with Professor McClinton, and neither he nor Tommy got a good vibe from the guy, so they were thinking they might have their man. As long as the fingerprints came back and backed them up.

Needless to say, the chief was thrilled to hear the news. If his detectives could wrap up a double murder in just three days, that was big. The sooner they could put this behind them, the better.

But first, the mayor was looking for a briefing. If nothing else, Charlie Oland did care about what was going on in his city. While he wasn't a micromanager, trying to force his way into every police matter that arose, he did want to be kept up-to-date on the big cases. And right now, a popular priest and a morning radio DJ being killed in their homes was big news.

"So... you think a Parker, Baker, Worthington, Tildon, or Moss is behind this? Are you just going to start questioning every member of one of those families? Hell, you'll have to talk to my wife then."

"That's not what I'm saying, Mr. Mayor," Ben said. "It's just a possible theory that has come up. In fact, it's a theory offered to Tommy…Detective Mason and me by someone we are looking at as a potential suspect."

"Good. I don't need to be stirring up more trouble with those families after everything that's happened over the last few years. I may have married into one of them, but you and your partner have certainly done a bang-up job of dismantling their grip on this city."

"That was never their intent," Chief Brent said. "But when someone commits a crime, it doesn't matter who you are or how many years ago your family founded the city. We're still going to arrest you."

"I understand that, Chief. And I didn't mean to imply that this was anything… Detective, you and your partner have done outstanding work. I just wish it didn't always seem like the bad guys were the ones in this town with all the money."

"Well, sir, that isn't something Detective Mason and I take into consideration. We just follow the evidence in whatever direction it leads us. And right now, we believe these two murders have something to do with this mysterious historic journal. There seems to be something in it that someone is willing to kill to get their hands on."

"I'm having trouble buying it. Aren't you?" the mayor asked, leaning back in his chair and kicking his feet up on his desk. "I mean, killing for a journal? And if it isn't to protect someone's reputation, what else could it be? Are there clues to finding a treasure in it?"

The mayor, completely joking, saw the look exchanged between Ben and the chief.

"You're kidding me? A hidden treasure?"

"Again, sir, that isn't the theory we're working with. It's just another one that's come up. You know, there are rumors that there's a hidden treasure map on the back of one of the maps over in the Historical Society right now." Ben just wanted the mayor to have all the facts. Even if they seemed too outlandish, it was better for him to hear it all.

"Who is this suspect you have?"

Chief Brent held up a finger before Ben could say anything. "Right now, Mr. Mayor, I think it best we not share that information. We're waiting on some forensics to come in. And I wouldn't want anyone to think we'd made up our minds before we had all the hard facts."

"Are you going to be putting out a statement? For the last two days, I've been bombarded by the press questioning me about Taylor and Moran. It would be nice to let them know you're narrowing in on the killer."

"We're just not entirely sure we are," Ben offered. "Until we have a fingerprint match, it's just a hunch right now. And if we tell the press we have a suspect, then turn around and say we were wrong, won't that look worse?"

The mayor only needed to think about that for a moment. "You're right. But the minute you have something definitive, I want everyone to know it. Put out a press release as you're on your way to cuff the guy."

"I'll certainly keep the chief up to speed, and I'm sure he'll keep you in the loop, Mr. Mayor."

"That's all I'm asking," Charlie Oland said with a weak smile. "And that you catch the guy."

Chapter Seventy-Four

1862 ...

Doctor Robert Crum's office, which also served as the county's morgue, was just down the street from the Courthouse. He saw patients out of the first floor of one of the newer three-story buildings, which had recently gone up in the Downtown part of Parker. It was simple red brick but stately. Inviting to the residents who required the doctor's attention to an ailment they found themselves suffering. As for the bodies he tended to in his official capacity as the county's coroner, they were kept in a section of the basement under lock and key.

Caleb's heart sank as he came to the front of Doc Crum's building and saw several wagons sitting there on the street. Two were empty, but he could only guess what they'd brought to the morgue. The third was filled with soldiers looking to see a doctor and have their wounds tended to. Some of the men Caleb passed on his way in didn't even look like they were conscious, just being propped up by the men seated on either side.

Understanding how important it was for the injured men to see a doctor, Caleb felt uncomfortable knowing he was about to take up some of Doc Crum's time with his questions. But the doctor might be able to help them figure out who at least one of the individuals was behind the kidnapping and murder of Eustace Drake. So he needed to make his inquiries regardless of the dire nature in which some of Crum's incoming patients found themselves.

Having been one of the county's preeminent doctors for as long as he'd been, Doc Crum's practice was one of the most successful around. He was able to hire on a pair of junior doctors and two nurses, as well as a couple of attendants to assist with his official coroner duties. Today, Caleb witnessed all of them working feverishly to handle the influx of patients.

Through his official capacity as a deputy sheriff, Caleb knew the men who worked for Doc Crum, the coroner. One's name was Hicks, and the other's Morris. Standing in the small waiting room, he saw both of them helping to move soldiers around from room to room as needed. Hicks was just taking a young Union fighter down the hallway to be examined by one of the doctors. As they passed him, Caleb asked where he could find Doc Crum.

"Last I saw, he was in his office," Hicks said, trying to take most of the weight of the soldier. "He was tryin' to figure out where to put all these men. We're runnin' outta room here. Once the doctors see 'em, we gotta send 'em somewhere. We're waitin' for some carts to take them over to the Saint Paul's. The sisters will be seeing to their recovery."

Making his way down the hall to Crum's private office, where he and the sheriff had visited the doc before, Caleb tried his best to stay out of the way of the people working to ease the pain of as many of the poor souls as possible. He counted a number of women and men who, like so many around the city, were volunteering to do whatever they could to assist with the constant flow of battered and bloody men who'd recently seen battle.

The door to the doctor's office sat wide open, so Caleb had no concern about interrupting him. Seeing the portly man sitting at his desk in the corner of the room, Caleb announced himself by rapping firmly on the doorframe.

"Excuse me, Doc."

Turning in his chair to see who was at the door, Crum's glasses perched precariously on his large round nose while a smoking pipe was firmly clenched in his teeth.

"Caleb. What brings you here? Don't say it's another dead body. I just don't have the time."

"No, sir. It's not another body. It's the one you already picked up today. Mr. Drake's."

"I told Sam when I had the opportunity, I would see if I could find anything that might help figure out what happened to Eustace. But I've been up to my ears all afternoon. I still haven't had time to eat lunch, and it's nearly supper."

"I understand. But I was just hopin' you could answer a couple questions. Real fast. Then I'll get outta your hair."

The doctor shifted in his chair, then took his glasses off and laid them on the desk. "Pull up a chair. If it were anybody but you, I'd send them packing."

"I really do appreciate it," Caleb said, pulling a stool over so he could sit next to the doctor's desk. "The sheriff and I were wonderin' about the bullet hole in Mr. Drake's stomach area."

"I saw it. What's troubling you?"

"The fact that it looked like someone tried to sew him up. Someone that might have known what they were doing."

Doc Crum tapped the lip of the pipe's stem against his teeth while he thought back to what he'd observed when he'd taken a look at Eustace Drake's body lying next to the river.

"I guess you could say whoever patched him up might have had some surgical experience. But I don't think they were trying to save him. Maybe just trying to stop the bleeding for a while. If I'm remembering correctly, I don't think there was much that could have been done for him. Judging by where he was shot."

"But fixin' him up like that would have kept him alive just a bit longer?" Caleb asked.

"The wound would have also needed to be cleaned, so it didn't get infected. But like I said, Eustace wouldn't have made it one way or the other." Pausing for a moment, Crum thought about what Caleb was asking. "Do you think a surgeon was involved?"

"Someone patched him up. And judging by the way it was done, it wasn't by any band of highway robbers."

The next question Caleb asked needed to be worded extremely carefully. Neither he nor the sheriff thought it best to tell Doc Crum outright what was happening and everything they'd learned in the last few days. Caleb certainly couldn't just come right out and ask if he knew of any doctors in Parker City who hated the government enough to try and help overthrow it.

"In our investigation into Mr. Drake's disappearance," Caleb began, "we learned he was doing some work with the government in Washington for the war."

"Everybody's involved in the war these days."

"The sheriff and I believe Mr. Drake may have been the target of someone who didn't like him helpin' the Union if they found out about it. And since it looks like a medical man worked on him, we were wondering if there were any doctors in town you know of who might be...."

"A Confederate sympathizer?" Doc Crum blurted out. "I've had words with a couple of my colleagues about this damn war. I can't deny that. But there's none of them that I think would be working against the Union and willing to kill a man like Eustace Drake."

"I understand. It was just an idea me and the sheriff had."

Caleb's hope of unmasking one of the conspirators was quickly dashed. Though the doctor agreed it looked like someone with some medical training tried to fix up Drake after he'd been shot, he had no idea who it could have been. Caleb knew enough about Doc Crum from the sheriff that he was not a man who would withhold important information from the law.

Feeling disheartened but knowing he was on the right track, Caleb thanked Doc Crum and started for the door. He'd need to find some other way to figure out who sewed up the wound on Drake's body.

Chapter Seventy-Five

"Caleb, I don't know if it will help," Doc Crum said, pushing himself to his feet, "but if you want to take a look at the body again, it's downstairs on the slab. You know the way."

It couldn't hurt, Caleb thought, thanking the doctor again for his time.

Taking the winding staircase at the back of the office down to the cellar made Caleb appreciate why there was a separate entrance to the morgue below from the outside. It would be extremely difficult to transport a body down the twisting stairs. Even without carrying anything in his hands, he felt as though he was about to lose his balance a couple of times.

When he finally reached the basement, the cold chill in the air immediately made him shiver. Rubbing his hands together and blowing hot air into them, he watched as his breath formed little white clouds that quickly disappeared. Another shiver ran down his spine when he realized the number of bodies that were stacked in the confined space. The most he'd ever seen there at one time was three. But now, he didn't even want to count the wrapped-up corpses piled on every flat surface.

Instead, he just focused on the one in the center of the room on the table Doc Crum used to examine them. It looked as though Drake was still covered by the same sheet he'd been found in. Mud stains from the river had turned the once-white piece of cloth various shades of brown. Carefully pulling the sheet back, he saw the pale figure that was once Eustace Drake. His long white beard was dirty and matted against his face and chest. What clothing he still wore was just as dirty as the rag he was wrapped in. Caleb didn't know what else he might be able to learn by examining the body a second time. The Tasker River mucked up any chance they had of finding a telltale clue of where he'd been for the last two days.

Through the small windows near the basement's ceiling, Caleb could see that the day was quickly becoming night. If he didn't light any of the lamps, very soon, he wouldn't be able to see his own hand in front of his face. Thinking that maybe Doc Crum would be able to find something interesting, Caleb began to replace the sheet over the body. As he was pulling it into place, he noticed on the end he was holding there was a line of black thread woven into the material running along what would have either been the top or bottom of the sheet when placed on a bed.

"I wonder," Caleb said to no one except the stacks of bodies that surrounded him.

Chapter Seventy-Six

The streetlamps were just being lit as Caleb departed Doc Crum's. The light cascading down from the flames cast an unusually sinister glow. The sky wasn't helping matters much, Caleb thought as he hurried down the street. As the sun set for the day, the blue sky was quickly replaced with a deep purple with tinges of red just over the mountains. In the short time he'd been in with the doctor, then downstairs reexamining Eustace Drake's body, the city outside had taken on a ghostly feel. The usual sounds of evening that he was so accustomed to had been replaced with loud rattling wagons coming into town carrying wounded soldiers, who in turn filled the night air with their groans and wails of pain and agony.

Dodging an elderly couple on the corner, Caleb tipped his hat as he scurried past. He was hoping he could make it to Mr. Upton's shop before he locked up for the day. He did live above the general store, though, so it wasn't as if Caleb wouldn't be able to find him if he had closed before he got there.

Coming around the next corner and seeing Upton's General Goods just down the road, Caleb quickened his step. Candlelight still flickered in the windows, so someone was still there. Racing to the front door, he saw Mr. Upton standing behind the counter, speaking with a customer. Taking a deep breath before opening the door, he did his best to not look like he'd just run the four blocks he had.

A little brass bell jingled as he pulled the door open and stepped into the shop. The smell of the cedar wood shelves and the various sundries on display filled his nose. It was a pleasant smell. Though not one he would ever be able to really describe to anyone. But it was a familiar one, as he visited the store quite frequently. Mr. Upton saw him enter and gave him a smile and a nod as he finished ringing up the purchases of the gentleman to whom he was tending.

As the shopper took his wrapped packages and bid the shopkeeper a good evening, Caleb stepped to the counter.

"Good evening to you, Deputy Post. Are you here for your shaving supplies?"

"I plum forgot about them," Caleb admitted.

"Well, I can understand that," Mr. Upton said with a look of melancholy. "There's been a lot going on around town the last few days. Terrible business, really. With all the wounded men comin' in, I'm all out of everything from quinine to tweezers. Doctor Haller even came in and bought my last two hand saws."

"I was just over at Doc Crum's, and he has patients still sitting outside in wagons waitin' to see him," Caleb said. "Not very pleasant at all."

Though Caleb usually enjoyed chatting, time was very much of the essence, so rather abruptly, he changed the course of the conversation. "Mr. Upton, I was wonderin' if you might be able to help me with something. I'm in the middle of an investigation, and I came across a sheet—looks like it could be a bedsheet—that has a single black thread across the top of it. Any chance you might carry something like that here?"

"I know exactly what you're talking about," the shopkeeper said, his mood brightening. "I did sell them. But I don't have any more if you're looking to buy some. They were an inexpensive piece of merchandise a salesman comin' through the area got me to try. Weren't that popular really. Sold a couple sets of the sheets, if I recall."

Caleb was excited by the prospect of learning the name of at least one person involved in the abduction and murder of Eustace Drake. It would be the first real solid bit of information if Mr. Upton could remember who bought the sheets.

"Do you happen to recollect who you sold 'em to?" Caleb asked, not wanting to sound as eager as he was feeling.

Closing his eyes and thinking for a minute, Mr. Upton said, "It wasn't all that long ago actually." Turning around, he took a large ledger from the shelf behind him and began flipping back through the pages. "Here we are. Last month I sold a set of that type of sheet to Mrs. Wimsley. Do you know her? She cooks for the sisters over at Saint Paul's. A lovely lady."

In fact, Caleb did know Harriett Wimsley. She was a dear soul in her early 60s who was involved with a number of civic organizations around town. After her husband passed, she began spending most of her time volunteering. Hardly the type involved with the Knights of the Golden Circle.

"And," Mr. Upton said, running his finger down the page a little further, "Mr. Trimble, the bookseller, down the street."

"I guess neither of 'em has any medical training," Caleb said under his breath, a sense of defeat washing over him, replacing the excitement he'd felt just moments before.

"Um, I don't rightly know. But my guess would be not," Mr. Upton answered. "Doctor Aspen has medical know-how, though."

"Pardon?"

"Well, when the sheets weren't selling, Doctor Aspen was in looking for supplies for his hospital out there. I made him a special deal to take them off my hands. He bought the whole lot."

Caleb had never met Joseph Aspen in person, but he'd heard stories about the man. Some people in town thought he was some sort of celebrity. Others thought he was Doctor Frankenstein. Though Caleb never quite understood that comparison after having read Mary Shelley's story recently. The only thing Caleb knew for certain was that Joseph Aspen would have had the knowledge to patch up a bullet wound, and he'd bought the same type of sheet they'd found Eustace Drake's body wrapped up in.

Doctor Joseph Aspen was not a name that was on the list Caleb found in Drake's office. But that didn't mean he couldn't be involved. Judging by what people thought of Aspen, Drake probably didn't associate with the man, so wouldn't have suspected him. But now Caleb suspected the doctor, and he needed to tell the sheriff what he'd learned.

Chapter Seventy-Seven

1984...

Parker City Hall was a stately building both inside and out. The county's former Courthouse had been renovated several times since the Civil War. The addition of restrooms had been an enormous undertaking, let alone wiring the entire building for electricity, then telephones decades later. Through all of it, the integrity of the building had been maintained. All of the original details that gave it character were painstakingly preserved during each of the renovations. Although much of City Hall had been taken apart, then put back together at one time or another, if someone living when it was first built walked into the elegantly appointed lobby today, they'd have a hard time seeing that anything had really changed.

Descending the grand staircase that led down from the mayor's office, Chief Brent and Ben found Tommy anxiously pacing the floor in front of the desk where visitors signed in upon their arrival. An off-duty officer from the PCPD was manning the desk, as they quite often did.

"I spoke with the guys sitting on McClinton's house and Tully's place," Tommy said, not even acknowledging the chief. "Nothing. Both places are nice and quiet. Tully's wife is still the only one at his house, and there was no break-in. The professor got home shortly after we talked to him last night, and there was no break-in there either."

"So the killer found this diary at Moran's?" the chief asked.

241

"Possibly. And it's technically a journal," Tommy corrected. "The other option is he knows we're looking for him because we *spoke* to him last night and decided to lay low."

"You think it's the professor?" Ben asked, trying to read his partner's expression.

"I didn't get a good feeling from him. I think maybe we bring him in and put him in an interview room for a while and see if we can shake him up a bit."

The chief shook his head. "I can't believe two people are dead because of something a guy wrote over a hundred years ago in a diary…journal. Is there a difference? Actually, I don't care. But is what the professor said…was it that important? Important enough to kill for?"

"That's just it. He said he believes it may name prominent members of the city who were part of the Knights of the Golden Circle." Ben shrugged.

"But he could also be lying to us," Tommy pointed out. "Who knows what's actually in the journal? Maybe there's an even bigger secret in there that someone doesn't want coming out."

"The information you got from the auction house didn't give you any hints about what was in the *journal*?" Brent asked as he ran a hand through his hair. "I thought it was a big deal for auction houses to keep detailed records and be able to prove something's authenticity."

"If you're in New York or L.A., sure," Tommy said. "But this was just some books someone had in a box in their attic. I'm sure no one thought there was going to be a truly historic find just lying around like that."

"There are all kinds of stories of people finding lost paintings and antiques in their attics worth fortunes. It can happen anywhere. It's never happened to me," the chief admitted.

Ben was now flipping through his notebook. "We haven't gotten the CSU catalogue from the Moran scene yet?"

"No," Tommy confirmed. "We also haven't gotten the results of the fingerprint test from the cigarette packet yet, either."

"It's still early," Ben said looking at his watch. "We did only drop it off last night…when no one in the forensics lab was working."

"I can make a call," the chief offered. "See if I can hurry things along."

"That would be helpful," Ben said, sticking the notebook back in his jacket pocket. "I think we might want to head back to the Moran crime scene and take a second look around like we did at Saint Paul's. You never know what we might find with fresh eyes."

As was the custom, Ben promised to keep the chief updated with any developments. But before the chief went back to the station and his detectives headed toward the last crime scene, they agreed that unless something unexpected came up in the next few hours, Ben and Tommy would be asking Professor McClinton to join them at headquarters to answer a few more questions. Maybe he could explain to them what kind of information could actually be in this journal that someone was willing to kill to get their hands on...or keep hidden.

Chapter Seventy-Eight

The yellow crime scene tape was still stretched across the front door of Mike Moran's townhouse when Ben pulled the car up to the curb. Everything looked exactly as it did when they'd left the day before. If he'd had his wish, there'd have been a patrol car stationed on the street in front of the townhouse. But he was always being reminded of the limited resources the department had at its disposal, specifically the number of officers needed to patrol the city. Taking an officer off patrol to babysit a crime scene—or any location for that matter—always caused a headache and required a great deal of rearranging shift assignments. That's why Ben was so happy when he'd been given officers to watch Tully and McClinton's places overnight.

"What exactly are we looking for here?" Tommy asked, getting out of the car and pulling his jacket tighter around him. It was a chilly morning, but the forecast was for it to warm up a bit in the afternoon. Typical Maryland weather, he thought. It could be snowing in the morning and then sixty degrees in the afternoon.

"We're looking for anything that…" Ben stopped. He wasn't actually sure *what* they were looking for. Something. Anything that could crack the case wide open. "It would be great if we found the journal."

"We don't have that kind of luck." Tommy unlocked the front door with the key he'd signed out from the station, opened it, and ducked under the crime scene tape.

"We need to look at all the books like we did at Taylor's place."

"Yeah. But we were able to match all of the books on the auction list with ones that were actually at Saint Paul's. Here, you're saying we should be looking for something that Moran shouldn't have had to begin with."

Ben slowly nodded. "That sounds about right."

"Man, do I need a vacation. I can't believe there is someone out there killing people over a book. I mean, seriously. A book!"

"It's a book that supposedly has a big secret in it. I thought you liked that kind of stuff. It could unravel a conspiracy that was going on here in Parker. You like conspiracy theories."

"Yeah. When they're mine," Tommy said, starting to look at the bookcase in the den where Moran's body was found.

The DJ had eclectic taste when it came to reading material. Plenty of biographies, non-fiction, mysteries, some science fiction mixed in. But of all the subjects, the largest number of books was on the Civil War. All of the books were ones he'd have gotten at the bookstore. No handwritten journals.

"Wait," Tommy said, running his finger along the spine of a leather-bound book that was obviously much older than the rest. Taking the book from its place on the shelf, he flipped through the first few pages. With a disheartened sigh, he replaced it. "It was just a book published in 1864. It looked old. I thought we might have gotten lucky."

Ben surveyed the room. According to the coroner's initial examination, Moran was killed sometime in the evening on Wednesday. The body hadn't been found until Thursday morning. Which meant the killer would have had more than enough time to search the entire house and find the journal if it had been there.

Did Moran have it? And that's why nothing occurred at either Walter Tully's or Henry McClinton's. Or was Tommy right, and the killer knew he needed to cool it for a while. Ben was getting frustrated with the whole investigation. He felt like they were nowhere. Even the working theory they had seemed ridiculous. But then he reminded himself anyone willing to kill another person wasn't thinking rationally, to begin with. So why couldn't the reason be totally outside of what *he* thought made sense? To the killer, it was probably part of a plan he, or she, saw crystal clear.

"Yeah," Ben finally said. "I think I agree with you. I need a vacation too."

"Wow. If you want to take a break from work, then I know we're in trouble. You're Mr. Workaholic. If you took a vacation…I mean, I can't even imagine the crime wave the city would be facing."

"I guess you're going to have to brace yourself for when Nat and I go on our honeymoon then."

"Hell no. I'm not gonna stick around and deal with it. I'm coming with you."

"You're coming on our honeymoon? Don't you think it might be a little crowded?"

"I think Natalie would love it if I came along. She loves me."

"You know, you're right. She was just saying to me last night how she didn't think we'd need a romantic honeymoon, just the two of us. She thinks the more people with us, the better. I'm sure she'd be happy to book you a hotel room right next to ours."

Tommy gave Ben a quizzical look. "What are you talking about? I don't need my own room. I'll stay in yours. Aren't you going to be getting the honeymoon suite? There should be plenty of space for all three of us."

Chapter Seventy-Nine

After spending another hour and a half meticulously going through Mike Moran's townhouse, Ben and Tommy admitted there was nothing there that was going to help them. Anything that was there to be found had already been found the day before. Not that they'd really thought they were going to find something that'd been missed. But it was better to make certain. And they didn't have any other leads at the moment. Until CSU was able to compare McClinton's fingerprints to the one found on the handle of the knife, there wasn't much more they could be doing there.

Feeling defeated, both detectives dropped into their chairs in their tiny office at the PCPD. Ben's spirits were slightly lifted when he found the report for the Moran crime scene was delivered while they were out. Unfortunately, there was no update about the fingerprint test.

With the report that arrived the day before on the Taylor crime scene and now Moran's, Ben and Tommy dove in, reading every line. If either came across anything of interest, they added it to the chalkboard in front of their desks, giving them a complete picture of both cases and how they were related.

When they'd both finished reading the pair of reports and had placed all the important details on the board, they sat back and took it all in. Ben was beginning to worry that they might have been too hasty in connecting the cases. If anything, finding the same auction catalog at both crime scenes might have just been a coincidence. Just because both men were Civil War buffs didn't *really* mean anything.

Ben didn't want to say it out loud, but he was thinking they might be on the wrong trail. Something wasn't feeling right about…

His thoughts were interrupted by the ring of the telephone on his desk. He'd been so deep in thought it took him a minute to realize what the sound was. Ben didn't know how long it had been ringing, but Tommy was already reaching over his own desk to answer when Ben's hand finally made it to the receiver.

"This is Ben Winters."

"Hey, Ben. It's Hirsh."

"What's up, Randy?" To Tommy, Ben mouthed *Dispatch*.

"We just rolled a unit over to one-oh-seven Ritchie Way. Possible break-in. Thought you might want to know."

Ben thought for a moment. Was he supposed to recognize the address? Repeating it back, he said, "One-oh-seven…."

"Yeah. It's the address of that professor you asked me to put a pair of eyes on last night."

"Henry McClinton. Wait, you got a call of a break-in?" Ben was already on his feet.

"Dunkin's en route now. Like I said. I thought you'd want to know."

"Thanks, Randy. I appreciate it," Ben said, hanging up the telephone and motioning for Tommy that they needed to go.

"Report of a break-in at McClinton's place."

"That's what I gathered," Tommy said, pulling his jacket on and following Ben out the door. "Do we have another dead body?"

"I didn't ask."

"That really needs to be one of the first questions from now on."

Chapter Eighty

1862...

Silas Moss's bulldog-like appearance always gave Joseph Aspen pause. The way his jowls drooped from the sides of his round head made it look as though his entire face was sagging. Even on the extremely rare occasions when he would smile, the folds fought to drag the ends of his mouth downward.

In the former mayor's hand, he held a message he'd received earlier in the day. President Abraham Lincoln was planning to travel north from Washington to Parker City, where he would meet with General George McClellan. It was to be a clandestine trip for the president's safety. But in trying to travel as inconspicuously as possible, he would have fewer guards surrounding him. Making it easier for anyone looking to do the man harm to get to him. Naturally, those in the War Department thought the secrecy of the trip would be its own form of protection. But the Knights of the Golden Circle had their sources, and now the group's agents in Parker City were preparing for the chance to send the most devastating message possible.

"Will your man be ready?" Moss asked Bloody Bill Anderson after revealing the details of the president's trip.

The Confederate soldier scratched the rough beard along his chin and smiled a nasty grin. For a moment, even the unmovable Moss felt uncomfortable.

Thaddeus Parker, sitting next to him at the table in the basement room at the Aspen House Hospital, refused to look at the lieutenant directly. He did not keep it a secret that he felt Anderson and the men who'd been assigned to the operation in Parker were beneath him.

"If we succeed, our business here will be concluded." Parker spoke to everyone in the room. "Lieutenant Anderson has seen to it that his men have moved the resources we've collected from our allies in the north on to Richmond. And while we would all gladly continue to provide a safe thoroughfare for information and funds to travel south, the death of Lincoln will trigger more scrutiny than we've ever had to deal with.

"I, for one," Parker continued, "think a trip to Europe may be a good idea. My wife has been saying she would like to return to Paris one day."

"You boys don't have t' worry none," Bloody Bill said, stretching his legs out under the table. "We'll keep ya squeaky clean. No one'll ever know what you've been up to. And on behalf of the whole Confederate army, we'd like t' thank you fer all the money yous raised fer the cause. Once we deal with old Abe, we'll git out of your hair, and yous can go back to living your fancy life while the rest of us keep plugging away."

"We've put everything on the line here," Moss protested, slamming his meaty palm down on the table. "We all want the same thing. But we have far more to lose, mind you."

Bloody Bill narrowed his gaze, ready to wade into the verbal battle of who stood to lose the most if their plan was discovered but bit his tongue. An unusually diplomatic move on his part. Instead, he turned to the nervous-looking clerk who always followed Moss and Parker around and asked, "What details do you have fer me?"

McClinton closed the book in which he'd been writing and took a piece of paper from his jacket pocket. "There has been a request made to the city for a special military train to make a stop at the station at twelve o'clock Noon tomorrow. General McClellan personally signed the request asking that there be no other trains allowed to move through Parker during that time. He also requested the station be shut down for several hours."

"They're jus' sayin' it's fer a *military* train?"

"We were not given any sort of manifest or information as to what was going to be on the train," McClinton confirmed.

"No one is supposed to know that Lincoln is even coming to Parker City," Moss pointed out. "So obviously, that's how he's getting here."

"Will the sheriff be providin' any type of security at the station?" Bloody Bill asked, picking at the dirt under his fingernails with a dagger from his belt.

"Not to our knowledge," Thaddeus Parker grumbled.

"So McClellan'll be usin' his men then." Bloody Bill drew an imaginary circle on the top of the table with his finger.

"Will that pose a problem?" Silas Moss questioned.

Anderson slowly began shaking his head. "Not at all. His boys jus' got through a terrible fight. They're bloodied, battered, tired. They're makin' it easy for us."

Chapter Eighty-One

"Jonathan says there's no way to convince the president not to make the trip. Lincoln is dead set on it. He and McClellan have been having some disagreements of late about a course of action, and he feels the only way to handle the matter is with a face-to-face sit down with the general," Sheriff Tildon explained to Caleb once they were safely shut away in his library.

They'd decided it was too dangerous to speak of the situation at the Courthouse, so they'd work out of the sheriff's home for the time being. They would have very much liked to enlist the assistance of some of the other deputies, but at the moment, they simply did not know whom they could trust.

The sheriff handed Caleb the most recent message he'd received from their secret friend in Washington, delivered that morning just before the young man arrived at the house. Between the messages Tildon was sending and the replies they were receiving, there was now a well-worn path between the War Department and the Parker County Courthouse. But since there was only one rider Jonathan trusted to carry the messages to and from Parker, and his horse could only make the trip back and forth once a day at most, they'd resorted to coded telegraph communications.

"This is hogwash! According to this," the sheriff shouted as he waved one of the other cables around in the air, "Stanton refuses to allow Lincoln to know his life could be in danger if he travels to Parker City."

"And the president's train arrives at Noon tomorrow?" Caleb asked.

"A *military* train arrives at Noon tomorrow. That's all that's been told,"

Tildon corrected.

"So, we have a little over twenty-four hours t' try and catch the members of the Golden Circle here in Parker."

"Are you asking me or telling me, my boy?" The sheriff stubbed out his cigar with such force Caleb thought the small side table next to his chair would collapse.

Leaning forward with his elbows on his knees, Tildon rubbed his eyes with the palms of his hands. He'd never felt so out of control and unprepared before. It was clear the president's life could be in danger. But there seemed to be no way to stop him from making the trip. According to part of one of the messages he'd received—Jonathan had become extremely forthcoming under the circumstances—the meeting was imperative because the president was preparing to give McClellan an ultimatum. He went no further to say what the nature of the ultimatum was, but that was neither here nor there as far as the sheriff was concerned. The inner workings of the War Department and the army were nothing for him to fret about.

"I believe I should pay a call on Doctor Aspen," Caleb offered. "If I do some pokin' around at the hospital, maybe I'll come across something."

"I'm worried about the danger. Especially now."

"There's a chance that the Golden Circle doesn't even know President Lincoln is comin' to Parker City," Caleb pointed out, though he wouldn't be willing to place a bet on it.

"As the sheriff, I cannot take that chance."

"Well, maybe if they think we're snoopin' around, they'll realize we're on to 'em, and that will make them think twice about...."

"Or, they'll do the same to you that they did to Eustace."

The thought hadn't crossed Caleb's mind. Until just a few days ago, he couldn't imagine a group out to do so much damage that they'd have the audacity to kidnap and kill one of the richest men in town. Let alone a sheriff's deputy. But the war really had changed everything. What was even more disturbing, the more he thought on it, was that the men seemingly behind all of it were the city fathers themselves. Which meant they could be almost unfettered in their actions. Unless he and the sheriff could figure out a plan.

"Have either Councilmen Moss or Parker said anything to you about this military train? Or that they know what's actually afoot?"

"I haven't spoken with either of them since the day Eustace disappeared. It was the chief clerk who informed me a request was made for the train station to be placed under military guard tomorrow. Naturally, Mayor Gladhill agreed. He had no choice. The request came directly from McClellan."

Whether the sheriff wanted him to or not, Caleb had made up his mind to visit the Aspen House Hospital. The fact that it used the same kind of sheets that Eustace Drake's body had been found wrapped in and that a medical man seemingly tended to the man's wound was enough for Caleb to suppose Joseph Aspen may be involved.

"I know I can't keep you from going to that hospital," Tildon said, as if he were reading Caleb's mind. "Sometimes you're as stubborn as a mule. But you need to watch yourself. If Aspen is involved in all of this, and these men are even half as dangerous as they seem... Just remember. Edie will kill me if anything happens to you."

Chapter Eighty-Two

Caleb had never once visited the Aspen House Hospital since it'd been built. There'd been no reason. He knew the sheriff had been there a time or two on city business, though. And, of course, he'd heard what everyone in town said about the place. Which made it all the more surprising when he finally got a look at the mammoth estate as he rode Dolly up the path to the front gates.

The hospital itself rivaled any of the majestic homes in Parker City. Quite possibly twice as big as any of them, if not larger, he thought. It was difficult to tell, with the main house sitting out by itself in the middle of rolling acres, surrounded by gardens.

Guiding Dolly to a clump of trees several yards from the main path, Caleb tied the horse in the shade where she could be hidden. He was aiming to approach the house unseen, so thought it wise not to ride straight up to the front door. The route he was going to take would be much more concealed. One side of the property was still very much a forested area, so he would make his way over the low stone wall that circled the hospital's grounds from that direction, under the cover of the fall foliage. Once over the wall, he'd be forced to cover open land with only bushes and flower beds between him and the main building. Though the yard was empty, he had no idea if there was anyone watching out the windows who could alert someone to a stranger on the premises.

If he was discovered, he simply needed to introduce himself as Deputy Post and inform whoever it was that'd intercepted him that he was there on official business from the sheriff. His badge would be his cover. Though he very much hoped he could scout out the hospital unseen.

Before leaving Dolly, he checked to make certain both his pistols were fully loaded. He was not intending to need them, but if he found himself in a tough spot, he might not have much choice. If Joseph Aspen or anyone in his employ was behind the abduction of Eustace Drake, they'd already shown they were willing to kill to achieve their goals. He needed to be ready for anything.

Pistols ready, Caleb quickly made his way along the side of the property into the trees. From his vantage point, he was able to see clear across the grounds, so if anyone were to appear, he could take cover behind one of the large hickories. But for now, he saw a clear path from his hiding spot to the hospital. Which prompted him to move as quickly as possible. The closer he got to the building, the louder he heard his heart thumping in his ears.

Carefully peering through the first window he came to, he saw a fierce-looking woman in a plain gray dress with a white apron covering it speaking to two other—much younger—women. Judging by their attire, they were nurses or female attendants at the hospital. The older woman was in charge. No question about that. And judging by the look on her face and the forceful hand gestures she was making, she was not too pleased about something.

Caleb was making his way toward the next window along the wall when he thought he heard the sound of a gunshot. A rifle, to be more precise. Reaching for one of his pistols, he crouched as low to the ground as he could get without laying himself flat out. After a moment, he heard the sound again. Seeing no one around, he began thinking the shots were coming from the other side of the hospital. It would account for the fact the blasts sounded more distant. With a giant house in the way, they were bound to be quieter than if someone was standing just a few feet away.

Scurrying in the direction from which he thought the shots had come, he was happy to see a large row of scrubs planted near the back corner of the hospital. He'd be able to nestle himself amongst the bushes. They'd provide the perfect spot for him to survey the back of the property.

Unfortunately, the bushes were more prickly than he'd anticipated, and Caleb found himself under attack by the edges of the thick, sharp leaves.

Uncomfortable though he was, the hiding spot allowed him a full view of the manicured lawn. Under different circumstances, he could see this as a beautiful place to picnic or spend the afternoon playing cricket or baseball.

A third shot rang out. Much louder this time. Off in the distance, Caleb was able to see a puff of smoke from the rifle. There looked to be two men in the field. One now reloading the rifle, the other holding up what looked to be a black or dark blue jacket. Further along, a stack of hay bales looked to be the shooter's target.

There was no way for him to get closer without being seen, so he needed to just let his eyes adjust to the distance. As he did, he thought he might recognize the men. Was it possible they were the two Confederate soldiers he thought were following him a few nights ago? Surely, they couldn't be? But then again, he thought, why not? That's when he realized the jacket the one man was holding was that of a Union soldier!

Chapter Eighty-Three

1984 ...

"She says she was out having lunch with a couple of friends, and when she got home, she found the side door from the carport there open," Officer Dunkin was relaying to Ben and Tommy the information he'd been given when he arrived at Henry McClinton's home. "The door was definitely forced open. Doorframe's broken, and there's a metal rod or something lying on the ground next to it. Don't worry. I didn't touch it."

Ben smiled.

"I took a quick look around inside. A couple of rooms look like they were tossed."

"Thanks, Stan," Ben said. "Where is Mrs. McClinton now?"

"She's at the neighbors. One of the ladies she was having lunch with."

"Okay. Stick around out here until CSU arrives. We're going to take a look around inside."

"You got it, Detective."

"Technically, it's Detective-Sergeant," Tommy said.

"What?" the uniformed officer asked, looking up from his notebook.

"Nothing. Ignore him, Stan. He's just being a pain," Ben said.

"It's true. I am." Tommy smiled.

"Keep an eye out for CSU," Ben said, starting toward the house.

The McClintons lived in a nice little neighborhood not too far from the mall, an area that was really beginning to see a lot of development. The house was a single-level brick rancher built back in the '60s. A couple of large windows looked out on the street, framing the front door, while the rest of the house spread out on either side. It was actually deceptively large. Ben realized as he started to walk around to the side where Mrs. McClinton had parked her station wagon in the carport.

When there'd been no activity at the house overnight, Ben wasn't able to convince the Patrol commander to keep a car parked out front. He said he couldn't spare the resources. Even though Ben didn't like it, he understood. But now he wished he'd pushed just a little harder.

One thing he knew was that they must be on the right track. He'd started thinking it was just a coincidence that both Father Taylor and Mike Moran both attended the same auction and bid on the same lot of books. All they really had was a copy of the same auction catalog at both crime scenes. Even the murders themselves were completely different, though they were still waiting on the official paperwork reporting cause of death. But it didn't take the coroner's report to see one had been beaten and the other stabbed. So Ben had begun questioning their working theory that someone was trying to get their hands on this mysterious journal. But now that a third person who'd been interested in the books had had their house broken into, it seemed reasonable to think their theory was sound and they'd figured out the killer's motive.

Unless...

"Any chance you think the good professor staged this little break-in while his wife was out to throw us off his trail?" Tommy asked just before the thought crossed Ben's mind.

"Ever the cynic," Ben said, crouching down so he could examine the broken door jam closer.

"Don't tell me the great Detective *Sergeant* Ben Winters wasn't thinking the same thing."

"I plead the Fifth."

"See. Now, who's the cynic?"

"You still are," Ben said, standing up and stepping through the open door into the house.

The detectives entered into a spacious kitchen, which, though it still had a distinctively 1960s design, was filled with modern appliances making it feel more like the '80s. It didn't look like there was a single thing out of place in the kitchen. Ben got the impression this was going to be a house where *everything* had its place, and it always stayed there. A stark contrast from what they'd seen in the professor's office at Hammermill. His controlled chaos did not carry over to his home.

Beyond the kitchen was a dining room that led into a living room. Both looked like they were pictures right out of a home design magazine. It wasn't until they caught a glimpse of what they assumed was McClinton's home office across the entry hall from the dining room that they saw anything out of place.

But once they walked into the wood-paneled study with its bookcases and file cabinets, they weren't sure if the place had been ransacked or if this was the one place in the house where McClinton could "organize" things as he liked. The room looked much like his office at the college. Papers were strewn everywhere. Books lay haphazardly on the floor and sat at random angles on the shelves.

It was the lamp broken on the floor that told them this wasn't the way things were supposed to be. As Ben walked behind the professor's desk, he found all the drawers had been pulled out and emptied onto the floor. He also found a picture frame, a spiderwebbed crack across its glass, at his feet.

"This lock's been jimmied," Tommy said, examining one of the file cabinets. Then using a handkerchief—something Ben encouraged him to carry for just this reason—he slid open the top drawer. It was empty. He looked in the next drawer. Empty. The third drawer down was still filled with papers and folders, but they were piled upside down and every which way. Same with the bottom drawer. "It looks like someone went through the drawers. Emptied out the top two. Didn't take anything from the bottom ones...that *I* can tell."

What about the other filing cabinets?" Ben asked.

"Hmmm. They're still locked."

"Sir, you can't go in there!" They heard Officer Dunkin's muffled voice from outside.

"It's my house!" Professor McClinton yelled back.

"Here we go," said Tommy as he quickly retraced their steps, intercepting an irate Henry McClinton in the kitchen.

Chapter Eighty-Four

"What's going on? Where's my wife? She called and said someone broke in!" McClinton was bordering on frantic.

"Sir. Just take a breath." Tommy was standing only inches away from him. He wasn't going to let McClinton get any further than he already had. Not until they asked him a few questions. Behind the professor, who was becoming more and more anxious with every passing second, Dunkin was standing in the open doorway, ready to assist if needed.

"Where's Judith?"

"Sir."

"I want to talk to my wife."

"Professor McClinton, your wife is at the neighbor's. You can talk to her just as soon as Detective Winters and I ask you some questions."

Ben was now standing behind his partner and gave Dunkin the sign that everything was under control and he could go back to watching for the Crime Scene Unit.

The detectives watched as McClinton pulled his glasses off and began rubbing his eyes. Knowing where his wife was calmed him down a bit. Just enough to focus. Now to find out if this was all an act or if he really was upset because someone *really* broke into his house.

"Professor, your wife told the officer outside she was at lunch with friends this afternoon. Where were you?"

"What? I was at the college. I had office hours this morning."

"And there would be people who could say they saw you there?" Ben asked. There was no way to make it sound any other way than he intended.

McClinton immediately understood the implication to the question.

"Of course, people saw me. I was there to meet with students. You think I broke into my own house? Why on earth would I do that?"

"Well…" Tommy started just before Ben cut him off.

"We just need to confirm your whereabouts. It's a standard question."

"You ask people where they were when their house has been broken into?"

"Yes." Tommy's voice was dry and emotionless.

"Well, I told you. I was at the school."

"And you were meeting with students?"

"That's what I said!" McClinton's temper flared.

Ben was trying to decide how far to push him. He was trying to calculate just how angry he needed to make the professor to get him to trip up. *If* he was going to trip up, that is. Then Ben made a snap decision. He was going to show him his study and see what kind of reaction he got.

"Professor," Ben lowered his voice, "I'd like to show you something. If you'd follow me. But please don't touch anything. The state's forensic team is on its way. We're going to have them look for fingerprints or anything that might help us identify the individual who broke in."

"My fingerprints are going to be all over everything," the professor pointed out. The condescension in his tone was not lost on neither Ben nor Tommy.

"That is true," Ben agreed, playing the good cop. "We just don't want you to add any more right now."

"Yeah," Tommy followed up. "If they find a fresh print that matches someone who isn't supposed to have been here on top of an old one of yours…then we've got our guy." He knew that wasn't exactly how it worked. But he was banking on McClinton being a History nerd, not a forensic expert.

After giving Tommy a long look, McClinton thrust his hands into his pockets. Ben then led the way to the study. The professor mumbled under his breath as they walked through the house.

In the living room, McClinton stopped and looked around. "I don't understand. Everything looks fine. Why did Judith think someone broke in?"

"Didn't you notice the broken door when you came in?" Tommy asked.

"I guess not," he confessed.

"And then there's this," Ben said, motioning toward the open door to the study.

The detectives carefully watched as McClinton crossed the foyer into his home office. At the door, the professor stopped dead in his tracks. Ben watched his eyes go wide. A look of abject horror took hold of McClinton's face.

"What...I..."

"Professor?" Ben asked, taking a step forward. "We know you have a *special* way of organizing your office, so we weren't really sure...."

"Yes. Someone's been in here," he said, crossing into the room and looking around frantically. "My work. Everything's been...."

McClinton stopped midsentence when he saw the two filing drawers sitting wide open. Ben and Tommy watched him cross to the cabinet and start searching around pointlessly in the empty spaces.

"Professor McClinton, please. Fingerprints," Ben reminded him. "We've already looked. The drawers are empty."

"Yeah. Someone popped the lock and cleaned them out," Tommy pointed out. "But the bottom drawers still have all kinds of papers in them. Any reason someone would just take what was in the top drawers?"

"What kind of papers did you keep in there," Ben immediately jumped in.

"Please. Just... Please. I need to think for a minute."

Ben shot Tommy a quick look and raised an eyebrow. The professor's reaction seemed pretty genuine. For as much as Ben thought he'd been holding out on them the first time they spoke in his office at Hammermill, McClinton was surrounded by none of the same airs or arrogance. He appeared legitimately shaken.

However, his reaction was almost too frantic. Ben had seen people react in many different ways when their homes were broken into and burglarized. It was a very emotional experience. So there really was no telling how someone would act. But something about McClinton's focus on the filing cabinet told Ben the good professor was still hiding something.

Chapter Eighty-Five

When the Crime Scene Unit arrived, Ben instructed the technicians to go through McClinton's home office with a fine-tooth comb. Anything that could be remotely useful, he wanted bagged and tagged. The study looked to be the only room in the entire house that had been touched.

Practically having to drag the professor from his study, the two detectives finally got him to walk through the rest of the house, all of the other rooms, to see if anything else had been disturbed. When he said that it all looked as it had when he left for work that morning, Ben asked Officer Dunkin to escort McClinton next door so he could see his wife, and to stay with them.

"What are you thinking?" Tommy asked Ben as they stood watching the state CSU team work its way methodically around the study.

Rubbing his eyes, Ben said, "I don't think he staged this."

"Damn. I was thinking the same thing. I was hoping you'd convince me otherwise."

Ben smiled. He could tell just how much his partner didn't like Henry McClinton. It wasn't as bad as the hatred Tommy still had towards the reporter Roger Benedict, but Ben got the feeling it was pretty close.

"Okay. Alright," Ben said, refocusing. "Three break-ins. I think we can safely say we know what the intruder was looking for in all three cases."

"The journal," Tommy answered.

"Right. He didn't find it at Taylor's, so he moved on to Moran's. When he didn't find it there, he came here."

"But in the first two instances, he was interrupted. Which led to us having two bodies on our hands."

"Yes. But since no one was here when he broke in, there was no threat to him. But, according to McClinton, he didn't have the journal. So, the guy wouldn't have found it here."

"Yet, he still cleaned out two file drawers. And the professor still hasn't told us what was in them."

"Right again. Does that mean Walter Tully is next? He could have bought the journal off Father Taylor."

"Or," Tommy suggested, "McClinton was lying to us. He had the journal, and now he doesn't."

"There's only one person who can answer that."

"And he's right next door," Tommy said.

"If he did, in fact, have the journal, why didn't he tell us that?"

"Because then we'd think he killed Taylor and Moran to get it," Tommy said, leading the way to the next-door neighbor's house.

"Even if he didn't actually kill them, and he bought it from Taylor after the auction?"

Tommy stopped and looked at Ben. "Well, I guess we'll never know what our reactions would have been since he didn't *actually* tell us that."

"Something about this just doesn't make sense to me. It's not adding up."

"Man, we're running around trying to find someone killing people to get their hands on a journal. *A journal.* Unless it has the answer to who shot J.F.K. in it, I don't understand the reason anyone would be killing to get hold of it."

"Even if it has a treasure map in it?" Ben asked, giving his friend a verbal jab.

"You told me that wasn't an option!" Tommy shouted, standing in the middle of the yard.

Chapter Eighty-Six

1862...

"I think I know how they're going to try and kill President Lincoln," Caleb managed to say as he stumbled into the sheriff's library, nearly out of breath.

"Caleb, my boy! Your coat's ripped, and you have scratches on your face," Tildon said, not hiding the deep concern in his voice. "Are you alright?" Then looking to Mr. Percy, who was standing next to him with a tray of bread and jam, he said, "Go fetch something to clean Caleb's face. And tell Mrs. May we're in need of her sewing skills."

Once Mr. Percy had hurried on his way with extra determination in his step, the sheriff hefted himself out of his chair and poured a brandy for his young protégé. "What have you, my boy?"

As Caleb shared what he'd seen on his reconnaissance mission to the Aspen House Hospital, Sheriff Tildon sat silent and stone-faced. It certainly seemed to confirm their fears that the institute's proprietor was somehow mixed up with the Confederacy. Especially if he was allowing two of its soldiers to use his property for shooting practice.

"Laying hands on a federal uniform would be simple right now. With so many soldiers in sickbeds, no one would notice a jacket disappearing," the sheriff pointed out after Caleb told him about seeing one of the men with what he thought was a uniform jacket.

"I think one of them is gonna disguise himself as a Union soldier to get in with the president's guards and then shoot him," Caleb finished. "You said the request for a military guard at the train station came directly from General McClellan? Do you think *he* could be involved with the Golden Circle, and he's settin' President Lincoln up?"

"Would that explain why he was so insistent on highway robbers being the culprits who abducted Eustace?" The sheriff paused before answering his own question. "It could. *However…*my gut tells me he's not. He may be many things. But a traitor isn't one of them."

"That doesn't mean his decision to use his own men isn't a bad one."

"True. *But*…since we can't be certain he isn't involved, I don't think we can safely take this information to him." The sheriff crossed the room and took a fresh cigar from a case on his cluttered desk. Lighting it, he stood staring out the window, considering their options.

"Is it possible for you t' send Jonathan a coded message? Tell him that one of the Union soldiers could be an assassin?"

"I'll most definitely try. But we need to have our own plan in place."

"We could…."

Caleb was interrupted by Edie Tildon pushing her way into the study with Mr. Percy and Mrs. May close on her heels. "Caleb, dear boy. What has happened to you? Mr. Percy said you'd been hurt."

"I actually said he needed t' be cleaned up a bit," the butler politely corrected.

"Tut tut. Hand me that cloth. Let me clean those scratches."

As the lady of the house fretted over attending to the minor scrapes left by the bushes in which he'd been concealing himself, Mrs. May and Mr. Percy pulled Caleb's long duster off so it could be mended.

"Really, I'm alright," Caleb tried to say between dabs of the soft cloth. "And my coat's fine. It's just a small tear."

"Nonsense," Mrs. May chided. "I will have this fixed up in no time. And I have some soup on the stove for you to put in your stomach. It will make you feel much better."

"But I feel fine," Caleb protested again.

The sheriff watched the commotion with a raised eyebrow. Serious business needed to be addressed. But he knew he could not interrupt his wife for fear of the damage that she may do to him if he did. The scratches on Caleb's cheeks would pale in comparison. So, he allowed the trio to work and minister to the boy. While they did, he sat and hastily scribbled out a coded message to send to Washington. Seeing that Caleb was in good hands, he left to find their houseboy, Billy, to have him take the message to the cable office.

Chapter Eighty-Seven

By nightfall, everything at the Tildon home had returned to normal. All things being considered. While the rest of the household went about their usual routines, and Edie sat cross-stitching in the parlor, Caleb and the sheriff finished discussing what was to happen the following day. Since sending the telegraph to Washington, they'd heard nothing in reply. Nor had Jonathan's trusted messenger arrived with any news or information.

"Maybe he's makin' arrangements to protect the president," Caleb suggested with a shrug.

"I surely hope. But if he's been unable to, you know what needs done. I will order Gimble, Ford, Cruthers, and Watson to take up positions outside the military cordon around the station at each of the four street corners," Tildon said, pointing to a sketch of the streets around the train station he'd drawn.

"What'll you tell them they're there for?"

"Just that they need to keep an eye on things and provide any assistance the military guard may require. But they will also be on hand if someone does make an attempt on the president and manages to get past the guards."

"Unless one of them is also in on it."

The sheriff exhaled. "I can only pray that the faith I put in those men when I hired them was not misplaced. Not a one of them has ever given me cause to doubt their honor. Oscar may be sour at times, and Ford doesn't have the sharpest wit, but I believe they're all good men."

Of all the deputies he worked with, he and Oscar Gimble were the ones that tended to rub each other the wrong way at times. But that was just because they both had different ways of doing things. He held no ill will toward Gimble, and he didn't believe Gimble did for him. At least their disagreements never seemed to last for very long. Taking all of the deputies as a whole, they were a dedicated group of lawmen, each one of whom he knew held the sheriff in the highest possible regard. So if the sheriff believed in his men, then so too did Caleb.

"Tomorrow, I will go about my day so as not to arouse any suspicions," Tildon continued. "I will remain at the Courthouse until shortly before Noon, then I take a stroll over toward the station...to exercise my legs."

"Doc Crum does say exercise is a good thing," Caleb said with a grin.

"I'm just sorry you won't have a comfortable night's rest," Tildon said, looking at his pocket watch. "But you will need to be going soon."

"One rough night will be worth it if it means we can get through tomorrow without any more bloodshed."

Chapter Eighty-Eight

As the sun rose the next morning, Parker City quickly came to life as it did every day. Mr. Upton was again sweeping in front of his shop before opening for business, Doc Crum was in early attending to patients, Moses Wilkins and his son were making their milk deliveries, and Deputy Caleb Post was concealing himself in a small luggage storage room at the Parker City train station.

After leaving the sheriff's house the night before, he made his way to the station so that he could take up a position that would allow him a clear view of the arriving train. He needed to be in place before General McClellan, and his men descended on the building early the next day. Which they had several hours earlier. From his hiding place, Caleb could hear soldiers passing along the platform, which was just on the other side of the door. Once, he heard McClellan himself talking to someone, giving him instructions as to where to position the men.

"I want at least four soldiers at each entrance," the general barked, "two on the inside and two outside. No one gets into this station without being personally approved by me. Understood, Lieutenant?"

It sounded as though McClellan was trying to secure the station as best he could. Caleb wondered how many soldiers were now securing the station. And if the man he saw at the Aspen House Hospital the day before was among their ranks.

Parker City's train station was a long, narrow two-story building. Inside, other than the ticketing booth and the manager's office, the ground floor was completely open, filled with benches and tables where travelers could pass the time waiting for their train to arrive. A balcony, looking down over the gallery below, ran along the second floor where the B&O Railroad kept several offices. Outside, a long platform ran the length of the station, dotted with porter stands and benches for those who liked to watch the trains pass by.

Caleb had decided the best place to hide was in a luggage room with a door on either end, one leading to the platform and the other to the first-floor gallery inside. Not much space for luggage, let alone Caleb, but through the slats in the doors, he could watch what was happening around him.

He'd quickly learned that the meeting that was to take place between General McClellan and President Lincoln was going to be right there in the station itself. Which might have been the smartest thing about this entire affair because it meant there was less moving around of the president. He would walk directly from the train into the station and be surrounded by Union troops the entire time. There'd be no traveling down a street out in the open where there would be a better chance of an attack. The president's movements, in addition to being secret, were being confined. Caleb wondered if that could be the work of Jonathan, his effort to protect the commander-in-chief during what could otherwise be seen as a fool-hearty trip.

These precautions would all be for naught, however, if one of the Union soldiers was an impostor. It wouldn't make much difference that the president was being kept in one place if the assassin was there as well.

As Caleb quietly paced the few steps it took for him to get from one side of the storage closet to the other, he continued to listen for any conversations he could hear from his hideaway. At one point, there was shouting coming from outside on the platform, but it was too far away for him to hear what was being said. When the shouts turned to boisterous laughter, he realized it was just some rowdy soldiers letting off steam.

Caleb's anxiousness grew as the closer to Noon it became. Then, just after Saint Joseph's bell finished announcing the midday hour, he heard the unmistakable rumble of a train off in the distance, followed by its high-pitched whistle. Abraham Lincoln was about to arrive in Parker City, and

Caleb was hiding in a closet because he and the sheriff were afraid someone was going to try and kill him.

Chapter Eighty-Nine

1984...

"Those papers are extremely important!" Professor McClinton yelled, standing only a few feet from Ben in the middle of his neighbor's living room. "Now they're gone!"

Trying once again to calm him down, Ben said, "I understand, Professor. We're trying to understand why someone would have taken your files, but you won't tell us exactly what was in those papers."

From the moment Ben and Tommy joined the McClintons and their neighbor next door, Henry McClinton had been irate, shouting and demanding to know what the police were going to do to catch the person who broke into his house. Even his wife wasn't able to calm him down, saying several times how ridiculous he was behaving.

"What difference does it make what was in the files? You just need to find them and get them back to me," he snapped.

"Well, sir," Tommy said, about to lose his cool. "Depending on what's in the files will determine which direction our investigation goes. If they were financial papers and we come to find out you owed money to someone, then we will start looking at them for the break-in. If they were secret love letters from your mistress, pardon me, Mrs. McClinton, just an example...then we'll start looking at her husband. See how this works?"

"I *am not* having an affair!"

"He was just trying to explain why we need to know what was taken,"

Ben explained, doing everything he could to not lose his temper. Only one of them could play the bad cop, and right now, Tommy was wearing that badge.

"Just tell them, Henry!" Judith McClinton shouted, taking everyone by surprise.

After several more seconds of pacing back and forth with his arms tightly crossed against his chest, the professor finally said, "It was research. They were notes and documents for a book I'm working on."

"Someone broke into your house to steal your research notes?" Tommy asked. The disbelief in his voice could not be hidden.

Before the professor could answer, Ben asked, "Do these papers...this research project...have anything to do with the journal we spoke to you about?"

McClinton didn't need to say a word. The answer was written all over his face. Everything that had happened over the last several days—the murder of two men and now the break-in at the McClintons's—was all connected to a mysterious journal from the Civil War. A journal whose content no one actually seemed to know.

Between Ben and Tommy, they knew Henry McClinton still was not ready to talk. Or at least tell them the truth, the whole truth, and nothing but the truth. He needed one final shove to get him over the line. Normally, Ben would want to work him and bring him around willingly. But his patience was wearing thin.

So, he turned to Tommy and said, "Detective Mason, will you please do the honors."

Tommy nodded as he reached around and pulled his handcuffs from the clip on his belt. "Professor Henry McClinton," he said very deliberately as he advanced on the man, "you are under arrest on suspicion of the murders of Father Roland Taylor and Michael Moran. Please put your hands behind your back."

"You can't do this! I didn't kill anyone."

"You have the right to remain silent. Anything you say can and will be used against you...."

Ben was quickly playing through things in his head as Tommy finished reading McClinton his rights. They had no hard evidence that he committed either of the murders. Nothing that would stand up in court, at least. And nothing the state's attorney would even consider filing charges with. But they had enough reasonable suspicion to bring him in, on good faith, and be a little more forceful with their questions. This was the push they needed to break him and get some answers.

As Tommy escorted the now handcuffed professor to the car, Ben had a few last words with Officer Dunkin, who was going to keep an eye on things as CSU finished its work.

"Are you arresting him for breaking into his own house?" Dunkin asked with a confused look on his face.

"No. We know he didn't stage this. But he has answers that can help us nail whoever killed Taylor and Moran. So, we're taking him in on *suspicion* of murder," Ben pointed out. "We just need to get him to talk. He's holding out on us."

"Won't his lawyer throw a fit?"

"Probably."

"And couldn't you and Detective Mason get in trouble?"

"We aren't doing anything wrong. There is no doubt in my mind Henry McClinton is involved in this whole mess, one way or another. If he will just answer a few of our questions, then that will be that, and he'll be out the door in a few hours."

"I guess this is better," Dunkin said.

"Better than what?"

"Your partner just threatening to shoot him like he does all the time."

Chapter Ninety

The interrogation room at the PCPD was—only partially by design—the most uncomfortable room in the entire station. Not only did it sit directly in the center of the first floor, right where the air conditioning and heating never seemed to work right, but it was painted with a hideous cross between light lime green and slate gray blue. That was the only way Ben was ever able to describe the color to anyone, and he knew full well it didn't make sense unless you actually saw it in person. The metal chairs around the metal table were cold and uninviting, immediately putting whoever sat in them on edge. Even more aggravating for a suspect who'd been brought in for questioning, the lights were just a little brighter than was necessary. Sort of the modern equivalent of the lamp police officers back in the day would shine directly into a perp's face.

Ben and Tommy hated the room and only used it when they felt it was absolutely imperative. Tonight, they needed Henry McClinton to realize his best option was to talk to them and hold nothing back. They needed him to be off his game, not the meticulous strategic thinker he considered himself. They needed the interrogation room.

From behind the one-way mirror, Tommy watched McClinton sitting in the room on the other side by himself. They'd uncuffed him once they got him to the station but hadn't allowed him to make any calls yet. If his wife had telephoned an attorney and directed him to the station, he hadn't arrived.

Stepping into the observation room, Ben was followed by Chief Brent. Both men were carrying cups of coffee.

"Gee. Thanks. I didn't want any," Tommy said when he saw the steaming cups in their hands.

"I'll buy you dinner when we're finished here to make up for it. How about that?" Ben said to placate his now pouting partner. "I've brought the chief up to speed. He knows why we brought McClinton in and just got off the phone with the state's attorney. We've been given some legal leeway because of who our victims are."

"Legal leeway," Tommy repeated. "Is that even a real thing?"

The chief took a sip of coffee and said, "It is for the next thirty minutes."

Chapter Ninety-One

Walking into the interrogation room, Ben and Tommy had one goal. To get answers. They also had a limited amount of time to do so. When the county's top prosecutor said they had thirty minutes to get what they needed and send McClinton on his way, they knew he meant it. After that, he wasn't going to give them any legal cover.

"I haven't gotten my phone call yet?" the professor said the minute the detectives walked into the room.

"There's a reason for that, Professor McClinton," Tommy said, taking the seat directly across the table from him. "If you call your lawyer, this all becomes a *thing*. We have to fill out forms and file all kinds of paperwork. You end up going down into the cells for the night. Or at least until you're arraigned. And since it's Friday night and the court is closed until Monday... that's the whole weekend."

"What my partner is trying to say," Ben said, picking up the baton and running with it, "is there is a way all of this goes away, and you walk out of here tonight."

"I didn't kill anyone."

"Okay," Ben said. "We can start there."

The one thing they needed to make sure McClinton didn't say was that he wanted a lawyer. The minute he said that, they would need to stop talking to him. Period. Criminal Defense Procedure 101. Not all cops followed that rule, but Ben did. Therefore, so did Tommy. But so far, all he said was he wanted his one phone call. He neglected to mention who he was going to call. Since neither Ben nor Tommy were mind readers, how could they know who he wanted to call?

They needed to make him think all of this was just a big misunderstanding, and if he just cooperated, he'd be free to go. Which he would be. In all honesty, if he hadn't been such a pain in the ass and just answered their questions the first time they spoke with him, he wouldn't even be there now.

"You say you didn't kill anyone," Ben repeated. "For the record, you're referring to Roland Taylor and Mike Moran, yes?"

"Yes. I mean, no. I mean…I *did not* kill either Roland Taylor or Mike Moran." The professor was flustered. This could work for them, Ben thought, taking a seat next to his partner and laying a notepad on the table.

"Again, for the record, you did know both men."

"Yes. Taylor was always getting his name in the paper. Everyone knew who he was. Just like Moran. I listened to his radio show like everyone else in the city."

"But you also knew them from your work as an historian?"

"They were hobbyists at best. But yes, they were interested in history. Specifically, the Civil War. An area I specialize in."

"See, this isn't hard," Tommy gibed. Even though he was talking, they needed to make sure he didn't get too comfortable.

Ben was scribbling some notes on his pad. It was all information they already knew, but he was using his notetaking as a way to time his questions and pace the interview. "Now, Professor, you, along with Taylor, Moran, and a Walter Tully, all attended an auction at Bensons Auctions and Antiques at which you all bid on a set of books. Correct?"

"Yes."

"But you did not win the auction. Father Taylor did."

"Yes."

"Did you ever have a chance to look at these books?"

"Not in detail. No."

"What made them so interesting to you?"

McClinton was doing his best to keep his temper in check. Ben could tell he was a man who didn't like repeating himself, and that is exactly what Ben was making him do right now. But it was to lay the groundwork for the rest of the questions he had planned. Questions that might finally tell them who was behind the murders and the break-in at the professor's house.

"There was only one book in the lot that I was actually interested in. A journal. I believe the journal belonged to my great...to one of my ancestors, William McClinton. He was a clerk for the city during the Civil War."

"The first time we spoke, you said you believed this journal contained information about something that happened in Parker City during the Civil War. Something that has been covered up in the years since. Is that correct?"

McClinton chewed on his lower lip for a moment. "Detective, you need to understand something. I am an historian. I do research. I can't share information freely because someone else may take my work and...."

"Beat you to the punch?" Tommy asked.

"Yes. I'm working on a book that could completely...that could reveal a secret people in Parker want to cover up."

Tommy shifted in his seat. "Professor, what could possibly have happened in Parker that was so scandalous?"

Turning red in the face, McClinton sat forward and said, "How about the attempted assassination of President Abraham Lincoln?"

Chapter Ninety-Two

"Excuse me?" Tommy asked, the confusion evident in his voice. "You think someone...in Parker City...tried to kill Abraham Lincoln? And then they covered it up?"

"I told you. I have journals that belonged to William. He never came right out and said it. Only made references to events and people. But there was one journal in his collection that was missing. The one that would cover the exact time period of the Battle of Antietam and the assassination attempt. I believe that was the journal Bensons sold and that it would have the rest of the information I needed to prove my theory."

Tommy looked to Ben for his next cue.

For his part, Ben sat with his pen frozen over the notepad. What the professor said was certainly not what he was expecting. Granted, he had to admit, he wasn't sure what he *actually* thought McClinton would tell them was in the journal. But a story about someone trying to kill President Lincoln wasn't even in his top ten guesses.

"I can see by the looks on your faces you don't believe me," McClinton said, sitting back in the metal chair and crossing his arms. "It doesn't surprise me. But if I could just find the last pieces of information to confirm my theory.... It will also explain how the Aspen House Hospital burned down."

"Okay! Hold on!" Tommy said, practically jumping out of his chair. "Wait. Stop. Back up. The Aspen House Hospital? The old insane asylum outside of town? That has something to do with this too?"

"Yes. I just need to prove it."

"I think we just need to lock this guy up for being crazy," Tommy said directly to Ben. "Now he's just making shit up. An assassination attempt of the president *in Parker City* somehow has something to do with the Aspen Hospital fire? Are you buying any of this? Don't you think if someone tried to kill Lincoln here in Parker, *everybody* would know about it? I mean, it's kind of a big deal.

"And the fire…" Tommy stopped to think for a minute. "The fire was caused by a patient. One of the loonies burned the place down."

"That's exactly what they want you to believe!" McClinton shouted, shooting up from his chair.

In a fraction of a second, both Ben and Tommy were on their feet, each reaching for his sidearm.

"Everyone, just take a deep breath," Ben said, trying to calm the situation and defuse some of the tension. "I will admit…this does sound a little… um…hard to believe. *But* I think we should hear the professor out."

The three men looked at each other for a moment, none of them moving.

"Why don't we take a moment? Professor, can I get you a cup of coffee? A soda?" Ben asked.

"Some water would be nice."

"We will be back in a few minutes. And then we will listen to your story."

"It's not a story."

"Your theory. You can tell us exactly what it is you think happened. And I promise. We will keep open minds."

As McClinton sat back down, Ben and Tommy exited the interrogation room to get themselves some coffee and the professor a glass of water. Tommy was wondering if he should go pop some popcorn because he was sure they were in for a whale of a story.

When the door to the interview room was closed, he turned to Ben with eyes the size of volleyballs and said, "Can you believe it? There was a conspiracy to kill Lincoln right here in Parker City? I knew it! I knew there was going to be some deep, dark conspiracy behind all of this. I knew it. I knew it. I knew it!"

Ben leaned his back against the wall and started rubbing his temples, trying to make sense of everything. "If it turns out to be true, there's going to be no living with you, is there? You're never going to let me live it down, will you?"

"Not...a...chance."

Chapter Ninety-Three

1862...

The giant steam engine roared into the station much like an elephant would charging into a barn. The couple pieces of luggage piled in the corner—seemingly forgotten by their owners—vibrated as the train thundered to a halt, its massive brakes producing a sound, so ear-piercing that it drowned out all others.

Carefully sliding one of the loose wooden slats in the door down, so he had a better view, Caleb watched as several soldiers, dressed in much nicer uniforms than the men General McClellan was currently commanding, disembarked from the train. These troops, most likely the president's personal guard, were followed by another group of men in fancy suits and hats. Amongst the distinguished-looking collection of men, speaking with an older gentleman with small round spectacles and a long, bushy gray beard was his and the sheriff's mysterious friend of many secrets. Caleb wondered if his presence was a good sign.

Finally, appearing in the train's doorway at the top of the steps, was the tall, slender frame of Abraham Lincoln. As he descended to the platform, Caleb was surprised by his height. He'd always heard that the president was tall, but to see him, it was very intimidating. And with his signature stovepipe hat atop his head, he looked downright giant. His presence was commanding, that point could not be argued. But as he came closer, Caleb saw in his eyes a sorrow he hadn't expected. The war was taking its toll.

Suddenly, Caleb's view was blocked by a swath of blue.

"Good afternoon, Mr. President." George McClellan had stepped forward to greet the commander-in-chief.

"Hello, General," Lincoln replied. His voice was more pinched and nasally than Caleb was expecting. "I must personally congratulate you on the outcome of the battle in Sharpsburg. I cannot help thinking, though, with Lee on the run as he was, it might have been beneficial if you'd given chase."

"With the casualties we suffered, if we had followed and Lee was able to regroup...I don't believe you'd be congratulating me," the general said, his tone betraying his feeling of annoyance.

"These are all matters we shall discuss today," Lincoln said, his tone the very opposite of McClellan's.

On that note, Caleb heard the sound of footfalls on the wooden platform, and then his view was restored as McClellan followed the president into the station. Stepping across the room to the other door, Caleb watched as the individual members of the assemblage took their places around a large table that had been set up in the middle of the gallery. Lincoln sat in the center on one side, with McClellan directly across from him. Both were flanked on either side by stern-faced men looking as though they were preparing to launch into verbal combat.

As the time passed, Caleb found himself struggling to stay focused. The gathering was just barely within his hearing, making it difficult to understand everything that was being said. Much of what he could hear, he didn't fully comprehend. The only thing he would be willing to bet his weekly pay on, though, was that President Lincoln and General McClellan were not fond of one another. To him, it even sounded like the general might be in some sort of trouble.

Several times, the meeting came to a halt so everyone could stand and stretch, use the necessary, and have private conversations away from the group. While others stood and roamed around during these intermissions, the president did not rise from his chair once. He remained seated, reading papers and making notes on them as he went. Caleb was impressed by his fortitude.

The meeting finally appeared to be coming to an end, just as the sunlight outside was turning a vibrant shade of orange. Caleb knew the sun would soon be setting. If the president was able to return to the train, the threat would be over. Wouldn't it?

Stepping out onto the platform, the president placed his hat back on his head, once again raising his height so he could be seen over the men standing around him. As his traveling party was beginning to make their way onto the train, Lincoln stopped and wandered down the platform a few paces. He was looking up to the sky, his hands firmly clasped together behind his back. Caleb couldn't even begin to imagine the thoughts a man such as the president was having at that moment.

For whatever reason, Caleb eased open the door and slid out onto the platform. Standing with his back to the station wall, he took his own deep breath of fresh air. The first he'd had since ducking into the storage room nearly twenty-four hours earlier.

What disturbed him the most was that no one noticed him there on the platform in full view. And if they had, they didn't raise an alarm. He was not dressed as a soldier, nor was he wearing the formal attire of the president's men from Washington. He did not belong.

The first person to catch Caleb's eye was actually Lincoln himself as he turned to make his way back to the train. A split second later, Caleb saw the president's gaze shift slightly higher over Caleb's head. At the same time, his eyes squinted, trying to see something. Following his eyes, Caleb turned and instantly saw the same thing as the president. A Union soldier standing on the roof of the train station, his rifle pointed directly at the president.

Chapter Ninety-Four

C aleb hated having to pull his pistols for any reason. But when they were necessary, they were necessary, and his draw was the quickest of all the sheriff's deputies. Only fractions of a second passed from the time he saw the rifleman standing on the roof of the station to his right hand reaching for his pistol, withdrawing it from its holster, and firing its first shot. At almost the same time, his left hand had done the same with the pistol on his other hip.

Both shots ran out, sending the station into chaos.

The soldiers whose responsibility it had been to protect the president snapped to. A dozen gun barrels now pointed in Caleb's direction. Even with his own life in jeopardy, he never took his eyes off the rifleman on the roof, who'd been struck by at least one of his shots. The would-be assassin was clutching his shoulder and hurrying to the far end of the roof where a ladder rested.

Taking aim again, Caleb released another shot. A burst of crimson exploded from the fleeing assassin's already wounded arm. The force of the bullet's impact forced him to stumble the last few steps before he regained his balance and started down the ladder.

As a wave of soldiers began to close in on Caleb, it was President Lincoln who shouted, "Stop *that* man!" All eyes turned in the direction he was pointing.

Confusion rapidly spread amongst the men on the platform. Some ran towards Caleb and the president, while others turned and started moving in the opposite direction, following Lincoln's orders. Everything was happening so quickly, but Caleb was trying to keep his eyes on his target. Though he knew if he moved, there was a good chance he would be shot.

It wasn't until he saw Jonathan and another man dressed in a dark suit holding a pistol emerge from the crowd that he figured he would be safe.

"Get the president on the train!" Jonathan shouted to the other man as he grabbed Caleb by the arm and hustled him toward a door leading into the station.

With a quick glance over his shoulder, Caleb watched as the president was enveloped by an onslaught of soldiers and quickly ushered onto the train. That was the last he saw of the action outside as the door closed behind him.

"Do you know where he might be heading?" Jonathan asked, now moving Caleb across the gallery floor toward the main entrance to the station.

It took a second for the question to fully register. Caleb's adrenaline was pumping so fast, he was trying to make sense of everything.

"Deputy Post! Do you know where he's running to?"

"Yes. I have an idea."

"Then go!"

"Will President Linc…"

"He'll be seen to. I promise. Make haste!"

Caleb felt Jonathan push him through the doors onto the street. A crowd had begun gathering outside after hearing the gunfire. It was odd enough seeing the building circled by Union soldiers, but then to hear shots. Human curiosity took hold of all those on the street. It was all Caleb could do to push through to the other side of the mass of people.

Gaining his bearings, Caleb began running in the direction of the Aspen House Hospital. It was a distance from the center of town, but the rifleman only had a short head start on him and was injured. There was a good chance Caleb could catch up to him.

His hopes disappeared as he reached the corner and watched a horse gallop past him. Riding atop the mighty thoroughbred that Caleb instantly recognized as one of the horses that used to pull Eustace Drake's carriage was the shooter from the train station. He'd removed the uniform jacket, but Caleb had seen his face. Even with a badly injured arm completely covered in blood, he maintained expert control of the beast as it charged down the street, throwing clouds of dust and dirt in all directions.

There'd be no way to catch up with him now, Caleb thought. He would just need to get to the hospital as quickly as his legs could carry him.

"Caleb!" He heard someone shouting his name from somewhere behind him. Turning, he saw Deputy Gimble racing in his direction, driving the sheriff's buggy. "Caleb!"

Bringing Dolly to an awkward halt, Gimble's tone was a combination of confusion and anger. "What is goin' on? There's all sorts of commotion at the train station, and the sheriff said to keep an eye out for you."

"Oscar, there's no time to explain. I need the rig. And you need to get the sheriff and all the deputies to the Aspen House Hospital as fast as you can. Bring the rifles!"

Caleb very nearly pushed Gimble out of the driver's seat and left him standing in the middle of the street with a bewildered look on his face.

"I'm sorry, girl," Caleb said to Dolly as he slapped the reins, "but we need to go as fast as you can manage. I promise you the best hay in the city if you pick up the pace." Whether it was his imagination or not, he felt Dolly jolt forward, pushing him deeper into the cushion of the leather seat. "That's a girl."

Chapter Ninety-Five

It wasn't until the Aspen House Hospital was in view that Caleb again caught sight of the fleeing soldier on horseback. Now, as the pursuit was coming to an end, Caleb realized he hadn't thought about what his plan was to be. Was he just thinking he could march into the hospital and arrest the man who tried to kill President Lincoln? Just the thought of it being that easy was a fantasy and cause to have his head examined.

Without concern for remaining unseen this time, Caleb guided Dolly up the path to the building. Through the shadows created by the sun's rapid descent, he could just make out the figure of a horse and its rider dismounting. As the horse trotted off, the man began running toward the side of the sanitarium on a pair of very unsteady legs. Jumping down from the driver's seat, Caleb followed suit. He knew Dolly wouldn't wander off on her own, and hopefully, the sheriff would be arriving momentarily and could have someone tend to her.

Following the dark figure around to the rear of the building, Caleb watched as he struggled to open a large iron door using only his good arm, then disappear inside. In a few long strides, Caleb was at the door, which sat partially open. A set of stairs on the other side led downward into a cellar. With a pistol in each hand and at the ready, Caleb started down the steps.

Even before he reached the bottom, he could hear muffled voices coming from somewhere at the end of the passage.

"Everyone needs to get out of here!"

"If they come looking...."

"Just go now!"

"William, leave the damn papers!"

"We can't be seen…."

"This was botched good, Anderson!"

"Go!"

Caleb's feet hit the stone floor, and he found himself in a long hallway. Doors ran along the walls on both sides. He noticed a thick trail of blood running down the stairs and along the passage into the room where the voices were coming from. Making his way toward the shouting, Caleb stepped into the doorway and raised his pistols.

"I am Deputy Caleb Post with the Parker County Sheriff's Department. Place all of your hands in the air. You are all hereby under arrest."

Frozen silence filled the room. Caleb took in the sight and quickly began calculating his next move. Standing around a large table were three men he knew well – Silas Moss, Thaddeus Parker, and William McClinton. The other man, neatly attired and extremely red-faced, he did not know. Next to him was a Confederate officer. And slumped motionless in a chair at the far end of the room was the man Caleb had put two holes in.

"Deputy, I'm Doctor Aspen. This is my hospital," the unknown man said. "There's been a terrible misunderstanding. I don't know what—"

"Hold your tongue!" the officer said only a moment before he raised a pistol and shot the doctor in the side of his head.

The men watched in stunned horror as the doctor's body fell to the floor unceremoniously.

"Good God, Anderson!" Thaddeus Parker shouted. "You're mad!"

Bloody Bill turned the gun on him in the next instant and was just about to pull the trigger again when Caleb put a bullet into his hand, sending the pistol clattering to the table. Moss, Parker, and McClinton took the opportunity to rush for the door. Colliding with Caleb as they pushed past, the young deputy was knocked to the ground, one of his pistols tumbling through the air. As he was struggling to get back on his feet, Anderson lunged out the door and pinned him to the wall, his good hand hammering into Caleb's stomach once, then a second time, and a third.

Fighting back, Caleb smashed the pistol he still held into his attacker's face, setting him off balance. But the force also knocked the gun from Caleb's hand.

With the two men facing off in the narrow corridor, neither with his gun, they were both looking for anything that could be used as a weapon. Anderson was the first to grab one of the oil lamp sconces from the wall and hurl it towards Caleb. Jumping out of the way of the flame, Caleb crashed into one of the other doors, sending it swinging open and him stumbling into the room. His momentum was only stopped when he struck a large wooden barrel.

His senses momentarily knocked out of him. It took a second to notice the black powder he'd been covered with when he landed on the barrel. Once he did, he looked around in horror to see more of the barrels containing gunpowder lining the walls.

In the doorway, Bloody Bill stood holding another of the burning oil lamps. "Looks like you picked the wrong door, *Deputy Post.*" And then, as casually as if he were tossing Caleb a ball to catch, he lobbed the lamp onto one of the barrels and then took off down the passageway.

Scrambling to his feet and running after the Confederate officer, Caleb was just about to reach the stairs leading to the outside when the last thing he heard was the roar of the cache of gunpowder as it erupted behind him.

Chapter Ninety-Six

1984...

B en and Tommy sat in stunned silence following the conclusion of Professor McClinton's wild, historic tale. To the detectives, it sounded like the plot of some action-adventure movie. But the professor assured them that he'd pieced the whole story together through research that included letters from eyewitnesses to the events, journal entries both in his relative's collection and others from the time, and random bits in newspaper articles. He was counting on the missing journal from William McClinton to tie everything together.

The only sound in the interrogation room was the ticking of the clock on the wall. McClinton looked from Ben to Tommy, waiting for one of them to speak. It was apparent that he was proud of his theory and was yearning for praise or recognition of his in-depth research. When none immediately came, he sat back in his chair and crossed his arms, pouting like a child told he could not have ice cream until he'd finished his dinner.

Tommy finally broke the silence. "So...what you're telling us is that just days after the Battle of Antietam, President Abraham Lincoln made a secret trip to Parker to meet with George McClellan, and during this visit, there was an assassination attempt made. And that the men behind all of it—the Knights of the Golden Circle operating in Parker City—were actually former mayors and members of two of the most powerful families in town—both then and now—as well as Doctor Joseph Aspen, whose hospital—that was being used as the conspirators' headquarters—burned to the ground because of it? Did I pretty much sum it up correctly?"

Impressed that his partner was able to get all of that out in one breath, Ben looked to McClinton for his answer. Which came in the form of one simple word.

"Yes."

"And then, on top of all that, it was completely covered up and forgotten about in the last…hundred and…" Tommy trailed off as he was doing the math.

"Twenty-two years," McClinton answered. "One hundred and twenty-two years since."

"And you think it's possible to rewrite history like that?" Tommy, the conspiracy-lover, was having a hard time buying it.

"Of course! It's not like it's the first time history has been rewritten, and some scandalous event has been covered up."

"Okay, I think we've heard enough here." Ben wasn't sure if they should have the academic committed or if what he was saying could have actually happened. There were times when the strangest theory made sense, weren't there? He couldn't believe he was starting to think like Tommy. "You certainly weave a good tale, Professor. I'm sure your students must love your lectures. But this sounds a little farfetched to me. Do you actually expect us to believe that someone is out there killing for this journal? A journal that would only seem to benefit *you* and your work."

"It could be someone in the Parker or Moss family who doesn't want it known that one of their ancestors tried to kill Abraham Lincoln!" McClinton's voice raised several octaves as he protested Ben's disbelief. "I *did not* kill Roland Taylor or Mike Moran."

"As much as we'd just love to take your word on that," Tommy said, "we're going to stick with the evidence."

"Which we're hoping will give us an answer one way or the other shortly," Ben said, referring to the fingerprint analysis they were waiting on. "While we're waiting, let's start at the beginning again, and you tell us where you were when Father Taylor was…."

There was a knock on the door, then Chief Brent stepped into the room. With a silent, subtle jerk of his head, he instructed Ben to join him in the corner. In the chief's hand was a file folder with the logo of the state police emblazoned on it. It was the CSU report on the fingerprints. If the analysis said what Ben expected it to, they'd be wrapping the case up in a matter of minutes.

"This was just delivered," Brent said, handing him the folder.

Ben quickly opened the cover and flipped to the summary. Reading through the lines, he found the section he was looking for. It wasn't until reading it the third time that he accepted he'd gotten his answer. None of the fingerprints lifted from the cigarette package matched the one found on the knife that killed Mike Moran. Henry McClinton was telling the truth. He wasn't the killer. Could that mean his story about what happened a hundred and twenty-some years ago was true? And if *he* wasn't the killer, who was?

Chapter Ninety-Seven

P lacing the CSU report in front of Tommy as he returned to his seat, Ben looked directly at McClinton and tried to decide how much of what he was saying could be legitimate. It was obvious the professor thought all of it was. He did say he had pieced the whole thing together through other resources. It hadn't just come from the journal, which he was still claiming to never have read.

"Alright, Professor. That report there tells me that you are telling the truth. Your fingerprints don't match the one we found on Mike Moran's murder weapon."

"I told you I didn't kill them...wait a minute. How did you get my fingerprints?"

"The cigarettes," Tommy and Ben said at the same time.

A look of indignation formed on McClinton's face. "How dare you!"

"Oh, spare me," Tommy said, smacking his hand on the table. "We're the police. We were investigating a double murder. You handed over the cigarette pack willingly."

"You tricked me!"

"Cry me a river."

"Guys," Ben said, putting his hands up to stop them. "Like I said. The test clears you. I think it's more important to figure out who actually is behind all of this."

"Fine. Professor, who else knew about the research you were doing?" Tommy asked, trying to sound as though he'd let his frustration go.

"No one. If I could prove what I told you, it would be huge...enormous.

Any historian would want to make a discovery like this. One that would change history."

"But is there anyone specific you told about what you were working on or that you actually had the journal?"

Thinking carefully, McClinton said, "Just Judith. But I don't believe my wife would be trying to steal my work."

"None of your students? No one at the college was assisting in your research?" Ben asked.

"No. I didn't want to take the chance of anyone finding out what I was working on."

"Let's try this a different way," Ben said. "Think back to the auction. We know you were there, along with Father Taylor, Moran, and Tully. Was there anyone else there who might in any way have any idea what the journal could contain?"

Again, the professor thought for a moment. "No...well...maybe."

Both Ben and Tommy sat forward in their chairs.

"And who would that be?" Tommy prodded when the professor didn't immediately offer the information.

"Teddy."

Ben looked over at Tommy and then back at McClinton. "Teddy?"

"Teddy Nestor. My teaching assistant. He was at the auction that night. But he works there part-time. His family owns Benson's."

"I thought the Osbournes owned the auction house," Tommy said.

"They do. Teddy is Ellen's son. When Ellen and Teddy's father got divorced, she went back to her maiden name."

Ben leaned his elbows on the table and put his head in his hands. Thinking back to the Spring Strangler case and the shootings earlier in the year, he now realized how straightforward both of those investigations were.

"Is Teddy as interested as you are in the Civil War period?" Ben asked.

"Quite. Though I feel he is sometimes more intrigued by the myths of the era."

"The myths?" Tommy wanted to jump over the table and shake the answers out of the man. He couldn't understand why McClinton didn't realize this wasn't a game and why he felt the need to drag out his answers. Suspense was one thing in a movie, but this was real life.

"He once wrote a paper about the treasure the Knights of the Golden Circle that was supposed to have hidden. I thought it was all nonsense."

"At any time," Ben asked very slowly, "did you ever mention William McClinton's missing journal to Teddy."

"I'm sure at some point I mentioned something about it. Just in passing."

"Do you remember what you said?"

"Well, maybe I said if I was able to find the journal...I'd be striking gold." Thinking about what he'd just said, the professor looked at Ben with wide eyes. "You don't think he took that to mean it was part of some treasure map?"

"Are you fucking kidding me!?" Tommy said, jumping to his feet. "All of this is because this kid is searching for hidden treasure!?"

Chapter Ninety-Eight

Ben, in his unmarked Crown Victoria, and Tommy, in his Bronco, arrived at Benson Auction and Antiques at the same time. Both pulling up in front of the building and parking at odd angles on the street. Before either was able to exit his car, two patrol cruisers glided toward them with their lights flashing. Additional units were on their way to Ellen Osbourne/Teddy Nestor's home and Hammermill College as well. Without knowing where the boy was, Ben wanted all three locations to be searched at the same time.

Grabbing a walkie-talkie from the car, he told the two uniformed officers to wait outside and that he'd radio if their assistance was needed. He didn't want to charge into the place and put everyone on the defensive because of a needless show of force. But that wasn't to say he wouldn't call in the cavalry if necessary. Ben was no cowboy. Backup was there for a reason.

"Don't let anyone in or out," were Ben's last words as he and Tommy stepped into the first-floor showroom of Benson's.

As before, Daniel Osbourne appeared from the office in the rear with a big smile. This evening, the jolly gentleman was wearing a red and white polka dot bowtie. Making his way around the glass display cases, his smile broadened when he saw the visitors were Ben and Tommy.

"Detectives! So good to see you again. How can we help you this time?"

"Mr. Osbourne, have you seen your grandson today?"

"Edward? Yes. He came in a few hours ago. There's a spare room upstairs—it's really more like the attic—where he goes to do his homework and study sometimes. I believe that's where he is now. He said he didn't want to be bothered because he was working on a big project for school."

"Thank you, Mr. Osbourne," Ben said while giving Tommy the signal to head upstairs. "There are two officers waiting outside. We're going to need you to stay down here, please."

"Is everything alright?" The smile had disappeared.

"We just need to talk to Teddy," Tommy said over his shoulder as he began climbing the stairs.

On the second-floor landing, both Ben and Tommy unholstered their guns and began moving in tactical form. Neither intended nor wanted to use force. Both were hoping the situation would be resolved peacefully, but they'd be ready just in case. After all, they were about to confront someone they believed had killed two people...to find hidden treasure. The odds were Teddy might not be as mentally sound as he appeared when they met him in McClinton's office back at the college.

Ellen Osbourne's office door was open, but there were no lights on in the room. Following the hallway down a few steps further, they came to a set of stairs leading to the attic space above. Ben motioned that he'd take point and keep his gun high, letting Tommy know to keep his aim low.

Halfway up the steps, they began hearing quiet groans of what they could only describe as frustration. At one time or another, each of the detectives could say they'd made the same sound when something wasn't making sense and irritating them.

"There has to be something here," they heard Teddy saying. "I know it is. I know I'm right. But I can't find anything. Where is it? None of these papers help!"

Was Teddy talking to himself, or was someone up there with him?

Before Ben's head cleared the top of the steps, he paused. Should he announce their presence and give Teddy a chance to arm himself if, in fact, he had a weapon in the attic with him? Or should they move quickly and take him by surprise? Either option could be risky. He wanted to see the space before charging in with their guns drawn.

Looking around for anything reflective, Ben could see nothing on the stairs of any use, and he wasn't going to backtrack to go looking for something now. Instead, he did something that he would have seriously chastised Tommy for if he'd done it. He slowly raised his head above the level of the floor so he could get a view of the room. Luckily, Teddy was sitting with his back to the stairs, so did not see the top of Ben's head emerge from the stairwell. Turning back to Tommy, he counted on his fingers one-two-three, then took the last few steps two at a time. Tommy was right behind him.

"Teddy," Ben said, trying to keep his voice as even as possible, "this is Detective Winters. We met in Professor McClinton's office. I'm here with my partner. We're going to need you to put your hands in the air and turn around slowly."

The boy was sitting on the floor with what Ben could only assume were the papers stolen from Henry McClinton's house strewn all around him. On the wall in front of him, there was a bulletin board with pictures of Confederate soldiers. Some Ben recognized from his History classes, like Robert E. Lee and Stonewall Jackson. Others, he needed to squint to read the names Teddy had written on them. The one that particularly caught his eye was of a bearded man with wild, untamed hair. In red marker, the name BLOODY BILL ANDERSON was written on it.

"Teddy? Did you hear me?" Ben asked when he did not move.

"I'm just working on a school project. Please leave me alone."

"I'm afraid we can't do that, Teddy. We need to ask you a few questions. Can you please turn around?"

"With your hands out so we can see them," Tommy added.

Slowly, Teddy began to adjust the position in which he was sitting. Both Ben and Tommy raised their guns, taking careful aim. As he turned toward them, they saw the journal that had been the cause of everything that happened over the last few days in Teddy's hands.

"Teddy, what is it you're looking for in there?" Tommy asked, genuinely curious.

"The treasure that was lost after the war ended. I thought, with everything Professor McClinton said about this journal, it would have the clues I needed. But once I read it, I couldn't figure them out. So I needed to see his notes to figure out how he'd found the treasure."

"So...you broke into his house this morning. But those papers don't say anything about a hidden treasure, do they?"

"No! But there are references to the Knights of the Golden Circle in some of the copies of letters he has. I just can't figure out the code."

"Teddy, there isn't any code. There isn't any treasure," Ben tried to convince him.

"Yes, there is. There has to be! There has to be a treasure. That's why I did this. That's why I...." He stopped before he said what Ben and Tommy needed to hear.

"Why you did what, Teddy?" Ben prompted.

It was almost like someone flipped a switch, the boys unfocused glassy eyes suddenly became sharp and narrow. Even his posture went from being slumped to ramrod straight. Ben wondered if he'd been having a mental break of some sort, and now he was back to being the Teddy they'd first spoken with. Ben could see the recognition in his eyes now. The recognition that he was in serious trouble.

What Ben hadn't been able to see was the Root Revolver, a Civil War-era pistol Teddy had in his lap under the journal. As the boy raised the gun, Ben instinctively bolted towards him. First, to put himself in front of Tommy so if Teddy fired, he could block the round from hitting his partner; and second, to put himself in front of Tommy so he would not shoot Teddy.

Ben tackled the boy just as the pistol went off, the blast echoing off the walls in the small empty space. Tommy was on them seconds later, pulling Ben away from Teddy to see if either had been hit. As Ben rolled to the side, he grabbed the antique revolver and took it with him, leaving Teddy lying on the floor stunned. To Tommy's relief, he saw a hole in the floor between his partner and the boy where the round had struck.

"You good?"

"Yeah," Ben said, catching his breath. "Did you see how I saved your life there?"

Rolling Teddy over and quickly cuffing his hands behind his back, Tommy said, "Dude, you are so under arrest."

Chapter Ninety-Nine

After the report of "shots fired" went out, all available units responded to Benson's, crowding the street in front of the auction house with patrol cars lighting the night with their emergency flashers. As Ben exited the building, one hand firmly gripping Teddy Nestor's arm, he realized that this was a scene he'd witnessed far too many times this year.

As he handed Nestor off to one of the uniforms to put in the back of a squad car, Ben saw the unmistakable form of Chief Brent silhouetted by the red and blue lights. He could see that the chief was moving toward him along with another man. When they were close enough to make out their faces, Ben saw that it was the mayor.

"Detective Winters, we heard that shots were fired. Are you alright?" the mayor asked.

"It's actually Detective *Sergeant* Winters, to be precise," Tommy said from behind Ben. "And it wasn't anything we can't handle. Some quick footwork on my part probably saved both of our lives but…."

"Tommy." The chief's stern voice told him it wasn't the time for his usual smartassedness.

"It will all be in our report, sir," Tommy concluded.

"But you caught him?" the mayor confirmed. "The man responsible for killing Father Taylor and Morning Mike?"

"More like a kid," Ben corrected. "A college student who…I think it's safe to say may have an insanity defense in the making."

"He thought he was searching for hidden Confederate treasure," Tommy clarified.

"The Knights of the Golden Circle?" Mayor Oland asked, visibly taking the three police officers by surprise. "I was a History major in college. I've always been fascinated by the Civil War."

"See, I told you. Everyone in Parker City is a Civil War buff," the chief said, referring back to his earlier statement when they were trying to come up with a list of potential suspects and their motives. "We could have been looking at the mayor here from the beginning."

"Well, if even half of what Professor McClinton said is true, there could be a lot of people implicated in what went on," Ben said. "Which is why I think we're going to have to seriously look at exactly what information we release about this case. Some serious feathers could get ruffled."

"Especially if the good professor has his way," Tommy interjected.

"In that case, I think it may be better if I remove myself from the situation," Charlie Oland said, literally taking a step back. "I just wanted to make sure you two were alright. And Chief, you'll keep me posted on whatever it is I *need* to know?"

"I will, sir."

"Thank you," Ben added as the mayor walked away.

"Nice guy," Tommy said. "He may be the only politician I've ever actually liked."

"So, what exactly went down here?" Brent asked, leaning against the hood of Ben's car.

Ben took the next few minutes to walk the chief through their interaction with Teddy and quickly explained how all the pieces of the puzzle were now fitting together perfectly. Of course, the full report would explain everything in detail, but it looked like they had a solid case against the college student. But as Ben had already pointed out, the chances of him claiming temporary insanity, or some variation thereof, was definitely a possibility.

"Well, for now, we've got him. And if this journal really is as explosive as you think, I'll make sure the state's attorney keeps it tied up in evidence for as long as possible."

"Thank you, Chief. That might be a good idea."

Thinking for a moment, the chief asked, "You say this kid says he got the journal from Moran's house?"

"That's what he said after I put the cuffs on him and started asking him questions," Tommy answered.

"*After* reading him his rights," Ben added.

"So…how did Moran come into possession of the journal?" Brent asked.

Ben and Tommy looked at each other.

"With Taylor and Moran dead," Ben said, "it looks like just one more mystery."

Brent shook his head and said, "Well, if you two head back to the station and at least file an initial report tonight, I think…."

"We can have tomorrow off?" Tommy asked with his trademark grin.

"I think that can be arranged, Detective Mason. You two could use the break."

"And how!" Tommy said, starting toward the driver's side of his truck.

"But if something comes up…" Ben began saying.

"Don't worry. I'll call you," the chief said with a smile.

Chapter One Hundred

1862...

Samuel Tildon and Jonathan had been locked away in the sheriff's study for most of the afternoon. The events from several days earlier weighed heavy on both men as they discussed how to proceed and what, if anything, there was to do now. The war was going to continue to wage on, and secret agents of the Confederacy were going to continue to try and undermine the Union. But as far as Parker City was concerned, its involvement with the Knight of the Golden Circle, now that their operatives had been uncovered, was at an end. However, there was a problem that had put Tildon in a rage.

"How can you stand there and say that we cannot do anything to these men?" the sheriff roared.

"Because we have no evidence any of them were actually involved in the plot," Jonathan answered, his cool demeanor not cracking for an instant. "Names on a list...a list that we no longer even have...mean nothing. And to that point, even if we did still have the list, did you not say your own name was on it?"

"Jonathan!"

"I understand your frustrations, Sam. Believe me. If there was anything I could do...if I had the power...I would make certain each and every one of the traitors swung in the town square."

"But Caleb..."

"Sam, what Caleb did makes him a hero. He saved the president's life."

"And you're saying no one will ever know it."

Jonathan sighed and leaned back in his chair, a look of sympathy on his face. "I was asked to deliver this message to you."

Withdrawing a folded piece of paper from his vest pocket, he handed it to the sheriff, who read:

I WILL FOREVER BE IN YOUNG DEPUTY POST'S DEBT FOR SAVING MY LIFE. I WILL SEE TO IT HE RECEIVES THE VERY BEST MEDICAL ATTENTION POSSIBLE.

A. LINCOLN

"Oh, my boy," Tildon sighed.

After a moment, Jonathan turned to his friend and said, "Right now, we have a great responsibility. We cannot let it be known just how close these conspirators came to achieving their goal. It would only embolden others. And the president has already said he wants to visit the Antietam battlefield himself. More attempts could be made on his life. We need Lincoln to see us through this damnable war. You know that. That is our job now. To keep everything that happened from coming to light. It will have to be up to someone else to sort all of this out in the future."

Knowing his friend was right and the damage that would be done if word of the assassination attempt spread, the sheriff rubbed his chin and thoughtfully said, "Hopefully, whoever that turns out to be, has the same wits as Caleb, and they are much smarter than you or me."

Forty miles away, as the sheriff said those words, Caleb lay in a bed in a private hospital in Washington, D.C. Outside his window, the dome of the Capitol building stood guard. He'd been in and out of consciousness the first few days after the explosion, but on the last day, had come to fairly well. Every inch of his body hurt worse than any pain he'd ever felt, but the doctors said they felt confident he would be able to recover from his injuries. Though they said there was not much they could do for the scars on his back and legs. For the time being, they were seeing to it that his wounds were tended to, and he was as comfortable as possible.

As Caleb stared out the window, his mind wondering, there was a knock at the door. Carefully turning his head, gritting his teeth to ward off as much of the pain as possible, he saw a burly-looking fellow standing there. Though he was dressed in a tailored suit, he still appeared slightly disheveled with a beard that could use a trim. Taking his bowler hat from his head, the stranger stepped into the room and looked Caleb over with a keen set of eyes.

When he finally spoke, his accent was not like anything Caleb had ever heard.

"I hear ya saved Old Abe's life, lad. Impressive. What you did takes gumption. I also hear you're pretty good at sleuthing. That's how ya uncovered the plot to put a bullet in the president."

"I have a good mentor," Caleb answered.

"Sam Tildon's something else, isn't he? I have a great deal of respect for that mentor of yours."

Seeing the slight look of apprehension on Caleb's face, the man smiled and said with a wink, "I'm here because we all have a mutual friend here in Washington."

Jonathan, Caleb thought.

"The name's Allan. Allan Pinkerton and I can use a lad like yourself in my organization. So, I'm gonna need ya to get better now. You hear me? Cause as soon as you are, President Lincoln has work for us to do. Sound like something yer interested in?"

For a brief moment, as Caleb fully realized the opportunity before him, all the pain disappeared. Forgetting why he was lying there recovering in the first place, he started raising himself up to get out of bed. Instantly, a searing jolt shot through his entire body forcing him back down.

"Easy there," Pinkerton said, seeing the expression flash on Caleb's face. "You've been through an ordeal, lad. You need to properly heal. There's gonna be a place for you when you're good and ready."

As much as he would have liked to spring from the bed and immediately join the Pinkerton Agency, he knew he needed time to fully recover. And then…then he'd be ready for his assignment.

About the Author

When not sitting in his library devising new and clever ways to kill people (*for his mysteries*), Justin can usually be found at The Way Off Broadway Dinner Theatre, outside of Washington, DC, where he is one of the owners and producers. In addition to writing the Parker City Mysteries Series, which includes *Now & Then* (Finalist for the 2022 Silver Falchion Award for Best Investigator) and *Vice & Virtue*, he is also the mastermind behind Marquee Mysteries, a series of interactive mystery events he has been writing and producing for over fifteen years. Justin and his wife, Jessica, live along Lake Linganore outside of Frederick, Maryland.

SOCIAL MEDIA HANDLES:
www.Facebook.com/JMKiska
www.Instagram.com/JMKiska
www.twitter.com/justinkiska

AUTHOR WEBSITE:
www.JustinKiska.com

Also by Justin M. Kiska

Now & Then

Vice & Virtue

www.ingramcontent.com/pod-product-compliance
Lightning Source LLC
Chambersburg PA
CBHW050134120726
47903CB00002B/347